拆解

James St. André
蘇正隆 編著

中式英文 增訂版

FIXING CHINGLISH (REVISED EDITION)

商務印書館

拆解中式英文（增訂版）*Fixing Chinglish (Revised Edition)*

編　　者：James St. André　　蘇正隆

責任編輯：黃家麗

封面設計：趙穎珊

排　　版：高向明

印　　務：龍寶祺

出　　版：商務印書館 (香港) 有限公司

　　　　　香港筲箕灣耀興道 3 號東滙廣場 8 樓

　　　　　http://www.commercialpress.com.hk

發　　行：香港聯合書刊物流有限公司

　　　　　香港新界荃灣德士古道 220–248 號荃灣工業中心 16 樓

印　　刷：寶華數碼印刷有限公司

　　　　　香港柴灣吉勝街勝景工業大廈 4 樓 A 室

版　　次：2024 年 7 月增訂版第 1 次印刷

　　　　　© 2024 商務印書館 (香港) 有限公司

　　　　　ISBN 978 962 07 0641 7

　　　　　Printed in Hong Kong

　　　　　版權所有　不得翻印

Publisher's Note 出版説明

學英文沒捷徑，卻有訣竅。

不下功夫練習聽、説、讀、寫，很難精通英文，但方法不當，再多花時間也徒勞無功。精通英語，關鍵在於方法。

本書將説寫英文常見的典型錯誤分類整理，先列出中文例句，之後英文正誤並舉，再附重點形式的解釋文字。透過錯誤分析，幫助讀者排除學習障礙，並指引迴避錯誤的方法。

受詞彙和句型影響，最難克服的英語錯誤是中式英語。全書注重分析中式英語形成的原因，強調分辨中英思維差異，引導讀者避免錯誤。

文字簡潔、舉例地道。我們衷心希望，本書有助初學者提升英文水平，掌握流暢自然的英文。

商務印書館 (香港) 有限公司
編輯出版部

Usage Note
使用説明

Step 1

做練習題測試自己的語法概念是否清楚。

> 7. 全國人民慶祝他們的勝利。　　(2.8)
> The whole nation celebrated (　　) victory.
> a) their　　b) its　　c) it's　　d) his

Step 2

看正文的中文例句，嘗試自己用英文表達該句意思，再比對英文正確例句，如無誤，不必細看説明文字，可直接跳到下一句。如有錯，需詳細看文字解釋。

> 3.120 暴君迫使他們從早工作到晚。
>
> ✔　The tyrant made them <u>work</u> from dawn till dusk.
>
> ✘　The tyrant made them <u>to work</u> from dawn till dusk.
>
> > feel, hear, see, let, make, have, watch 等動詞後面複合受詞中的不定詞符號 to，照例必須省去。

Step 3

看每個例句之前的符號。✔ 正確符號，表示例句語法正確，外國人就是這樣説的。✘ 錯誤符號，表示例句含嚴重語法或用字錯誤。✘ 半對符號，表示語法正確，但用字不精確，易引起誤解。

> 3.117 昨天他必須上市場去。
>
> ✔　He <u>had</u> to go to the market yesterday.
>
> ✘　He <u>needed</u> to go to the market yesterday.
>
> ✘　He <u>need</u> go to the market yesterday.

Contents 目錄

Say goodbye to Chinglish
向中式英語説再見

中國人説、寫英文時，往往受中文語法習慣以及學過的英文單字短語的中文意思所左右，造句上受到很大的束縛，一不小心就説、寫出中式英語（Chinglish），有時文法上也説得通，但往往不是以英語為母語者所能了解，即或能了解，也會覺得怪異。

導致中式英語的原因有很多，以下舉出其中幾個：

1　忽略中英文化差異

　　中英文對各種事物的區分往往因文化、社會背景不同而有明顯差異。有時中文一詞可以涵蓋好幾種東西，英文却分得很細，有很豐富的詞彙。譬如，肉類中文很簡單，動物名稱加上肉字就成了。英文就複雜多了，豬肉叫 pork，鹿肉稱 venison，禽肉叫 poultry，包含 chicken, duck, goose, turkey 等。牛、羊則長幼有序，成牛（cow）的肉叫 beef，小牛（calf）的肉叫 veal；大綿羊的肉叫 mutton，小羔羊的肉叫 lamb。此外，red meat 指牛羊類的肉，white meat 指雞及火雞之類，game 指山珍野味。這些詞彙常會令人眼花撩亂，不知從何入手。

2　忽略假同源詞 (false friends)

　　假同源詞往往會引起許多混淆，比如將 a miss is as good as a mile 誤為 "失之毫釐，謬以千里"，把 at the end of the day 當成 " 一天結束時 ",technically speaking 譯成 " 技術上說來 " ……等,有些字面上很像中文,如 green bean ,卻不是綠豆,而是 " 四季豆 "。

3 誤將中英文對號入座

正文內 1.49 舉出實際例子:這兒交通很方便。

✔ It is quite easy to get anywhere from here.

✘ The traffic is very convenient here.

traffic 主要指的是來往的車輛。關於誤句我們曾經做過一項調查,詢問了十幾位以英語為母語的人士,沒有人懂得誤句的意思。以下是他們的反應:"Too weird to understand."、"Not certain."、"Too strange."、"Unintelligible."。經過解釋後,他們表示除了上面所舉的正句外,可視情況說:

Transportation / Travel is convenient here.

The traffic conditions are good.

Getting around is easy.

It's a good location for public transportation.

因此,我們應認清一個事實,那就是我們在課本或英漢辭典上看到的英文單字短語的中文意思與英文原意並不完全相等,大多只有局部的交集,用法上更往往有很大的出入。所以我們在學習時只能各個擊破,一個單字、一個短語個別去了解其定義及用法,無法速成。一廂情願想以英文單字短語的中文意義來類推英文用法是很危險的,是造成中式英語的主要原因之一。

避免之道在多模仿句型,多查英文用法詞典,沒有把握時盡量不要自己杜撰句子,以免習非成是,難以改正。

**Chinglish vs natural English
中式英語 vs 地道英語**

1.1　王老師很負責，每天都準時到學校。

✔　Miss Wang is <u>conscientious</u>. She comes to school on time every day.

✘　Miss Wang is <u>responsible</u>. Every day she comes to school on time.

> 一個人很認真、負責、敬業，英文通常用 conscientious 來表達，它的名詞是 conscience（良心）。responsible 接在 be 動詞之後是指對某事負責，也可指做錯事時該負的責任，因此"她該負責"英文是 She is <u>responsible</u> for it.。如果某人很負責、值得信賴，可以託付重任，可説 She / He is a <u>responsible</u> person.。

1.2　她身體不舒服所以不能來。

✔　She cannot come because she is <u>sick / ill</u>.

✘　She cannot come because she is not <u>comfortable</u>.

> 不舒服如果程度輕微，可説 She isn't feeling well.。如果是中文裏生病的委婉説法（身體不舒服），不能按字面直接翻成英文，否則理由顯得牽強可笑。

1.3　這些蘋果是甚麼顏色？

✔　What colour <u>are</u> the apples?

✘　What <u>is</u> the colour of the apples?

> 第二句合乎文法，但不夠自然。母語人士通常會用第一句。

1.4　現在是三點鐘。

✔　<u>It</u> is three o'clock (now).

✘　<u>Now</u> is three o'clock.

now 用作名詞時，前面應有介詞，如 from now on, by now，且通常不可作主詞。表示時日、天氣、距離等，主詞要用 it。除加強語氣，如：Now it's three o'clock. 等情況，now 用作副詞應放在句尾，才合乎英語習慣。

1.5　他個子不高。

✔ He is not <u>tall</u>.

✔ He is not <u>a tall man</u>.

✘ His <u>body</u> is not tall.

✘ He is not <u>high</u>.

high 通常指 "物" 的高大，tall 則指 "人或細長物" 的 "高"。但講人的高度，有數字時可以説 He is six feet <u>high</u>. 或 He is six feet <u>tall</u>. 。

1.6　我能佔用你幾分鐘嗎？

✔ Can you <u>spare</u> me a few minutes?

✘ May I <u>occupy</u> you a few minutes?

spare：騰出，省下。不顧句型及前後文，只把學過的英文詞彙的中文解釋任意還原為英文時很容易造出這種中式的英文句子。

1.7　讓我想想看。

✔ Let me think <u>it over</u>.

✔ Let me think <u>about it</u>. (以上兩句表示考慮)

✔ Let me <u>see</u>. (想一時忘記的事物時用此句)

✘ Let me think <u>over</u>.

"Let me think over." 語法上似乎通順，但不合習慣。參考以下兩句：
<u>Let</u> me see. What should we do now?
<u>Let</u> me think a moment. (= Give me time before I answer.)

1.8　這輛車價格多少？（這輛車多少錢？）

✔ What is the <u>price</u> of the car?

✔ How <u>much</u> is the car?

✔ How much does the car <u>cost</u>?

✘ How <u>much</u> is the <u>price</u> of the car?

> How much 已有 "多少錢" 的意思，不須再重複 the price。

1.9　你覺得這部電影怎樣？

✔ <u>What</u> do you <u>think of</u> the movie?

✔ <u>How</u> do you <u>like</u> the movie?

✘ <u>How</u> do you <u>think of</u> the movie?

> What do you think of ＝ What is your opinion of。think 的賓語是 what，不能用 how。

1.10　我不知道怎麼辦。

✔ I did not know <u>what</u> to do.

✘ I did not know <u>how</u> to do.

> 中文裏的 "怎麼辦"，實際意義是 "做些甚麼"，因此應該用代名詞 what，而不用副詞 how。只有在 "我不知道怎樣來做這件事" 等句子中才說 "I <u>do not know</u> how to do it."。注意：do 後面的賓語 it，與正句中的 what 作用相同。

1.11　他想再學一種樂器。

✔ He wanted to learn <u>another</u> instrument.

✘ He wanted to learn an instrument <u>again</u>.

> 中文裏的 "再" 並不完全等於英語的 again。這裏 "想再學一種樂器" 實際上是指在他已學的樂器之外的另一種樂器，在英語裏應為 another instrument。比較下列中英文句子：
>
> 我想再買本筆記本。
>
> ✔　I want to buy <u>another</u> notebook.
>
> ✘　I want to buy a notebook <u>again</u>.
>
> 我在他論文中又發現了一個錯誤。

> ✔ I found <u>another</u> mistake in his paper.
> ✘ I found a mistake <u>again</u> in his paper.

1.12 你認為哪一個歌星唱得最好？

✔ <u>Which</u> singer do you <u>think</u> is the best?

✘ Do you <u>think which</u> singer is the best?

> 英語中 which singer 似乎是 do you think 的賓語，實則 do you think 是
> 插入語，其他例子如下：
>
> 你以為他喜歡誰？
> <u>Who</u> do you <u>think</u> he likes?
> 你以為我住在哪裏？
> <u>Where</u> do you <u>think</u> I live?
> 你想我昨天在公園裏碰到了誰？
> <u>Whom</u> / Who do you <u>think</u> I met in the park yesterday?

1.13 謝謝你的幫忙。

✔ Thank you <u>for</u> your assistance.

✘ Thank <u>your</u> assistance.

> 感謝的對象是人，不是事，所以應以 you 為賓語。其他如 praise,
> punish, criticize 等詞也可用動詞＋人＋for... 這一種結構。試比較下列
> 中英句子：
>
> 老師稱讚李先生工作做得出色。
> The teacher praised Mr. Li <u>for</u> his excellent work.
> 老師批評他太粗心。
> The teacher criticized him <u>for</u> being too careless.

1.14 他急忙到醫院去。

✔ He hurried <u>to</u> the hospital.

✘ He hurried <u>to go to</u> the hospital.

> hurry 有 "趕着去"、"急忙去" 的意義，所以不必再用 to go。

1.15 她正在做她的工作。

✓ She is doing her job / work.

✗ She is making her job / work.

do 通常含有“做”、“幹”之意；make 含有“製造”之意。前者含義較廣，例如：to do one's homework, to do exercises / one's best 等；to make a mistake / a bookcase / a report / a speech / a bed 等。

1.16 在這場友誼比賽中，我們可以勝過 B 班。

✓ We can win the friendly match with Class B.

✓ We can beat Class B in the friendly match.

✓ We can defeat Class B in the friendly match.

✗ We can win Class B in the friendly match.

✗ We can win over Class B in the friendly match.

win 用作及物動詞是“贏得”，不是“勝過”，可以説 to win a game / a battle / the war / a victory / fame / the first place，但不能以對手作為賓語。win 用作不及物動詞，是“得勝”，如：I win.“我贏了”。to win a person over 意為“把某人爭取過來”。“You have won me.” 意為“你的話使我信服”。

1.17 他喜歡那個女孩子嗎？

是的，他喜歡。

✓ Does he like that girl?

Yes, he likes her.

✓ Does he like that girl?

Yes, he does.

✗ Does he like that girl?

Yes, he likes.

一般疑問句 (interrogative sentence) 的回答有完全和簡略兩種形式，完全回答要回答整個句子，其公式是：

Yes, + 肯定陳述句

No, + 否定陳述句

對行為動詞的一般疑問句的簡略回答是：
Yes, + 主詞 + do / does / did 或其他助動詞
No, + 主詞 + do / does / did + not

助動詞的一般疑問句的簡略回答是：
Yes, + 主詞 + 助動詞
No, + 主詞 + 助動詞 + not

1.18 他們查過你的護照沒有？
　　 是的，剛查過。

✔ Have they checked your passport?
　 Yes, they <u>have</u>.

✘ Have they checked your passport?
　 Yes, <u>just checked</u>.

參見例 1.17。

1.19 王先生不在嗎？
　　 對了，他不在。

✔ Mr. Wang is not here, is he?
　 <u>No</u>, he isn't.

✘ Mr. Wang is not here, is he?
　 <u>Yes</u>, he isn't.

中文裏回答"是"或"否"，須視問句的口氣而決定，但在英語裏，如果回答是肯定的，就用"Yes"，如果回答是否定的，就用"No"，不管問句原來的口氣如何。此外，請讀者特別注意，"is he?"和"isn't he?"之類的句尾附加疑問句 (tag question)，相當於中文的"嗎"或"吧"字，許多書上將之譯為"是嗎？"和"不是嗎？"太過生硬，不妥。

1.20 她今天不離開吧？
　　 不，她會離開的。

✔ She won't leave today, will she?
<u>Yes</u>, she will.

✘ She will not leave today, will she?
<u>No</u>, she will.

> 參見例 1.19。

1.21 爸，把車子借給我好不好？
抱歉，車子不能借你。

✔ Would you mind lending me the car, Dad?
I'm sorry. I <u>can't</u>.

✘ Would you mind lending me the car, Dad?
<u>Yes</u>.

> 以 Do you（或 Would you）mind... 開頭的請求語，如果答語表示拒絕，
> 習慣要用 I am sorry... 如果答語表示應允，就説 Certainly not，或 Of
> course not，或 Not at all。

1.22 澳大利亞的領土約為 7,700,000 平方公里。

✔ Australia <u>has a territory</u> of about 7,700,000 square kilometres.

✘ The <u>territory</u> of Australia <u>is</u> about 7,700,000 square kilometres.

> be 動詞所承接之兩端的名詞意義上通常是相等的，territory 本身不等於
> square kilometres，第二句之 "territory" 若改為 "territorial area"（領土
> 面積）則是自然的句子。

1.23 我們彼此認識很深。

✔ We <u>know each other</u> well.

✘ We <u>each other know</u> well.

> "彼此" 在中文裏是副詞，但在英語裏 each other 是代名詞，只能用作
> 賓語。

1.24 他不論到甚麼地方，總是帶着一把雨傘。

✔ <u>No matter where</u> he goes, he always takes an umbrella.

✔ <u>Wherever</u> he goes, he always takes an umbrella.

✘ <u>No matter wherever</u> he goes, he always takes an umbrella.

> 説 no matter wherever，不合習慣，應説 no matter where, no matter how, no matter what, no matter when...。用了 wherever, however, whenever 等詞，就不用 no matter。試比較：
>
> <u>No matter</u> when you come, I will be waiting for you.
> <u>Whenever</u> you come, I will be waiting for you.

1.25 那天，法國人民的心裏充滿了悲哀。

✔ <u>The hearts</u> of the French people were full of sorrow that day.

✘ <u>In the hearts</u> of the French people were full of sorrow that day.

> 錯句中的 were 沒有主詞，應以 hearts 作主詞，改動句子結構。

1.26 這張桌子的價錢太貴了。

✔ This table is too <u>expensive</u>.

✔ The <u>price</u> of this table is too <u>high</u>.

✘ The <u>price</u> of this table is too <u>expensive</u>.

> 説到東西的貴賤，用 expensive 或 cheap，形容 price 通常用 high 或 low，間或用 dear 形容 price。例如：
>
> Twenty dollars for a pencil? That's too <u>dear</u> (a price)!

1.27 她想再買一輛車子。

✔ She <u>wants</u> to buy another car.

✔ She <u>is thinking</u> of buying another car.

✘ She <u>thinks to</u> buy another car.

> think to 有 intend to 的意思，用在這裏不妥。

1.28 我們星期二考化學。

✔ We <u>will</u> (/ are going to) <u>have a test</u> in chemistry Tuesday.

✔ We <u>are having an</u> <u>examination</u> in chemistry Tuesday.

✘ We<u>'ll examine</u> chemistry Tuesday.

> "參加考試" 美語通常用 have / take an examination, have / take a test；
> 在英國則用 sit for an examination. 但是不能説 *join an examination,
> *join a test。表示老師考學生英文，可以説：
>
> The teacher <u>gave</u> the students <u>a test</u> in English.

1.29 王教授（對學生）講授古代希臘文學。

✔ Professor Wang <u>lectured</u> (to the students) <u>on</u> ancient Greek literature.

✘ Professor Wang <u>lectured the students on</u> ancient Greek literature.

> lecture 為不及物動詞時，作 "講授" 解。lecture 為及物動詞時，作 "訓
> 誡" 解。例如：
>
> The teacher <u>lectured</u> one of his students for his being late.
> The student <u>was lectured</u> for being late.

1.30 他不顧困難把工作完成了。

✔ <u>In spite of</u> difficulties, <u>he</u> got the job done.

✘ <u>He</u> was <u>in spite of</u> difficulties and got the job done.

> heedless of, instead of, in spite of, regardless of, in place of... 等都
> 用作副詞，不用作形容詞。例如：He completed his work <u>in spite of</u>
> difficulties. 不可説 *He was in spite of difficulties and completed his
> work.。

1.31 我臥病三天。

✔ I <u>stayed in</u> bed for three days.

✔ I <u>kept to my</u> bed for three days.

✗ I <u>slept in my</u> bed for three days.

> 動詞 sleep 通常作 "睡眠" 解。例如：
> Usually we sleep eight hours a day.
> "因病臥床" 應用 to stay in bed 或 to keep to one's bed.。

1.32 她夢想總有一天會去巴黎。

✓ She dreamed <u>of going</u> to Paris someday.

✓ She dreamed <u>that</u> some day she <u>would go</u> to Paris.

✗ She dreamed <u>to go</u> to Paris some day.

> 動詞 dream 作 "夢見" 或 "夢想、幻想" 解。後面接 of + 名詞或動名詞，
> 或接用 that 引導的賓語從屬句，但不可以接不定詞。例如：
> I dreamed <u>of</u> revisiting my hometown.
> I dreamed <u>that</u> I revisited my hometown.

1.33 約翰的這個老朋友是個木匠。

✓ This <u>old friend of John's</u> is a carpenter.

✗ This <u>John's old friend</u> is a carpenter.

> 現代英語裏，所有格前面不可用指示形容詞，須仿照 a friend of mine
> 的形式改成 this old friend of John's。參見例 3.23、3.24。

1.34 彼得容易傷風。

✓ Peter <u>catches</u> cold <u>easily</u>.

✓ Peter is <u>liable to</u> colds (/ to catch cold).

✓ Peter is <u>subject to</u> colds.

✗ Peter is <u>easy to catch</u> cold.

> easy 常用於事，可以說 English is easy to learn. 或 It is easy to learn
> English. ，但不可以說 *I am easy to learn English. 。因為 easy 很少用
> 於人，尤其用來指 "容易" 的場合。除非用在 an easy person 中，easy
> 在此意思是 "隨和"。另外，可以說 "It is <u>easy</u> to misuse the article."
> 或 "The article is <u>easily</u> misused." ，不可以說 "*The article is <u>easy</u>

to misuse."。類似的形容詞有 difficult, hard, possible, impossible, dangerous 等。

1.35　他單獨處理這項工作很困難。

✔　It is difficult for him to do this job alone.

✘　He is difficult to do this job alone.

> 參看例 1.34。difficult 用以指人時，作 "執拗的"、"難以應付的"、"易於生氣的" 等解。例如：
>
> He is a rather difficult person to get along with.
> He is difficult to deal with.（他不易對付。）

1.36　那個顧客再也無法掩藏他的怒氣。

✔　The customer could no longer conceal his rage.

✔　It was impossible for the customer to conceal his rage.

✘　The customer was impossible to hide his rage any longer.

> "他不可能（做甚麼）"，英語中不可說 *he was impossible，只能說 he could not (do) 或 it was impossible for him to (do)。impossible 在英語中一般是形容事物，如 "The task / work was impossible."（那任務〔工作〕當時沒有完成的可能）。如果說 "You are impossible." 則只有解釋為 "你這個人簡直不可理喻" 或 "你這個人簡直不可救藥"。"The mistake is simply impossible." 意為 "這個錯誤簡直荒謬"。

1.37　他一個人去爬山很危險。

✔　It is dangerous for him to go mountain climbing alone.

✘　He is dangerous to go mountain climbing alone.

> "危險" 是指 "他一個人去爬山" 這件事。誤句意指 "他本人是危險人物"。

1.38　醫生對他說："你已經沒有危險了。"

✔　The doctor told him,"You are out of danger."

✔　The doctor told him,"You are no longer in danger."

✘　The doctor told him,"You are <u>no longer dangerous.</u>"

> 參看例 1.37。

1.39　我背痛。

✔　I have a <u>pain</u> in my back.

✘　I am <u>painful</u> in my back.

> painful 用於事物，意為 "痛苦的"。例如：
> Did you have a <u>painful</u> experience?
> We are apt to reject <u>painful</u> truths.
> 類似的形容詞有 shameful, dangerous, frightful, wonderful, harmful 等。

1.40　人人都必須為自由而努力。

✔　<u>Every one</u> of us must work hard for freedom.

✔　<u>We</u> must all work hard for freedom.

✘　<u>Everybody all</u> must work hard for freedom.

> everybody 不可與 all 連用。可以説 we all, you all, they all, it all; all of you, all of them, all of it; us all, you all, them all, it all。

1.41　他們個個都説他騙你。

✔　<u>They all</u> say he is lying to you.

✔　<u>All of them</u> say he is lying to you.

✘　<u>Every one of them all</u> says he is lying to you.

> 參見 1.40。

1.42　我太太批評我不應該這麼笨。

✔　My wife criticized my <u>stupidity</u>.

✔　My wife criticized my <u>stupid behaviour</u>.

✔　My wife criticized me <u>for behaving</u> so stupidly.

✘　My wife criticized me <u>that I should not</u> behave so stupidly.

動詞 criticize 的對象一般是人、文章等，不可接以 that 引導的賓語從屬句，也不可接抽象名詞。試比較下列中英句子：

我們批評他不應遲到。
We criticized him for being late.
他批評約翰違反學校紀律。
He criticized John for violating school discipline.

1.43 今年比去年生產更多的糧食。

✔ More grain was grown this year than last year.

✔ This year we grew more grain than last year.

✘ This year will grow more grain than last year.

中文裏的無主詞的句子在英語裏往往用被動語態表達。"今年"在句中作為副詞，不能作主詞。

1.44 為了在最短期間精通日文，他非常用功。

✔ He is working very hard (in order) to master Japanese in the shortest possible time.

✘ He is working very hard for mastering Japanese in the shortest possible time.

用 for + 動名詞表示目的，是不合習慣的，應改用不定詞。請看下列句子：

為了保衛鄉村，農夫們拿起了武器。
The farmers took up arms to defend their village.
為了改進工作，我們修改了部分計劃。
We made some changes in our plan (in order) to improve our work.

for 作 "為了" 解，後面跟名詞則是通順的。例如：

我們為國家建設辛勤工作。
We are working hard for national construction.
我們正在為下一代創造更幸福的生活。
We are building a happier life for our children.

1.45 全校老師領導學生共同打掃校園。

✔ All the teachers led the students <u>in cleaning</u> up the school grounds together.

✘ All the teachers led the students <u>to clean</u> up the school grounds together.

> lead + 賓語（人）+ 不定詞作 " 使人⋯⋯ " 解，例如：What <u>led</u> you to think so?。lead 作 " 領導 " 解時，後接賓語，可用副詞短語修飾，但不接不定詞，如 " 工程師領導我們重建大橋 " 一語不應譯為 *The engineer <u>led</u> us to reconstruct the bridge. ，應改為 The engineer <u>led</u> us in the reconstruction of the bridge. 。

1.46 感謝你的好意，但我不能接受。

✔ I appreciate your kindness, but I cannot <u>accept</u> your <u>offer</u>.

✘ I appreciate your kindness, but I cannot <u>accept</u>.

> accept 是及物動詞，後面通常接賓語。

1.47 她給她叔叔幾塊蛋糕，說：" 你要嗎？剛出爐的。"

✔ She offered her uncle some cakes, saying, "Do you <u>want any</u>? They're hot out of the oven."

✘ She offered her uncle some cakes, saying, "Do you <u>want</u>? They're hot out of the oven."

> 參見例 1.46 。

1.48 他很怕冷。

✔ <u>The cold</u> bothers him.

✔ <u>Cold weather</u> bothers him.

✘ He is <u>afraid of</u> the cold.

> 我們在英漢詞典或中學課本中所看到的英文字詞的中文解釋，和它的英文原義往往只有局部相等。中文的 " 怕 " 只有在表達恐懼時，才能用

fear 或 be afraid of，不能隨便套用，請參考下面兩個例子：

這錶防水。
The watch is <u>waterproof</u>.
我不怕熱。
The heat <u>doesn't bother</u> me.

1.49 這兒交通很方便。

✔ It is quite <u>easy to get anywhere</u> from here.

✘ The traffic is very <u>convenient</u> here.

traffic 主要指的是來往的車輛。關於誤句我們曾經做過一項調查，詢問了十幾位以英語為母語的人士，沒有人懂得誤句的意思。以下是他們的反應："Too weird to understand."、"Not certain."、"Too strange."、"Unintelligible."。經過解釋後，他們表示除了上面所舉的正句外，可視情況說：

<u>Transportation / Travel</u> is convenient here.
The <u>traffic conditions</u> are good.
<u>Getting around</u> is easy.
It's a good location for <u>public transportation</u>.

1.50 增進英文最好的方法之一是遇到生字就查詞典。

✔ One of the best ways to <u>improve</u> your English is to consult the dictionary when you encounter a new word.

✘ One of the best ways to <u>promote / grow</u> your English is to look up the dictionary when you meet a new word.

提高、增強英文能力，要用 improve your English，不能用 promote 或 grow。查字典是 look up the meaning (/ the word) in the dictionary 或 consult the dictionary，不能說 *look up the dictionary。遇到生字可說 come across (/ encounter) a new word，但不能從中文直接翻成 *meet a new word。以上這些錯誤都是由於不了解英文的慣用搭配（collocation）所造成。

Self-test 自測

I.　選出一個正確的答案

1.　吳老師很負責，照顧學生很周到。　(1.1)

Miss Wu is (　　). She takes good care of all her students.

a) responsive　　　b) dutiable　　　c) conscientious　　　d) rigid

2.　芬妮身體不舒服，所以不能來。　(1.2)

Fanny cannot come because she is (　　).

a) uncomfortable　　b) sick　　c) discomfort　　d) not comfortable

3.　這是甚麼顏色？　(1.3)

a) Which is the colour?　　　　b) Which colour is this?
c) What is the colour?　　　　d) What colour is this?

4.　現在是九點鐘。　(1.4)

a) It is nine o'clock now.　　　b) Now is nine o'clock.
c) At present is nine o'clock.　　d) It's at present nine o'clock.

5.　她個子很高。　(1.5)

a) She is very high.　　　　b) She is very tall.
c) Her body is very tall.　　d) She is a high woman.

6.　我能佔用你幾分鐘嗎？　(1.6)

(　　) a few minutes?

a) Can I take you　　　　b) May I occupy you
c) Can you spare (me)　　d) May I use you

7.　讓我想一下。(想一時忘記的人或事物)　(1.7)

Let me (　　).

a) think over　　　b) think it　　　c) think about it　　　d) see

8.　這本書的價錢是多少？　(1.8)

a) How many is this book?
b) How many does this book cost?

c) What is the price of this book?

d) How much is the price of this book?

9. 他想再買一輛自行車。　(1.11)

He feels like buying (　　).

a) another bicycle b) a bicycle again

c) an other bicycle d) a bicycle once more

10. 你認為他的演講怎麼樣？　(1.9)

(　　) his speech?

a) How do you think of b) What do you think of

c) What do you like d) What are your opinion of

11. 你媽媽不在家吧？　(1.19)

對，她不在。

Your mother isn't at home, is she?

(　　).

a) Yes, she isn't. b) Yes, she is.

c) No, she isn't. d) No, she is.

12. 她急忙到車站去。　(1.14)

She hurried (　　) the station.

a) to b) to go to c) going to d) for

13. 他們彼此信任對方。　(1.23)

They (　　).

a) each other trust b) each have trust other in

c) have trust each other d) trust each other

14. 在這場友誼賽中，我們可以勝過 A 班。　(1.16)

We can (　　) Class A in the friendly match.

a) win b) win over c) fight d) beat

15. 她喜歡她的新工作嗎？　(1.17)

是的，她喜歡。

Does she like her new job?

Yes, she (　　).

a) like b) does c) do d) like

16. 他今天不會來這裏吧？ (1.20)

   不，他會來。

   He won't be here today, will he?

   (   ).

   a) Yes, he will.   b) Yes, he won't.

   c) No, he will.   d) No, he will come.

17. 不論你去哪裏，我都要跟着你。 (1.24)

   (   ) you go, I will follow you.

   a) Where   b) No matter wherever

   c) No matter where   d) No matter

18. 你做完你的家庭作業了嗎？ (1.18)

   是的，剛做完。

   Have you finished your homework?

   Yes, (   ).

   a) just finished   b) I have

   c) just have   d) I did

19. 這張桌子的價錢太貴了。 (1.26)

   The price of this table is (   ).

   a) dear over   b) too expensive   c) too much   d) too high

20. 我們星期一考經濟學。 (1.28)

   We'll (   ) Monday.

   a) have a test in economics   b) test economics

   c) examine economics   d) have examination in economics

21. 喬治容易感冒。 (1.34)

   George (   ) catch cold.

   a) is subject to   b) is easy to

   c) is liable to   d) is easily to

22. 珍妮臥病了兩天。 (1.31)

   Jenny (   ) for two days.

   a) stayed in bed   b) kept in her bed

   c) slept in her bed   d) stayed to bed

23. 我夢想有一天能重遊故鄉。　(1.32)

I dreamed (　　　) my hometown.

a) on revisiting　　　　　　　b) of revisiting

c) to revisit　　　　　　　　 d) that I revisit

24. 當我遇到生字的時候就立刻查詞典。　(1.50)

When I (　　) a new word, I (　　) the dictionary at once.

a) meet; look up　　　　　　 b) encounter; consult

c) encounter; look up　　　　 d) meet; consult

25. 老師批評亨利不應遲到。　(1.42)

The teacher criticized Henry (　　　).

a) on being late　　　　　　　b) for being late

c) late　　　　　　　　　　　 d) that he should not be late

26. 他很難抗拒誘惑。　(1.35)

(　　　) to resist the temptation.

a) It is difficult for him　　　　b) He is difficult

c) He is hard　　　　　　　　 d) It is difficult to him

27. 人人都必須為自由而努力。　(1.40)

(　　　) must work hard for freedom.

a) Everybody all　　　　　　 b) Everyone all

c) All we　　　　　　　　　　d) Every one of us

28. 她晚上一個人回家很危險。　(1.37)

(　　　) to go home alone at night.

a) She is dangerous　　　　　 b) It is dangerous to her

c) It is dangerous for her　　　d) She is risky

29. 這裏交通很方便。　(1.49)

(　　　) is very convenient here.

a) The traffic condition　　　　b) The traffic

c) Communion　　　　　　　　d) Transportation

30. 工程師領導我們重建大橋。　(1.45 註)

The engineer led us (　　　) the bridge.

a) in the reconstruction of　　 b) to reconstruct

c) to rebuild　　　　　　　　 d) in construction

31. 是甚麼使你們相信你們會獲得最後的勝利？ (1.45 註)

    What led you (　　) that you would win in the end?

    a) believe　　　b) believing　　　c) in believing　　　d) to believe

32. 為了改進工作，他們修改了部分計劃。 (1.44)

    They made some changes in their plan (　　) their work.

    a) for improving　　　　　　b) to improve
    c) in order to improving　　　d) improving

33. 他們個個都説他對你是忠心耿耿的。 (1.41)

    (　　) he is loyal to you.

    a) All of they say　　　　　　b) Every one of them all says
    c) They all say　　　　　　　d) All of them says

34. 她不顧困難把工作完成了。 (1.30)

    She completed her work (　　) difficulties.

    a) instead of　　　b) in spite of　　　c) heedless to　　　d) in place of

II.　翻譯填空

1. 你認為這部電影怎樣？ (1.9)

   (　　) do you like the movie?
   = (　　) do you think of the movie?

2. 謝謝你的幫助。 (1.13)

   Thank you (　　) your assistance.

3. 李老師很負責，每天都準時到學校。 (1.1)

   Mr. Lee is (　　). He comes to school on time
   every day.

4. 在這場友誼賽中，我們可以勝過 B 班。 (1.16)

   We can (　　) Class B in the friendly match.

5. 他很怕冷。 (1.48)

   The cold (　　) him.

6. 我不知道怎麼辦。 (1.10)

I did not know (　　) to do.

7. 她身體不舒服，所以不能來。　(1.2)

He cannot come because she is (　　).

She cannot come because she is (　　).

8. 讓我想一想。(表示考慮)　(1.7)

Let me think (　　) it.

= Let me think it (　　).

9. 你認為哪一個歌星唱得最好？　(1.12)

Which singer (　　) you (　　) is the best?

10. 他想再學一種樂器。　(1.11)

He wanted to learn (　　) instrument.

11. 他不顧困難，把工作完成了。　(1.30)

In (　　) of difficulties, he got the job done.

12. 增進英文最好的方法之一是遇到生字就查詞典。　(1.50)

One of the best ways to (　　) your English is to (　　)
the dictionary when you (　　) a new word.

13. 我能佔用你幾分鐘嗎？　(1.6)

Can you (　　) (me) a few minutes?

14. 這輛車價錢多少？　(1.8)

How (　　) is the car?

= How (　　) does the car (　　)?

= What is the (　　) of the car?

15. 王先生不在吧？

對，他不在。　(1.19)

Mr. Wang isn't here, is he?

(　　), he (　　).

16. 她今天不離開吧？

不，她會離開的。　(1.20)

She won't leave today, will she?

(　　), she (　　).

17. 他不論到甚麼地方，總是帶着一把雨傘。 (1.24)

    (　　) (　　) where he goes, he always takes an umbrella.

    = (　　) he goes, he always takes an umbrella.

18. 這張桌子的價錢太貴了。 (1.26)

    The price of this table is too (　　).

    = The table is too (　　).

19. 王教授講授古代希臘文學。 (1.29)

    Professor Wang (　　) (　　) ancient Greek literature.

20. 我臥病了三天。 (1.31)

    I stayed (　　) bed for three days.

    = I kept (　　) my bed for three days.

21. 她夢想總有一天會去巴黎。 (1.32)

    She dreamed (　　) (　　) to Paris someday.

22. 傑克容易傷風感冒。 (1.34)

    Jack (　　) (　　) easily.

    = Jack is (　　) (　　) colds.

    = Jack is (　　) (　　) colds.

23. 那個顧客再也無法掩藏他的怒氣。 (1.36)

    The customer (　　) no longer conceal his rage.

24. 他一個人去爬山很危險。 (1.37)

    (　　) is dangerous (　　) (　　) to go mountain climbing alone.

25. 醫生對他說：“你已經沒有危險了。” (1.38)

    The doctor told him, "You are (　　) (　　) danger."

    = The doctor told him, "You are no longer (　　) danger."

26. 我背痛。 (1.39)

    I (　) a pain (　　) my back.

27. 我太太批評我不應該這麼笨。 (1.42)

    My wife criticized me (　　) behaving so (　　).

28. 全校老師領導學生共同打掃校園。 (1.45)

All the teachers (　　　) the students (　　　) cleaning up the school grounds together .

III. 改錯

1. Miss Lin is <u>conscious</u>. She comes to <u>school</u> <u>on time</u> every day. (1.1)
   　　　　　　　A　　　　　　　　　　B　　　C

   (　　　)＿＿＿＿＿＿＿

2. She cannot <u>come</u> to class <u>because</u> she is <u>not comfortable</u>. (1.2)
   　　　　　　A　　　　　　B　　　　　　　　C

   (　　　)＿＿＿＿＿＿＿

3. He <u>hurried</u> to <u>go to</u> the <u>hospital</u>. (1.14)
   　　　A　　　　B　　　　C

   (　　　)＿＿＿＿＿＿＿

4. We can <u>win</u> Class B <u>in</u> the <u>friendly</u> match. (1.16)
   　　　　　A　　　　　B　　　C

   (　　　)＿＿＿＿＿＿＿

5. <u>Have</u> they <u>checked</u> your passport?
   　A　　　　　B
   Yes, <u>just checked</u>. (1.18)
   　　　　　C

   (　　　)＿＿＿＿＿＿＿

6. The <u>territory</u> of Australia <u>is</u> about 7,700,000 <u>square</u> kilometres. (1.22)
   　　　A　　　　　　　　　B　　　　　　　　C

   (　　　)＿＿＿＿＿＿＿

7. <u>In the hearts</u> of the French people were <u>full of</u> sorrow <u>that day</u>. (1.25)
   　　A　　　　　　　　　　　　　　　B　　　　　C

   (　　　)＿＿＿＿＿＿＿

8. She <u>dreamed</u> <u>to go</u> to Paris <u>someday</u>. (1.32)
   　　　A　　　B　　　　　C

   (　　　)＿＿＿＿＿＿＿

9. The <u>customer</u> <u>was impossible</u> to hide <u>his rage</u> any longer. (1.36)
   　　　A　　　　B　　　　　　　　C

   (　　　)＿＿＿＿＿＿＿

10. He <u>is working</u> very hard <u>for mastering</u> Japanese in the shortest
        A   B
    <u>possible</u> time. (1.44)
        C
    (   )_____

IV. 請改正下列句子的錯誤

1. How much is the price of the car? (1.8)
2. He wanted to learn an instrument again. (1.11)
3. Let me think over. (1.7)
4. I appreciate your kindness, but I cannot accept. (1.46)
5. Now is three o'clock. (1.4)
6. How do you think of the movie? (1.9)
7. We'll examine chemistry Tuesday. (1.28)
8. His body is very tall. (1.5)
9. Does he like that girl?
    Yes, he likes. (1.17)
10. She is making her work. (1.15)
11. We each other know well. (1.23)
12. Professor Lee lectured the students on ancient Greek literature. (1.29)
13. The traffic is very convenient here. (1.49)
14. My wife criticized me that I should not behave so stupidly. (1.42)
15. This John's old friend is a carpenter. (1.33)
16. Andrew is easy to catch cold. (1.34)
17. The price of this table is too expensive. (1.26)
18. He is difficult to do this job alone. (1.35)
19. He was in spite of difficulties and got the job done. (1.30)
20. Thank your assistance. (1.13)

2 Sentences 句法

i. Agreement 一致關係

2.1　你哥哥住在舊金山嗎？

✔ <u>Does</u> your brother live in San Francisco?

✘ <u>Do</u> your brother live in San Francisco?

> 此句的主語是 brother，是第三人稱單數，一般現在式助動詞應該用 does。

2.2　幫助鄰居是每一個人的責任。

✔ It is everyone's duty to help <u>his or her</u> neighbour.

✘ It is everyone's duty to help <u>their</u> neighbour.

> everyone 是單數，在正式的寫作裏所有格以用單數為宜。

2.3　我們會發給大家識別證。

✔ We'll give each of you <u>a badge</u>.

✘ We'll give each of you <u>badges</u>.

> 代名詞 each 是單數，所以 badge 該用單數。

2.4　他們兩人都會做。

✔ Either of them <u>is</u> capable of doing this.

✘ Either of them <u>are</u> capable of doing this.

> either 指兩者之一，是單數，所以動詞該用單數。

2.5　他倆誰都不該責怪。

✔ Neither of them <u>is</u> to blame.

✘ Neither of them <u>are</u> to blame.

neither 指 "既不是這個，也不是那個"，是單數，動詞該用單數。

2.6 有人忘了關煤氣。

✔ Somebody <u>has</u> forgotten to turn off the gas.

✘ Somebody <u>have</u> forgotten to turn off the gas.

somebody 是單數，動詞該用單數。

2.7 屋子裏有幾張吸引人的畫。

✔ There <u>are</u> several attractive paintings in this room.

✘ There <u>is</u> several attractive paintings in this room.

帶有引導詞 there 的句子，單複數的形式決定於動詞後面的名詞，因為它是句中真正的主語。如果名詞是複數，動詞應該用 are 或 were。當兩個或兩個以上的單數主語用 and 連接時，或第一個主語是單數時，通常用 there is。例如：

There were two pencils and a notebook on the table.

There was a notebook and three pencils on the table.

2.8 全國人民哀悼他們死去的英雄。

✔ The whole nation mourned <u>its</u> dead heroes.

✘ The whole nation mourned <u>their</u> dead heroes.

"nation" 是一個整體，代名詞所有格須用所有格單數。

2.9 我們這樣做有益於我們的健康。

✔ What we are doing <u>is</u> good for our health.

✘ What we are doing <u>are</u> good for our health.

以關係代名詞 what 引導的作為主語的子句，動詞一概用單數。如：
<u>What</u> he said is true.。

2.10 七減四是三。

✔ Seven minus four <u>is</u> three.

✘ Seven minus four <u>are</u> three.

> minus 是介詞，Seven minus four 後面的動詞一般用單數。同樣 What <u>is</u> twice three? 以及 Five plus three <u>is</u> eight. 動詞也用單數。

2.11 能做的事都做了。

✔ All that could be done <u>has</u> been done.

✘ All that could be done <u>have</u> been done.

> all 指事情或抽象概念時當作單數。例如：
>
> <u>All</u> is well that ends well.
> （結果好就是好的。）
> <u>All</u> is over with him.
> （他已經沒希望了。）
> That's <u>all</u> for today.
> （今天到此為止。）
>
> all 指人時應當作複數。例如：
>
> <u>All</u> of us are interested in his proposal.
> <u>All</u> of us are doing our best.

2.12 錢已經用了一半。

✔ Half of the money <u>is</u> gone.

✘ Half of the money <u>are</u> gone.

> Half of... 作主語時，動詞與介詞 of 後面的名詞或代名詞相一致，即名詞或代名詞是單數時，動詞該是單數；若為複數，則動詞也該是複數，例如：
>
> <u>Half of</u> the story is interesting.
> <u>Half of</u> the stories are interesting.
> <u>Half of</u> it is interesting.
> <u>Half of</u> them are interesting.

2.13 許多人走過這條路。

✔ Many a man <u>has</u> travelled this road.

✘ Many a man <u>have</u> travelled this road.

> many a 意義上雖然作 many 解，但後面應跟單數名詞，動詞也是單數。

2.14 敵人被迫投降。

✔ The enemy <u>were</u> forced to surrender.

✔ The enemy <u>was</u> forced to surrender. (美式英語)

> 敵人作為總稱，前面必須有定冠詞，作為句中的主語時，動詞通常用複數形式，但美語中動詞用單數亦很普遍。

ii.　Co-ordination 句子的連接

2.15 他走出門，左右看一下，就過了馬路。

✔ He walked outside, looked left and right, <u>and</u> crossed the road.

✘ He walked outside <u>and</u> looked left and right, crossed the road.

> 並列連接詞 and 在這句中連接三個述語。一般的結構是 x, y, and z。x and y and z 是加強語氣的結構。x, y, z 極少見。x and y, z 是不可以的。

2.16 他們知道自己的弱點以及如何趕上其他競爭者。

✔ They saw where their weak points lay and <u>how they could</u> catch up with the other competitors.

✘ They saw where their weak points lay and <u>how to</u> catch up with the other competitors.

> and 一般連接同等的成分，即結構相等的單詞、短語或子句。誤句中 and 的前面是子句，後面是不定詞短語，兩者成分不同，不能用 and 連接，必須把不定詞短語改為子句，and 前後的結構就相等了。

2.17 從他的口音判斷，他一定是德州人。

✔ Judging by / from his accent, he must be from Texas.

✘ Judging by / from his accent <u>that</u> he must be from Texas.

> Judging by / from his accent 是獨立成分，用逗號與獨立子句分開。其他類似的獨立成分有 honestly / generally / strictly speaking 等。

2.18 當時他只曉得叔叔是錯的。

✔ At that time all he knew was <u>that</u> his uncle was wrong.

✘ At that time all he knew was his uncle was wrong.

> 連接詞 that 引導賓語從屬句時可以省略，引導作為補語的從屬句通常不省略。例如：
>
> The fact was <u>that</u> both of them were sick.
> What I heard was <u>that</u> he would soon be back at work.
>
> 當主語是 fact 時，在口語化的結構中 that 往往省略。例如：
>
> The <u>fact</u> is, I have no idea.
> All I know is, he likes it.
>
> 注意：is 後面有逗點。

2.19 她坐上計程車，直接到機場。

✔ She took a cab, <u>which</u> took her straight to the airport.

✔ She took a cab <u>and it</u> took her straight to the airport.

✘ She took a cab, <u>and which</u> took her straight to the airport.

> She took a cab 是主句，which took her straight to the airport 是從屬句，which 已經是連接詞，不能再用 and 連接。下列句子的錯誤屬同類性質：
>
> 昨天我去看一位朋友，他借我這張唱片。
>
> ✔ I went to visit a friend yesterday <u>and</u> he lent me this record.
> ✔ Yesterday I went to visit a friend, <u>who</u> lent me this record.
> ✘ I went to visit a friend yesterday <u>and who</u> lent me this record.
>
> 第二句裏的 who lent me this record 是非限定（non-restrictive）附屬子句，即附加補充說明的，因此與主要子句間要用逗點分開，以下是含有

限定附屬子句的句子，who 之前不用逗點：

Yesterday I went to see a friend who just came back from England.
（昨天我去看一位剛從英國回來的朋友。）

2.20 我們一位鄰居，她是律師，進來閒談了一會兒。

✔ Our neighbour, who is a lawyer, dropped in for a chat.

✔ Our neighbour, a lawyer, dropped in for a chat.

✘ Our neighbour she is a lawyer, dropped in for a chat.

有修飾作用的從屬句應用關係代名詞與主句連接，不能用人稱代名詞連接，但可把從屬句改為同位語，如第二句。

2.21 和別人告訴我們的正相反，他不大會彈鋼琴。

✔ Contrary to what we were told, he isn't a good pianist.

✘ Contrary to that we were told, he isn't a good pianist.

what = that which，作 were told 的主語，what 所引導的從屬句又作 contrary to 的賓語。that 引導名詞性從屬句，是連接詞，在從屬句中不起其他作用。觀察下列句中 what 的作用，都不可改作 that：

I don't know what happened.
He is not what he used to be.

2.22 這一章描寫牧人們怎樣在草原上跟自然搏鬥。

✔ This chapter describes how the shepherd struggled with nature on the grasslands.

✘ This chapter describes how the shepherd to struggled with nature on the grasslands.

賓語從屬句中動詞不能用不定詞表示，必須把 to struggle 改為 struggled。疑問副詞 how, when, where, why 等可以跟不定詞構成不定式短語，作為句中主語、賓語、補語等作用。例如：

He showed me how to use a compass.
Where to go is the question that puzzles all.

> The point is <u>when</u> to start the work.

2.23 我昨天看的書很有教育意義。

✔ The book I <u>read yesterday</u> is very instructive.

✘ <u>Yesterday</u> I <u>read</u> the book is very instructive.

> 中文裏的 "書" 是句子的主語,"昨天我們看的" 用以修飾 "書",在英語中應以 "書" 在前,後接限定性形容詞子句。

2.24 我常常想起那些不幸的同胞。

✔ I often think of / about those people in our country <u>who</u> are leading a miserable life.

✘ I often think of those people in our country are leading a miserable life.

> to think of / about 作 "想到"、"思及"、"念及" 解,後面接名詞、名詞短語或用疑問詞 (who, what 等) 引導的名詞從屬句。to think 接 that 引導的從屬句,沒有 of,作 "以為"、"認為"、"相信" 等解。例如:
>
> I <u>think that</u> many people in our country are less fortunate than myself.

2.25 大家同意他的建議:在下星期舉行一次派對。

✔ Everyone agreed to his suggestion <u>that</u> we (should) have a party next week.

✘ Everyone agreed to his suggestion <u>which</u> we should have a party next week.

> "下星期舉行一次派對" 是同位語從屬句 (appositive clause)。同位語從屬句主要用連接詞 that 引導,尤其是在 fact 和 suggestion 之後。另外也有用疑問詞 how, when, where, why, what, which 等引導的。例如:
>
> I have an idea <u>that</u> he will not come tomorrow.
> He has no idea <u>how</u> he is going to do it.
> I have no idea <u>when</u> he will be ready.
> There arose the question <u>which</u> way we should take.

> 注意以下兩句中 which 的句法功能與誤句中 which 的差異：
> a.　Everyone agreed to the proposal <u>which</u> Mr. Li put forth at the meeting.
> b.　Everyone agreed to the proposal <u>that</u> we (should) have an outing this weekend.
> a 句中的 which 子句是限定性形容詞子句，用來指明是哪個 proposal。
> b 句中的 that 子句是 the proposal 的同位語從屬子句，說明此 proposal 的內容。
> 另外，同位語從屬句中的動詞可用原形或原形前加 should。

2.26　我們必須修改原定本月完成這項方案的計劃。

✔　We'll have to revise the plan <u>that</u> we complete this project this month.

✘　We'll have to revise the plan <u>which</u> we complete this project this month.

> 參見例 2.25。

2.27　我們最小的女兒瑪麗成為一個聰明勇敢的女子。

✔　Mary, our youngest daughter, grew into an intelligent and brave woman.

✘　Mary, our youngest daughter, <u>she</u> grew into an intelligent and brave woman.

> Mary...she... 等主語重疊在中文裏偶或出現，但在英語中每個句子一般只有一個主語。

2.28　我父親是退休教師，他和兩個朋友開始做生意。

✔　My father, a retired teacher, and two of his friends launched a business.

✘　My father, a retired teacher, <u>he</u> and two of his friends launched a business.

參見例 2.27。

2.29 是殖民者來美洲破壞了美洲印地安人的文化。

✔ It was the colonists <u>that</u> came to America and destroyed the American Indians' civilization.

✘ It was the colonists came to America and destroyed the American Indians' civilization.

強調句中的主語、賓語或副詞最常用的方法是改成 It is...that... 的結構。被強調部分，就放在 It is 之後，其餘的部分放在 that 之後。若是將 that 省略則不合文法，因該句將多出一個動詞來。縱使 It is 之後的名詞是人，最好還是用 that，不要用 who。

It was my uncle <u>that</u> brought us this happy life.
（強調 My uncle brought us this happy life. 句中的主語。）
It was after independence <u>that</u> we led a happy life.
（強調 We led a happy life after independence. 句中的副詞。）

2.30 只有專家才能做這件事。

✔ Only specialists can do this.

✔ <u>It is</u> only specialists <u>that / who</u> can do this.

✘ <u>It is</u> only specialists can do this.

參見例 2.29。

2.31 我們打算買你去年住過的房子。

✔ We will buy the house where you lived last year.

✘ We will buy the house where you lived <u>there</u> last year.

用關係副詞 where 引導有修飾限定作用的從屬句，where 即是從屬連接詞，又是副詞，説明地點，因此不能再用副詞 there。

2.32 我那天買的微波爐花了我六百塊錢。

✔ The microwave oven that I bought the other day cost me six hundred dollars.

✘ The microwave oven that I bought the other day <u>it</u> cost me six hundred dollars.

> 關係代名詞 that 在句中有雙重作用，即連接主要及從屬句，本身又在從屬句中兼作主語或賓語。因此從屬句中出現的 it 是多餘的，應該刪去。句中的關係代名詞 that 在口語中通常也都省略。

2.33 他打了她，因此感到很羞愧。

✔ He was ashamed <u>that</u> he had hit her.

✔ He was ashamed <u>to</u> have hit her.

✔ He was ashamed <u>of</u> hitting (/ having hit) her.

✘ He was ashamed <u>of that</u> he had hit her.

> to be ashamed of 後面跟名詞，或用 what 引導的從屬句，如：He <u>is ashamed of</u> what he has done.；不能直接跟用 that 引導的從屬句，應刪去 of，或直接把 mistake 作 of 的賓語，同時變換句子的結構。例如：
>
> He <u>is ashamed that</u> he has made such a mistake.
> He <u>is ashamed of</u> the mistake he made.

2.34 我們因賽跑贏得冠軍而感到自豪。

✔ We are proud <u>that</u> we won first place in the race.

✔ We are proud <u>of</u> having won first place in the race.

✔ We are proud <u>to</u> have won first place in the race.

✘ We are proud <u>of that</u> we have won first place in the race.

> 參見例 2.33。

2.35 我怕明天會下雪。

✔ I am afraid <u>that</u> it will snow tomorrow.

✘ I am afraid <u>of</u> that it will snow tomorrow.

> 參見例 2.33。

2.36 起初我發覺這書很難懂。

✔ At first I found it very difficult to understand this book.

✘ At first I found very difficult to understand this book.

> 當複合賓語中第一部分不是一個名詞或代名詞而是一個不定詞、動名詞或從屬句時，通常要用 it 代替它，把這不定詞、動名詞或從屬句放在句尾。這裏 it 代替不定詞短語 to understand this book。

2.37 我覺得要我們兩人合作是不可能的。

✔ I felt it impossible for us to work together.

✘ I felt impossible for us to work together.

> it 代替不定詞複合結構 for us to work together。參見例 2.36。

2.38 他沒來，你不覺得奇怪嗎？

✔ Don't you think it strange that he didn't come?

✘ Don't you think strange that he didn't come?

> it 代替 that he didn't come，參見例 2.36。

2.39 她嫁給他，你覺得奇怪嗎？

✔ Do you think it strange that she should marry him?

✘ Do you think strange that she should marry him?

> it 代替從屬句 that she should marry him。參見例 2.36。

2.40 我講明白，每星期五都有一次測驗。

✔ I made it very clear that there would be a test every Friday.

✘ I made very clear that there would be a test every Friday.

> it 代替從屬句 that there would be a test every Friday。參見例 2.36。

2.41 資訊產業是本國經濟的基礎,這一點大家已有認識。

✔ As everyone admits, IT industry is the foundation of our nation's economy.

✘ As everyone admits <u>that</u> IT industry is the foundation of our nation's economy.

> 這裏 as 作關係代名詞,引導從屬子句。誤句把 IT industry is... 改成從屬句,使全句缺了主句,結構上錯誤。又如:
>
> <u>As</u> my friend pointed out, necessity is the mother of invention.
> <u>As</u> is known to all, grammar is not the only important thing in language study.

2.42 這本新書已經銷售一空,令他大為驚訝。

✔ To his great surprise, every copy of this newly-published book has been sold out.

✘ To his great surprise <u>that</u> every copy of this newly-published book has been sold out.

> 錯句中沒有獨立子句,應把 that 刪去。to his great surprise 是結果副詞。類似的結構有:to one's joy / sorrow / grief / disappointment / astonishment / embarrassment 等。

2.43 這狗好像懂得人話似的。

✔ The dog <u>looks as if</u> it understood speech.

✘ <u>As if</u> the dog understands speech.

> as if 是從屬連接詞,後面接從屬句,構成表示比較的副詞從屬句,不是一個完整的句子。必須加上一個主句 the dog looks,才能表達完整的思想。因為狗懂人話與事實不符,所以用過去式。

iii.　Word order 詞序

2.44 她心情總是非常好。

✔ She <u>is always</u> in a good mood.

✘ She <u>always is</u> in a good mood.

> always, often 一般放在行為動詞之前，連繫動詞、助動詞之後：
>
> He <u>always</u> behaves well.
>
> He is <u>always</u> happy and gay.
>
> He is <u>always</u> reading.
>
> 其他用法類似的副詞，還有 still、also、hardly、seldom、never 等。

2.45 你看！他還在寫信呢。

✔ Look! He <u>is still</u> writing letters.

✘ Look! He <u>still is</u> writing letters.

> still 用作修飾行為動詞當副詞時，其位置與 also 相同。試觀察下列句子並與中文作比較：
>
> He <u>still</u> remains here.
>
> He is <u>still</u> reading that novel.
>
> He is <u>still</u> very healthy.

2.46 由於腦部受傷的結果，他甚至不記得自己的名字。

✔ As a result of brain injury, he <u>cannot even</u> remember his own name.

✘ As a result of brain injury, he <u>even cannot</u> remember his own name.

> even 若用作修飾動詞時，放在行為動詞之前，但放在連繫動詞、助動詞之後。試比較：
>
> He <u>even</u> forgot his own address.
>
> He did not <u>even</u> know the first thing about integrals.
>
> She cannot <u>even</u> remember her own birthday.

2.47 下面的聲明，他看了沒有？

✔ Did he read the <u>statement below</u>?

✘ Did he read the <u>below statement</u>?

> the above statement 很普通，但不可説 *the below statement，只可以
> 説 the statement below 或 the following statement。

2.48 我不夠快。

✔ I wasn't <u>fast enough</u>.

✘ I wasn't <u>enough fast</u>.

> enough 用作副詞時，一般放在它修飾的形容詞或其他副詞後面。例如：
> The tea is hot <u>enough</u>.
> （茶是夠熱。）
> He did not work hard <u>enough</u>.
> （他不夠用功。）
> 但 enough 用作形容詞時，前置或後置都可以。例如：
> There is <u>enough</u> food (/ food enough) for us.

2.49 今晚七時我們將開董事會。

✔ We are having a board meeting <u>at seven o'clock this evening</u>.

✔ We are having a board meeting <u>this evening, at seven o'clock</u>.

✘ We are having a board meeting <u>this evening at seven o'clock</u>.

> 如果有幾個時間副詞，按照一般規則，單位大的應放在單位小的後面。
> 例如：
> I was born <u>in May 1939</u>.
> The meeting was held <u>at five o'clock yesterday afternoon</u>.
> 但如果小的單位是後來想起來的，則放在後面。例如：
> He arrived <u>yesterday afternoon, at about five o'clock</u>.
> （注意：afternoon 後面有逗號，表示有停頓。）

2.50 我生於麻州波士頓。

✔ I was born in <u>Boston, Massachusetts</u>.

✘ I was born in <u>Massachusetts, Boston</u>.

按照一般規則，地點副詞的位置，範圍大的應放在範圍小的後面。例如：

Before 1949 I lived in <u>a small cottage in Keelung</u>.

This machine was made <u>in Thailand</u>.

但有時為求句子結構均衡起見，範圍小的也可以放在後面。例如：

They spent the summer holidays <u>in Keelung in a large house near the beach</u>.

2.51　我昨天在維多利亞公園遇見你的一位同事。

✔　I met a colleague of yours in <u>Victoria Park</u> <u>yesterday</u>.

✔　<u>Yesterday</u> I met a colleague of yours in <u>Victoria Park</u>.

✘　I met a colleague of yours <u>yesterday</u> in <u>Victoria Park</u>.

時間副詞常放在句尾或句首。

2.52　他是一個有名的中國作家。

✔　He is a <u>famous Chinese</u> writer.

✘　He is a <u>Chinese famous</u> writer.

一個名詞有幾個修飾詞時，在句中的順序應遵從習慣。Chinese 靠近名詞，China's 離名詞最遠，如 China's territorial rights、ancient Chinese history，又如 a distinguished Japanese writer（一個日本優秀作家）不説 *a Japanese distinguished writer。

2.53　我明白了，原來如此。

✔　(Oh,) I see.

✔　<u>So</u> I see.

✘　I see <u>so</u>.

可以説：I believe so.

但不説：I see (/ notice) so. 應改作 So I see.

2.54　他們假裝不知道那件事。

✔　They pretended <u>not to</u> know about it.

✔ They pretended <u>that</u> they didn't know about it.

✘ They pretended <u>to not</u> know about it.

> not 和 never 通常放在不定詞的前面。例如：
>
> I told him <u>not</u> to waste my time.
> I left early so as <u>not</u> to miss the plane.
> I trained myself <u>never</u> to lose my temper.

2.55 他認為自己很誠實。

✔ He considered himself to <u>be strictly honest</u>.

✘ He considered himself to <u>strictly be honest</u>.

> strictly 在句中修飾 honest，不是修飾 be honest，因此不應放在 to be 之間，而且不定詞 to be 中間也不可以插入其他字。正句中的 to be 可省略。

2.56 以前沒見過他，我當然認不出他。

✔ <u>Not having</u> met him before, of course I did not recognize him.

✔ <u>As</u> I <u>had not</u> met him before, of course I did not recognize him.

✘ <u>Having not</u> met him before, I of course did not recognize him.

> 不可以説 *having not，該説 not having；也不可以説 *being not，該説 not being。例如：
>
> <u>Not having</u> received an answer, he wrote again. (或 <u>Having</u> received no answer, he wrote again.)

2.57 你們應該把它鎖起來。

✔ You should lock <u>it up</u>.

✘ You should lock <u>up it</u> .

> 我們可以説：We must <u>lock up</u> the house. 或 We must <u>lock</u> the house <u>up</u>.。但賓語是代名詞時，只可以説：We must <u>lock</u> it <u>up</u>.。同一類型的句子如下：

Hand it over.	Put it on.	Take it down.
Turn it on.	Turn it up.	

2.58 只有這樣，他才能確定他們不會傷害他。

✔ Only by so doing <u>could he</u> be sure (that) they wouldn't harm him.

✘ Only by so doing <u>he could</u> be sure (that) they wouldn't harm him.

> 用 only by + 動名詞句型時，主語與動詞要倒置。

2.59 他們只有推翻極權制度，才能恢復自己的權利。

✔ Only by overthrowing the totalitarian system <u>will they</u> be able to regain their rights.

✘ Only by overthrowing the totalitarian system <u>they will</u> be able to regain their rights.

> 參見例 2.58。

2.60 煽動份子以為這樣就能摧殘波蘭人民的民主了。

✔ The demagogues thought that by so doing <u>they could</u> trample on the democratic rights of the Polish people.

✘ The demagogues thought that by so doing <u>could they</u> trample on the democratic rights of the Polish people.

> 只有用 only by + 動名詞短語時才需要顛倒主述語次序；如單用 by + 動名詞短語，就不必倒置。

2.61 他體力很弱，不能做粗重工作。

✔ <u>As</u> he was <u>weak</u> in health, he could not do heavy work.

✘ <u>Weak as</u> he was in health, he could not do heavy work.

as 作連接詞，表示 "因為" 時，絕不能倒置，習慣上以 as 引導的詞序倒置的從屬句，是用來強調兩種意義相反的情況。例如：

Strong <u>as</u> he was, he could not lift that rock.
（儘管他的身體強壯，他還是舉不起那塊石頭。）
Weak <u>as</u> he was, he lifted that rock easily.
（儘管他身體很弱，他還是能不費力地舉起那塊石頭。）

2.62 母親在我書桌上放了些水果，我下班後就把它們吃了。

✔ <u>After work</u>, I ate the fruit which my mother put on my desk.

✘ My mother put some fruit on my desk which I ate <u>after work</u>.

作限定形容詞從屬子句應盡可能緊接所修飾的先行詞。

2.63 在落後國家裏，有很多婦女遭到這樣悲慘的結局。

✔ <u>In underdeveloped countries</u> there are many women who end up in similar tragic ways.

✔ There are many women <u>in underdeveloped countries</u> who end up in similarly tragic ways.

✘ There are many women who end up similarly tragic ways <u>in underdeveloped countries</u>.

錯句中把 in underdeveloped countries 放在限定性形容詞子句之末，易使人誤解為修飾 end up，因此應放在句首或緊接修飾的對象。

2.64 在極權國家裏，統治者甚麼都有，老百姓甚麼都沒有。

✔ <u>In totalitarian states</u> the rulers have everything, but the common people have nothing.

✔ The rulers have everything <u>in totalitarian states</u>, but the common people have nothing.

✘ The rulers have everything but the common people have nothing <u>in totalitarian states</u>.

"在極權國家裏"修飾"統治者……",也修飾"老百姓……"。第一個錯句 in totalitarian states 只修飾 the rulers have everything；第二個錯句 in totalitarian states 又好像只修飾 the common people have nothing，必須把這一修飾語放在句首，才不致影響句子思想內容的正確性。

2.65 我清楚記得我第一次去海邊的事。

✓ I remember <u>well the first time</u> I went to the beach.

✗ I remember <u>the first time</u> I went to the beach <u>well</u>.

well 放在句末，易使人誤會為修飾 went；如放在 the first time 後會把形容詞子句與先行詞分隔，因此應放在 the first time 前面。如果要使語勢更為強調，可以説 Well do I remember...

2.66 他昨天告訴我們，他已經寫完了他的第一本書。

✓ He told us <u>yesterday</u> that he had finished writing his first book.

✓ <u>Yesterday</u> he told us that he had finished writing his first book.

✗ He told us that he had finished writing his first book <u>yesterday</u>.

按一般規律，時間副詞應放在句末。但本句如把 yesterday 放在句末，會使人誤解為 yesterday 修飾從句中的 had finished。為了不致與原意不合，yesterday 可以放在中間或句首。

2.67 從他的談吐中，我們可以看出他是個受過良好教育的人。

✓ We can tell <u>from his speech</u> that he is a well-educated man.

✓ <u>From his speech</u> we can tell that he is a well-educated man.

✗ We can tell that he is a well-educated man <u>from his speech</u>.

第三句不算錯，但 from his speech 放在句末，易被人誤解為修飾從屬句中的動詞，最好放在句首或主句動詞之後。

2.68 他訪問澳洲時印象最深的是澳洲人民的環保意識。

✓ What impressed him most <u>when he visited</u> Australia was the people's awareness of the importance of environmental protection.

✘ What impressed him most was the people's awareness of the importance of environmental protection <u>when he visited</u> Australia.

> 參見例 2.65、2.66、2.67。

2.69 我不明白你為甚麼不信任他。

✔ I don't understand why <u>you don't</u> trust him.

✘ I don't understand why <u>don't you</u> trust him.

> why, what, how, when 所引導的疑問性賓語從屬句的詞序與一般陳述句相同，不能以問句的詞序出現。

2.70 我不懂為甚麼你這樣做。

✔ I don't understand why <u>you are</u> doing it this way.

✘ I don't understand why <u>are you</u> doing it this way.

> 參見例 2.69。

2.71 消息傳來，我們的人員受困在海灘。

✔ The news <u>came</u> that our men were stranded on the beaches.

✘ The news that our men were stranded on the beaches <u>came</u>.

> "that..." 這一同位語從屬句，按常例應緊接被它所說明的詞 the news，但這裏從屬句過長，把主語與動詞隔得太遠，而主句中的動詞又僅僅是 came 一個字，讀來非常不順，遇到這種情況，要把從屬句往後移。

2.72 謠傳他中了大獎。

✔ Rumour <u>has it</u> that he won a grand prize.

✘ The rumour that he won a grand prize runs.

> 參見例 2.71。

2.73 他到這裏不是來幫你的。

✔ He did <u>not</u> come <u>here</u> to help you.

✘ He came <u>here</u> not to help you.

> 按習慣用法，這裏 not 應與助動詞 did 結合。正句也可理解為 "他沒有來這裏幫你"。只有在含有對照的敍述中，才用其他否定形式。如：
>
> He came here <u>not</u> to ask for your help, but to give you some information.（對照）
>
> In any discussion, we should start <u>not</u> from definitions, but from actual facts.（對照）

iv. Direct and indirect speech 直接引語和間接引語

2.74 她說她很高興認識我。

✔ She said <u>that</u> she was glad to meet me.

✔ She said<u>,</u> "I am glad to meet you."

✘ She said <u>that</u> "<u>she</u> was glad to meet me."

> 間接引語不用引號，引號只用於直接引語。

2.75 聽了這話，那人笑說：" 你弄錯了。"

✔ On hearing this, the man said, laughing, "<u>You</u> are mistaken."

✘ On hearing this, the man said, laughing, <u>you</u> are mistaken.

> you are mistaken 是主語 the man 說的話，並非別人複述或轉述 the man 的話，應作直接引語而加引號。

2.76 她問他，喜不喜歡跳舞。

✔ She asked him if he liked to dance<u>.</u>

✘ She asked him if he liked to dance<u>?</u>

> 一般疑問句變為間接引語時，用 if 或 whether 來引導。疑問句變為間接引語即間接問題時，後面不能再用問號。

2.77 在訪問中鋼期間，我們問廠裏人員：你們是怎樣提高鋼鐵生產的。

✔ During our visit to C.S.C., we asked the personnel how <u>they</u> raised the steel production.

✘ During our visit to C.S.C., we asked the personnel how <u>you</u> raised steel production.

> 錯句中的 you 指 personnel，應改為 they。

2.78 他說我可以第二天來。

✔ He said that I could come <u>the next day</u>.

✘ He said that I could come <u>tomorrow</u>.

> 在間接引語中，如敍述者的地點和時間與說話者的地點和時間不同，則時間副詞、地點副詞和指示代名詞要作相應的變動。如 tomorrow 改為 the next day；yesterday 改為 the day before。同樣，today, tonight, last night, now, ago 應改為 the day, that night, the night before, then, before that time；here 改為 there；this, these 改為 that, those。反之，則不需變動。例如：
>
> He said that he <u>would</u> come <u>tomorrow</u>.
> （說話者的時間與敍述者的時間相同。）
> He said he <u>would</u> come <u>here</u>.
> （說話者的地點與敍述者的地點相同。）

2.79 她說她在前一天已把報告寫好了。

✔ She said that she had finished writing the report <u>the day before</u>.

✘ She said that she had finished writing the report <u>yesterday</u>.

> 參見例 2.78。

2.80 我問他，他的母親有甚麼問題。

✔ I asked him <u>what was</u> wrong with his mother.

✘ I asked him <u>what's</u> wrong with his mother.

間接引語中動詞的時態應與報告動詞（或稱先導動詞）一致。若報告動詞是過去式，則被引用句中的各種現在式變成相應的各種過去式，過去式變成過去完成式，將來式變成過去將來式。若報告動詞為現在式或將來式，則間接引語的動詞時態可以不受上述限制。例如：He is telling me that he was born in 1940. 。表示習慣、常例或普遍真理的時態也不受上述限制。例如：He said that facts <u>speak</u> louder (than words). 。

2.81 他的父母要他不要再犯這樣嚴重的錯誤。

✔ His parents <u>told</u> him <u>not to</u> make such serious mistakes again.

✔ His parents <u>suggested</u> that he should not make such serious mistakes again.

✔ His parents <u>told</u> him <u>that</u> he should not make such serious mistakes again.

✘ His parents <u>told</u> him <u>do not</u> make such serious mistakes again.

直接引語如果是一個祈使句，變成間接引語時，通常用一個複合賓語表達。試比較下列直接引語和間接引語：

"Be careful," he advised.

He advised me to be more careful.

He said to me, "Don't do this again."

He told me not to do that again.

"Get it ready," he ordered us.

He ordered us to get it ready.

在這種句子裏用甚麼詞作述詞，要根據所引句子的口氣來決定。在 tell, suggest, order 等後面也可以接賓語從屬句。

2.82 我問他那漂亮女孩是誰。

✔ I asked him who <u>that beautiful girl was</u>.

✘ I asked him who <u>was that beautiful girl</u>.

特殊疑問句變為間接引語，即是間接問題。間接問題用原來問句的疑問詞引導，其餘部分的詞序通常與陳述句同。例如：I don't know who the author is. 。

2.83 他問他們到哪裏去。

✔ He asked them where <u>they were</u> going.

✘ He asked them where <u>were they</u> going.

> 參見例 2.82。這裏 they 與 were 不可對調。

2.84 他問她為甚麼看起來這麼不快活。

✔ He asked her why she looked so sad.

✘ He asked her <u>that</u> why she looked so sad.

> 特殊疑問句變為間接引語時,用原來問句的疑問詞來引導,不能再用連接詞 that。在這種複合句中,why, when, where, how 等本身就有連接的作用,不能再用連接詞 that。

2.85 我知道學習英語是多麼重要。

✔ I know how important it is to learn English.

✘ I know <u>that</u> how important it is to learn English.

> 參見例 2.84。

v. Question tags 反義疑問句

2.86 你是他的朋友,是不是?

✔ You are his friend, <u>aren't you</u>?

✘ You are his friend, <u>is it</u>?

> 附加問句是由一個陳述句和一個簡化的一般疑問句構成,中間用逗號分開。如果陳述部分用肯定式,則疑問部分是否定式;如果陳述部分用否定式,則疑問部分是肯定式。疑問部分的主語應與陳述部分主語相同,述詞應在時態、人稱及單複數上與陳述部分之述詞一致。
>
> 錯句中的反義部分,與陳述句中的結構毫無相同之處,因此是錯誤的。反義疑問句在翻譯成中文時,往往可以在陳述句句尾加上"吧"、"嗎",用以代指"是不是?"或"是嗎?"等呆板的譯法。

2.87 你一直向她借錢，不是嗎？

✔ You always borrow money from her, <u>don't you</u>?

✘ You always borrow money from her, <u>isn't it</u>?

> 參見例 2.86。

2.88 他們已經把這塊地開闢來種菜了，是不是？

✔ They have cleared this plot of land to make a vegetable garden, <u>haven't</u> they?

✘ They have cleared this plot of land to make a vegetable garden, <u>didn't</u> they?

> 參見例 2.86。

2.89 唱歌的人唱得不錯，是不是？

✔ The singers are singing well, <u>aren't</u> they?

✘ The singers are singing well, <u>don't</u> they?

> 參見例 2.86。

2.90 金錢可不能買到友誼吧？

✔ Money can't buy friendship, <u>can</u> it?

✘ Money can't buy friendship, <u>isn't</u> it?

> 若附加問句陳述部分有助動詞時，其疑問部分只用助動詞。此句陳述部分是否定的，所以疑問部分應是肯定的。

2.91 我總不能希望他在運動方面勝過一般人吧？

✔ I can hardly expect him to be better than others at sports, <u>can</u> I?

✘ I can hardly expect him to be better than others at sports, <u>can't</u> I?

因 hardly, never, scarcely 等副詞有否定的意義，則其疑問部分應該是肯定式。

2.92 他要講南非現狀嗎？

✔ He will speak about the current situation in South Africa, <u>won't</u> he?

✔ He will speak about the current situation in South Africa, <u>will he not</u>?

✘ He will speak about the current situation in South Africa, <u>will not he</u>?

附加問句中疑問部分是否定式時，"not"應放在代名詞後，若放在代名詞前，則與助動詞連結，成為 isn't, aren't, doesn't, didn't, shan't 等。will he not 是書面語，口語中不普遍。

vi.   Negative sentences 否定句

2.93 所有的學生都不對。

✔ <u>None</u> of the students are / is right.

✘ <u>All</u> the students are <u>not</u> right.

"All... not..."並非全部否定，例如：All that glitters is <u>not</u> gold.（亮光閃閃的並非全是金子。）中文裏的"都不"、"都沒有"，在英語中習慣用 none of...（指兩個以上時）。

None of them attended the meeting.
（他們都沒有出席會議。）
None of the boys were / was interested in this game.
（孩子們對這項遊戲都不感興趣。）

若是要用 All 的話，則補語要用一個本身已是否定意義的詞，如 wrong 或 absent。例如：

All the answers are <u>wrong</u>.
All of the students were <u>absent</u>.

2.94 大家都爬不上來。

✔ No one could climb up.

✘ Everyone could not climb up.

> 在有 every 的句中的否定語氣也和 all 一樣，只是部分的否定，意謂 "非人人……"；若 not 放在 every 之前，也是一樣。例如：
>
> Not everyone can do this.（這不是人人都能做的。）
>
> 中文 "大家都不……"、"大家都沒有……"、"任何＋名詞＋都不……"，在英語往往用 no one、nobody 或 no＋名詞來表達。例如：
>
> No one can help him.（大家都無法幫助他。）
>
> No country has the right to interfere in the internal affairs of other countries.（任何國家都無權干涉他國內政。）

2.95 這兩本小説，我一本也不喜歡。

✔ I don't like either of these novels.

✘ I like neither of these novels.

✘ I don't like both of these novels.

> both 用在否定句中，是部分的否定。在意義上，錯句＝I like only one of the novels.，即 "這兩本小説我不是都喜歡的"，亦即 "我只喜歡這兩本小説中的一本"。在表示全部否定意義時，both 要用 neither 或 not...either 來代替。

2.96 他們兩位都沒有病。

✔ Neither of them is sick.

✘ None of them are sick.

> none of 後面的名詞或代名詞指三個以上的人或物，不可只指兩個，所以應該改為 neither of them，謂語動詞應為單數。

2.97 會議進行中，任何人都不得入內。

✔ No one will be admitted while the meeting is in progress.

✘ Anyone will not be admitted while the meeting is in progress.

否定句中作主語的只有 no one, nobody, nothing，用 anyone, anybody, anything 不合慣用法。例如，不可説 "*Anybody cannot do it."，應該説 "Nobody can do it."。不可説 "*Anything is not interesting"，該説 "Nothing is interesting."。

2.98 她變了很多，我幾乎認不得她。

✔ She has changed so much that I <u>can hardly / scarcely</u> recognize her.

✘ She has changed so much that I <u>almost cannot</u> recognize her.

almost 可以修飾 no, none, nothing。例如：
You've made <u>almost</u> no mistakes.
There is <u>almost</u> nothing left.
<u>Almost</u> none is left.

但不可修飾 not，也不可被 not 修飾。
"幾乎不"應用 hardly, scarcely 表達。請參考下列句子：
I could <u>hardly</u> stand.（我幾乎站不住了。）
I could <u>hardly</u> see anything in the swirling snow.
（在漫天大雪中我幾乎甚麼都看不見。）

2.99 我們永遠不會忘記老師給我們的臨別贈言。

✔ We shall <u>never forget</u> our teacher's parting advice.

✔ We shall <u>always remember</u> our teacher's parting advice.

✘ We shall <u>always not forget</u> our teacher's parting advice.

✘ We shall <u>forever not forget</u> our teacher's parting advice.

用 always not 表示 "永遠不" 或 "在任何時候都不" 是錯誤的。不能説 "*I shall always not forget it."，應説 "I shall <u>never</u> forget it." 或 "I shall <u>always</u> remember."。不可説 "*Always nobody was absent."，應説 "<u>Nobody</u> was ever absent."。

not always 作 "並非經常" 解。例如英語格言：
Crows are <u>not always</u> black.（烏鴉未必皆黑。）（借喻事情不可一概而論。）

2.100 她答應她父母今後決不輕舉妄動了。

✔ She promised her parents that she would <u>never</u> act so rashly <u>again</u>.

✘ She promised her parents that she would <u>not</u> act so rashly <u>forever</u>.

> forever 作 always 解時，它的全部否定語是 never，不是 not forever。

2.101 我們不可隨處亂畫。

✔ We must not write graffiti <u>anywhere</u>.

✘ We must not write graffiti <u>everywhere</u>.

> 錯句 *We must not write graffiti everywhere. 意味 We may write graffiti somewhere.。

2.102 我的練習裏有幾個錯誤。

✔ There are <u>a few</u> mistakes in my exercise.

✘ There are <u>few</u> mistakes in my exercise.

> few＝少到幾乎沒有，a few 才有肯定的意思，表示 "有幾個"。"He has few friends." 意為 "他幾乎沒有朋友"。little 與 few 一樣都是否定的意思，表示 "幾乎無"，a little 表示 "有一些"。
>
> He has <u>little</u> money. 表示他幾乎沒錢。little 跟 a little 是用來修飾不可數的名詞，few 跟 a few 是用來修飾可數的名詞。

2.103 他沒有姊妹。

✔ He has <u>no</u> sister. (He doesn't have a sister.)

✘ He has <u>not a</u> sister.

> no 加在單數普通名詞之前，表示 "沒用……"。例如：
>
> Has he a son? (英式英語)
> (= Does he have a son?) (美式英語)
> No, he has <u>no</u> son.

> (= No, he doesn't have.)
>
> 注意：在 have, there (/ here) is 後面，通常用 no，而不用 not。
>
> 例如：He has <u>no</u> wife.
>
> 但下面的句子中可以用 not a：
>
> He has twelve sisters and <u>not a</u> single brother.

2.104 我沒有這一種詞典。

✔ I <u>do not</u> have <u>such</u> a dictionary.

✔ I have <u>no such</u> dictionary.

✘ I have <u>not such</u> dictionary.

✘ I have <u>no such</u> a dictionary.

> such 後面接可數名詞單數時，必須加不定冠詞 a 或 an，dictionary 是
> 可數名詞單數，所以要説 such a dictionary。
>
> 但 no such = not such a，本身就包含不定冠詞，所以不可再加不定冠
> 詞。又如：
>
> There's <u>no such</u> thing in the world.
>
> <u>No such</u> thing has ever happened.

2.105 他不受利誘，也不屈服於威脅。

✔ He succumbs <u>neither</u> to bribery <u>nor</u> to threats.

✔ He doesn't succumb to <u>either</u> bribery <u>or</u> threats.

✘ <u>Not only</u> he doesn't succumb to bribery <u>but also</u> not succumb
to threats.

✘ He doesn't succumb to <u>both</u> bribery and threats.

> 當兩個子句都是否定句時，應用否定連接詞 neither... nor... 或在否定動
> 詞後接 either... or... 。至於 not only... but also... 則通常用來連接兩個肯
> 定句。

2.106 他跟他弟弟無論在相貌上或性格上都沒有相似之處。

✔ There is <u>not</u> the slightest resemblance between him and his brother in <u>either</u> appearance or character.

✘ There is not the slightest resemblance between him and his brother in <u>both</u> appearance and character.

> both...and... 用在肯定的場合。在否定的場合應用 neither...nor... 或 not...either...or... 。

2.107 他沒有任何痛苦的表示。

✔ He showed <u>no</u> sign of pain (at all).

✔ He didn't show <u>any</u> sign of pain (at all).

✘ He showed <u>no any</u> sign of pain.

> no ＝ not any。There will be no difficulty. ＝ There won't be any difficulty.。no any 是不合英文習慣的。正句之後可用 at all 加強語氣。

2.108 在第三世界國家裏，有很多人既沒有工作，也沒有房子住。

✔ In third world countries many people <u>have neither</u> jobs nor houses to live in.

✘ In third world countries many people <u>neither have</u> no job nor no house to live in.

> 連接詞 "neither... nor..." 的意義是 "既不……又不……"，它本身就是兩個否定的意義，不能再加否定詞 no。

vii.　Illogical sentences 不合邏輯的句子

2.109 學習滑雪應當循序漸進。

✔ To learn to ski, one <u>must go</u> step by step.

✘ To learn to ski <u>is</u> step by step.

> "循序漸進" 是指學習滑雪的方式，錯句中以 step by step 等於 to learn to ski，顯然是不合邏輯的。step by step 是慣用語，只能作副詞短語用。

2.110 那騙徒使老王失去工作，幾乎使他淪為乞丐。

✔ The con man made Mr. Wang lose his job and <u>reduced</u> him <u>almost</u> to beggary.

✔ The con man made Mr. Wang lose his job and <u>almost become</u> a beggar.

✘ The con man made Mr. Wang lose his job and <u>almost became</u> a beggar.

> 這裏主語 The con man 並沒有淪為乞丐，所以要變更第二個述語，或把 became 改為原形，承受使役動詞 (causative verb) made 的結果，維持全句統一的主語。

2.111 她的心往下一沉，簡直站不住了。

✔ Her heart sank and <u>she</u> could hardly remain standing.

✘ Her heart sank and could hardly remain standing.

> Her heart 可以做 sank 的主語，但不能做 could hardly stand 的主語，要在連接詞後面加主語 she。

2.112 蓋世太保把他關進牢獄，嚴刑拷打。

✔ The Gestapo arrested him and <u>tortured him cruelly</u>.

✔ The Gestapo put him in jail, where <u>he was cruelly tortured</u>.

✘ The Gestapo arrested him and <u>was cruelly tortured</u>.

> 錯句中有兩個述語，第一個 arrested him 是主動語態；第二個 was tortured 突然變為被動語態，它的主語並不是 the Gestapo。

2.113 我把自行車修理過了，可是還是不能騎。

✔ I have had my bicycle repaired, but <u>it is</u> still unusable.

✘ I have had my bicycle repaired, but still unusable.

> 錯句中 but 所連接的前一部分是子句，後一部分卻是短語，結構不完整，而且 still unusable 是指 my bicycle 而言。

2.114 我們的制度是每一個公民都享有發言的權利。

✔ Our system is <u>one under which</u> every citizen enjoys freedom of speech.

✔ <u>Under</u> our system every citizen enjoys freedom of speech.

✘ Our system <u>is that</u> every citizen enjoys freedom of speech.

> "每一個公民都享有發言的權利" 並不是制度本身，而是在這制度下發生的情況，因此不能把 that 引導的從屬句作為補語從屬句，應改用 under which...。

2.115 林先生出生於貧困農家，十歲時父親就死了。

✔ Mr. Lin is from a poor peasant's family. When <u>he was</u> ten years old, <u>his father died</u>.

✔ Mr. Lin is from a poor peasant's family. When ten years old, <u>he lost his father</u>.

✘ Mr. Lin is from a poor peasant's family. When ten years old (/ at ten), <u>his father died</u>.

> 錯句中副詞從屬句的省略結構意義很含糊，好像是說 "他的父親在十歲時死了"。如果保留原來的主句，從屬句不能用省略結構，應加 he was。如果保留原來的省略結構，則應改變主句的主語和動詞。

2.116 譯成英語後，句子的詞序就完全不同了。

✔ The syntax of the sentence is entirely different <u>when the sentence</u> is translated into English.

✔ <u>When the sentence</u> is translated into English, its syntax is entirely different.

✘ The syntax of the sentence is entirely different <u>when</u> translated into English.

> 譯成英語的並非 "句子的詞序"，而是 "句子"，所以從屬句中的 the sentence 不應省略，正句二則語意清楚，不致造成這種困擾。

2.117 做這件事時，他們碰到不少困難。

✔ While doing the job, they <u>met</u> many difficulties.

✔ While doing the job, they <u>came across</u> many difficulties.

✘ While doing the job, <u>there were</u> many difficulties ahead.

> 做工作的是 they，而不是 difficulties，所以應該用 they 作主句的主語，句子其他部分作相應的調整。

2.118 他們擺出一副好像對國家已有卓越貢獻的姿態。

✔ They <u>behaved</u> as if they had performed some meritorious service for the country.

✘ Their <u>action</u> is as if they had performed some meritorious service for the country.

> as if 可以引導補語性質的從屬句，但只能接在 it seems, it looks, he looks 等結構後面。例如：
>
> It looks / seems <u>as if</u> it were going to rain.
>
> He looked <u>as if</u> he had been ill for a long time.
>
> as if 通常與行為動詞連用，以引導副詞從屬句。例如：
>
> He acted <u>as if</u> he knew nothing about it.

2.119 我們應該多學習一點餐桌禮儀，以免人家覺得我們沒禮貌。

✔ We should learn more about table manners, so that <u>people</u> will not think us ill-mannered.

✘ We should learn more about table manners, so that <u>they</u> will not think us bad-mannered.

> 錯句的 they 是 table manners 的代名詞，table manners 不是人，不會認為我們失禮，所以應改為 people。"沒禮貌"英文最好說 ill-mannered，不要說 *bad-mannered，"有禮貌"比較地道的說法是 well-mannered，不是 *good-mannered。

Self-test 自測

I. 選擇題

1. 他們差不多都已經離開了。 (2.11 註)
   Almost all of them ( ).
   a) leave   b) is left   c) has left   d) have left

2. 這個故事有一半是有趣的。 (2.12 註)
   Half of the story ( ) interesting.
   a) is   b) are   c) has   d) have

3. 書桌上有一本筆記簿和三支原子筆。 (2.7 註)
   There ( ) a notebook and three ball-point pens on the desk.
   a) has   b) have   c) was   d) were

4. 他們兩人都會做。 (2.4)
   ( ) is capable of doing this.
   a) Both of them   b) Either of them
   c) Both of they   d) Either of they

5. 他們現在所做的是荒謬可笑的。 (2.9)
   What they are doing ( ) ridiculous.
   a) is   b) are   c) was   d) were

6. 他們兩人都不喜歡游泳。 (2.5)
   Neither of them ( ) swimming.
   a) do not like   b) does not like   c) like   d) likes

7. 全國人民慶祝他們的勝利。 (2.8)
   The whole nation celebrated ( ) victory.
   a) their   b) its   c) it's   d) his

8. 十二加十四是二十六。 (2.10)
   Twelve plus fourteen ( ) twenty-six.
   a) has   b) have   c) is   d) are

9. 許多人走過這座小橋。 (2.13)

Many a person (　　) crossed this little bridge.

a) has　　　　　b) have　　　　　c) is　　　　　d) have

10. 我所聽到的是他很快就會返回工作崗位。 (2.18 註)

What I heard (　　) he would soon be back at work.

a) was　　　　　b) was that　　　　c) were　　　　d) were that

11. 我昨天去看一位朋友，他借我這本書。 (2.19 註)

Yesterday I went to visit a friend, (　　) lent me this book.

a) whom　　　　b) and who　　　　c) whose　　　　d) who

12. 大家同意她的提議：本週末去郊遊。 (2.25)

Everyone agreed to her proposal (　　) we have an outing this weekend.

a) what　　　　b) which　　　　c) that　　　　d) who

13. 大家都不同意賽門先生在會議中所提出的建議。 (2.25 註)

Everyone objected to the proposal (　　) Mr. Simon put forth at the meeting.

a) what　　　　b) which　　　　c) when　　　　d) who

14. 他高聲唸出他的作文，好像發瘋了一般。 (2.43)

He read his composition, roaring as if he (　　) mad.

a) was　　　　　b) were　　　　　c) is　　　　　d) are

15. 和他們所聽說到的正相反，她一點也不懂西班牙語。 (2.21)

Contrary to (　　) they heard, she does not understand Spanish at all.

a) that　　　　　b) x　　　　　c) which　　　　d) what

16. 我昨天晚上看的電影很精采。 (2.23)

(　　) is very exciting.

a) The film I saw last night　　　b) Last night I saw the film
c) I saw the film last night　　　d) Last night the film saw I

17. 是我的舅舅為我們帶來了快樂的生活。 (2.29)

It was my uncle (　　) brought us this happy life.

a) who　　　　　b) whom　　　　c) which　　　　d) that

18. 他打算賣掉他去年住過的那個房子。 (2.31)

He plans to sell the house (　　) he lived last year.

   a) which   b) where   c) that   d) whose

19. 他對於自己犯了如此的錯誤感到很羞愧。 (2.33)

He is ashamed (　　) such a mistake.

   a) of that he has made   b) that he has made

   c) to making   d) of have made

20. 我恐怕他會遲到。 (2.35)

I am afraid (　　) he will be late.

   a) that   b) for   c) of that   d) what

21. 我發覺攀爬這座小山很困難。 (2.36)

I (　　) to climb the hill.

   a) found very difficult   b) found it very difficult

   c) found that very difficult   d) found its very difficult

22. 不要干擾她！她還在寫作文呢。 (2.45)

Don't disturb her! She (　　) writing her composition.

   a) still does   b) is still doing   c) still is   d) is still

23. 路易斯不夠用功。 (2.48 註)

Lewis did not (　　).

   a) enough study hard   b) study enough hard

   c) study hard enough   d) studied enough hard

24. 他很虛弱，甚至無法走路。 (2.46)

He is very weak. He (　　).

   a) cannot walk even   b) even cannot walk

   c) cannot even walk   d) cannot even walks

25. 你們必須遵守上列的聲明。 (2.47 註)

You must abide by (　　).

   a) the statement up   b) statement the above

   c) the statement over   d) the above statement

26. 林教授是一位中國古代史專家。　(2.52)

    Prof. Lin is a specialist in (　　).

    a) Chinese ancient history　　　b) ancient Chinese history

    c) Chinese history ancient　　　d) ancient China's history

27. 他告訴我不要浪費他的時間。　(2.54 註)

    He told me (　　) his time.

    a) not to waste　　b) to not waste　　c) not waste　　d) waste not

28. 她認為自己很漂亮。　(2.55)

    She considered herself (　　).

    a) be very pretty　　　　　b) to very be pretty

    c) to very pretty　　　　　d) to be very pretty

29. 由於沒有收到回信，她再寫一次。　(2.56)

    (　　) an answer, she wrote again.

    a) Having not received　　　b) Not received

    c) No having received　　　d) Not having received

30. 只有這樣做，他才能獲得他們的支持。　(2.58)

    Only by so doing (　　) get their support.

    a) he will　　b) he would　　c) could he　　d) he could

31. 儘管她身體很弱，她還是能不費力地舉起那張椅子。　(2.61 註)

    (　　), she lifted that chair easily.

    a) Weak as she was　　　b) As weak she was

    c) As she was weak　　　d) She was as weak

32. 我不明白為甚麼他這樣做。　(2.70)

    I don't see why (　　) doing it this way.

    a) is he　　b) does he　　c) he is　　d) he

33. 他到那裏不是去幫助他們的。　(2.73)

    (　　) help them.

    a) He went there not to　　b) He did not go there to

    c) He did go there not to　　d) He went there to not

34. 他説這個消息是假的。　(2.74)

He said, "The news (　　) false."

a) has　　　　　b) were　　　　　c) is　　　　　d) are

35. 他説他前一天己經把那本書歸還圖書館了。　(2.79)

He said that he (　　) the book to the library the day before.

a) had returned　　　　　b) has returned
c) have returned　　　　　d) was returned

36. 他的老師要他不可以再遲到。　(2.81)

His teacher told him (　　) be late again.

a) that he would not　　　　　b) that he should not
c) to not　　　　　d) for not to

37. 我問她為甚麼缺席。　(2.84)

I asked her (　　) why she was absent.

a) for　　　　　b) that　　　　　c) x　　　　　d) of

38. 我問她那挺帥的男孩子是誰。　(2.82)

I asked her who (　　).

a) that handsome boy was　　　　　b) was that handsome boy
c) that handsome boy seems　　　　　d) is that handsome boy

39. 你知道晚上一個人走過那片森林有多麼恐怖嗎？　(2.85)

Do you know (　　) to walk through that forest alone at night?

a) that how terrible it is　　　　　b) how terrible is it
c) it is how terrible　　　　　d) how terrible it is

40. 你一直花錢花得太兇，不是嗎？　(2.87)

You always spend too much money, (　　)?

a) isn't it　　　　　b) aren't you　　　　c) don't you　　　　d) not you

41. 我總不能要求她借一點錢給我吧？　(2.91)

I can hardly ask her to lend me some money, (　　)?

a) can I not　　　　b) can I　　　　c) can't I　　　　d) I can

42. 所有的答案都錯了。　(2.93 註)

a) None of the answers are wrong.

b) All the answers are wrong.

c) All the answers are not right.

d) All the answers is not right.

43. 他們兩位都沒有來。 (2.96)

( ) of them is present.

a) Either   b) None   c) Neither   d) All

44. 這兩具枱燈她都不喜歡。 (2.95)

She doesn't like ( ) of these desk lamps.

a) both   b) neither   c) all   d) either

45. 大家都猜不出這個謎的謎底。 (2.94)

( ) figure out this riddle.

a) Everybody could not   b) Everyone could not

c) No one could   d) Not anyone could

46. 在濃霧中他幾乎甚麼也看不見。 (2.98)

He ( ) see anything in the thick mist.

a) hardly could   b) almost could not

c) could hardly   d) could not almost

47. 她除了你之外幾乎沒有朋友。 (2.102註)

She has ( ) friends besides you.

a) few   b) a few   c) little   d) a little

48. 他沒有這一種詞典。 (2.104)

He has ( ) dictionary.

a) not such   b) no such   c) no such a   d) none such a

49. 這瓶子裏沒有果汁。 (2.107)

The bottle did not contain ( ) fruit juice.

a) some   b) any   c) a   d) no

50. 她既不喜歡物理也不喜歡化學。 (2.108)

She likes ( ) physics ( ) chemistry.

a) either; or   b) both; nor   c) neither; or   d) neither; nor

II. 翻譯填空

1. 他們兩人都會做。　(2.4)

   (　　) of them is capable of doing this.

2. 許多人走過這條路。　(2.13)

   (　　) (　　) man has travelled this road.

3. 能做的事都做了。　(2.11)

   All that could be done (　　) been done.

4. 當時他只曉得叔叔是錯的。　(2.18)

   At that time (　　) he knew was (　　) his uncle was wrong.

5. 和別人告訴我們的正相反，他不大會彈鋼琴。　(2.21)

   Contrary to (　　) we were told, he isn't a good pianist.

6. 只有專家才能做這件事。　(2.30)

   It is only specialists (　　) can do this.

7. 他打了她，因此感到羞愧。　(2.33)

   He was ashamed (　　) he had hit her.

   = He was ashamed (　　) have hit her.

   = He was ashamed (　　) having hit her.

8. 我覺得要我們兩人合作是不可能的。　(2.37)

   I felt (　　) impossible for us to work together.

9. 我講明白，每星期五都有一次測驗。　(2.40)

   I made (　　) very clear that (　　) would be a test every Friday.

10. 這狗好像懂得人話似的。　(2.43)

    The dog looks (　　) (　　) it understood speech.

11. 他們假裝不知道那件事。　(2.54)

    They pretended (　　) to know about it.

    = They pretended (　　) they didn't know about it.

12. 以前沒見過他，我當然認不出他。 (2.56)

(   ) (   ) met him before, of course I did not recognize him.

= (   ) I had not met him before, I did not recognize him.

13. 謠傳他中了大獎。 (2.72)

Rumour (   ) (   ) that he won a grand prize.

14. 她說她在前一天已把報告寫好了。 (2.79)

She said that she had finished writing the report (   ) day (   ).

15. 我知道學習英語是多麼重要。 (2.85)

I know (   ) important (   ) (   ) to learn English.

16. 所有的學生都不對。 (2.93)

(   ) (   ) the students are right.

17. 這兩本小說，我一本也不喜歡。 (2.95)

I don't like (   ) of these books.

= I like (   ) of these books.

18. 她變了很多，我幾乎認不得她。 (2.98)

She has changed so much that I can (   ) recognize her.

19. 我們永遠不會忘記老師給我們的臨別贈言。 (2.99)

We shall (   ) forget our teacher's parting advice.

= We shall (   ) remember our teacher's parting advice.

20. 我沒有這一種詞典。 (2.104)

I do not have (   ) (   ) dictionary.

= I have (   ) such dictionary.

21. 他跟他弟弟無論在相貌或性格上都沒有相似之處。 (2.106)

There is not the slightest resemblance between him and his brother in (   ) appearance (   ) character.

22. 我們的制度是每個公民都有發言的權利。 (2.114)

Our system is one under (   ) every citizen enjoys freedom of speech.

23. 做這件事時，他們碰到不少困難。　(2.117)

  While doing the job, they (　　) (　　) many difficulties.

24. 我們應該多學習一點餐桌禮儀，以免人家覺得我們沒禮貌。 (2.119)

  We should learn more about table (　　), so that people will not think
  us (　　).

25. 有人忘了關煤氣。　(2.6)

  Somebody (　　) (　　) to turn off the gas.

III.　改錯

1. What we <u>are doing</u> <u>are</u> good <u>for</u> our health.　(2.9)
  　　　　　　　　A　　　　B　　　　C

  (　　)＿＿＿＿＿＿＿＿

2. They saw <u>where</u> their weak points <u>lay</u> and how <u>to catch</u> up with
  　　　　　A　　　　　　　　　　　B　　　　　　C
  the other classes.　(2.16)

  (　　)＿＿＿＿＿＿＿＿

3. She <u>took</u> a cab, <u>and which</u> took her <u>straight to</u> the airport. (2.19)
  　　　　A　　　　　　B　　　　　　　C

  (　　)＿＿＿＿＿＿＿＿

4. This chapter <u>describes</u> how the shepherd <u>to struggle</u> with <u>nature</u>
  　　　　　　　　A　　　　　　　　　　　　B　　　　　　C
  on the grasslands.　(2.22)

  (　　)＿＿＿＿＿＿＿＿

5. Everyone <u>agreed to</u> his suggestion <u>which</u> we should <u>have</u> a party
  　　　　　　A　　　　　　　　　B　　　　　　　C
  next week.　(2.25)

  (　　)＿＿＿＿＿＿＿＿

6. We'll <u>have to</u> revise the plan <u>which</u> we complete this <u>project</u> this
  　　　　A　　　　　　　　B　　　　　　　　　　　　C
  month.(2.26)

  (　　)＿＿＿＿＿＿＿＿

7. My father, <u>a retired teacher</u>, <u>he and</u> two of his friends <u>launched</u> a
                           A   B   C
business. (2.28)

( )_____

8. The microwave oven <u>that</u> I <u>bought</u> the other day <u>it cost</u> me six
                         A   B   C
hundred dollars. (2.32)

( )_____

9. We are <u>proud of</u> that we <u>won</u> <u>first place</u> in the race. (2.34)
                  A   B   C

( )_____

10. He <u>considered</u> <u>himself</u> to <u>strictly be</u> honest. (2.55)
          A   B   C

( )_____

11. <u>Only by</u> overthrowing the totalitarian system <u>they will</u> be able <u>to</u>
  A   B
<u>regain</u> their rights. (2.59)
  C

( )_____

12. <u>Weak as he was</u> in health, he <u>could not</u> do <u>heavy work</u>. (2.61)
          A   B   C

( )_____

13. I asked him <u>what's</u> wrong <u>with</u> his mother. (2.80)
              A   B

( )_____

14. <u>His parents</u> told him <u>do not</u> make <u>such</u> serious mistakes
    A   B   C
again. (2.81)

( )_____

15. They have cleared <u>this plot of</u> land <u>to make</u> a vegetable garden,
                     A   B
<u>didn't they</u>? (2.88)
  C

( )_____

16. I can hardly expect him <u>to be</u> better than others <u>at</u> sports,
                                     A   B

   <u>can't I</u> ? (2.91)
     C

   (   )_____

17. The <u>con man</u> made Mr. Lin <u>lose</u> his job and almost <u>became</u> a
            A   B   C

   beggar. (2.110)

   (   )_____

18. He doesn't <u>succumb to</u> either bribery <u>nor</u> <u>threats</u>. (2.105)
                A   B C

   (   )_____

IV. 請改正下列句子的錯誤

1. He asked them where were they going. (2.83)
2. Neither of them are to blame.. (2.5)
3. Anyone will not be admitted while the meeting is in progress. (2.97)
4. Seven minus four are three. (2.10)
5. Her heart sank and could hardly remain standing (2.111)
6. The singers are singing well, don't they?. (2.89)
7. The news that our men were stranded on the beaches came. (2.71)
8. He asked her that why she looked so sad. (2.84)
9. I don't understand why don't you trust him. (2.69)
10. He pretended to not know about it. (2.54)
11. The whole nation mourned their dead heroes. (2.8)
12. They will go to see the house where you lived there last year. (2.31)

3 Words 詞法

i. Nouns 名詞

3.1 許多聽眾出席那次會議。

✔ A large <u>audience</u> attended the meeting.

✘ A large <u>number of audience</u> attended the meeting.

> audience 為聽眾或觀眾的總稱，不是個別的人。"聽眾多"應説 a large audience，"聽眾少"應説 a small audience。

3.2 他的衣服快穿破了。

✔ His clothes <u>are</u> almost worn out.

✘ His clothes <u>is</u> almost worn out.

> clothes 這一名詞統指衣服，只有複數而且不能與數詞連用。具體表示某一種衣服的名詞，如 garment, dress, coat 或 overcoat 等，可有單複數。"一套衣服"應該用 a suit of clothes。

3.3 你們是日本人，他們是英國人。

✔ You are Japanese. They are <u>English / Britons</u>.

✘ You are Japanese. They are <u>Englishman</u>.

> 表示民族的名詞，其單複數因習慣而不同，舉例如下：
>
> | 單數 | 複數 | |
> |------|------|------|
> | a Chinese | Chinese | 中國人 |
> | a Japanese | Japanese | 日本人 |
> | a Russian | Russians | 俄國人 |
> | a German | Germans | 德國人 |
> | an American | Americans | 美國人 |
> | an Englishman | Englishmen | 英國人 |
> | a Briton | Britons | 英國人 |
> | a Dutchman | Dutchmen | 荷蘭人 |

注意：Englishman 一詞現已逐漸少用。另外有一種趨勢是多用民族的形容詞來代替其名詞，如：説 I'm Jewish.（我是猶太人。）而不説 I'm a Jew.。同理，平常我們應説 I'm Chinese. 或 I'm American.，不宜説 I'm a Chinese. 或 I'm an American.。

3.4 她沒有叫多少菜。

✓ She did not order too <u>much</u> food.

✗ She did not order too <u>many</u> foods.

food 是不可數名詞，應與量詞一起用，如 three pieces / articles of food（三樣菜），a few bits of food（幾樣菜）或 a table of food（一桌菜）。

3.5 昨天我買了六塊肥皂。

✓ Yesterday I bought six <u>cakes of</u> soap.

✗ Yesterday I bought six soaps.

英語中的 soap, chalk, furniture, bread, information 等為不可數名詞，需要計數時，前面要加表示單位的量詞，如 a cake / tablet / bar of soap, three pieces of chalk, five pieces of furniture, a loaf of bread 等。

3.6 請給我兩張紙。

✓ Please hand me two <u>sheets of</u> paper.

✗ Please hand me two papers.

paper 作物質名詞 "紙張" 解時，沒有複數形式，前面只可加補充意義的字；作 "學術性的報告"、"報紙"、"考卷" 或 "論文" 等解時，可有複數形式。

3.7 祖母的頭髮已經變灰白了。

✓ Grandmother's hair <u>has</u> already turned grey.

✗ Grandmother's hairs <u>have</u> already turned grey.

hair 統指頭髮（或毛）時，只用單數。hairs 指多根頭髮（或毛），例如：She has several grey hairs.。另外，英文裏提到白頭髮習慣上多以 grey 一詞來代替 white，較為委婉含蓄。

3.8 他沒有多少工作要做。

✔ He doesn't have a lot of <u>work</u> to do.

✘ He doesn't have a lot of <u>works</u> to do.

> work 若指 "工作" 是不可數名詞，總是用單數，且不用不定冠詞。work 的複數形式表示下列幾種意義：(1) 著作，如 Chaucer's works；(2) 工廠，如 China Steel Works；(3) 機器的轉動部分，如 the works of a watch；(4) 工程，如 public works。

3.9 做完這些作業以後，他要做甚麼？

✔ What does he want to do after he finishes (/ has finished) <u>his</u> homework?

✘ What does he want to do after he finishes (/ has finished) <u>these</u> homeworks?

> homework 指學生的 "家庭作業"，偶或指 "工人在家替工廠做的工作"，一般不用複數，前面也不用複數的指示代名詞。

3.10 經過幾年的自學，他獲得不少知識。

✔ After studying several years on his own he acquired a great deal of <u>knowledge</u>.

✘ After studying several years on his own he acquired a great deal of <u>knowledges</u>.

> knowledge 屬不可數名詞，很少用複數形式，但可和 a 連用，後接 of。例如：He has a good <u>knowledge</u> of the English language.。

3.11 這是一個好消息。

✔ This is <u>very good</u> news.

✔ This is <u>great</u> news.

✘ This is <u>such a</u> good news.

> news 是不可數名詞，具有複數形式，但只有用作單數，前面不可加 a，
> 後面的動詞也應用第三人稱單數，如：Bad <u>news</u> travels quickly.。像
> 這類的名詞還有 politics, economics, physics, mathematics 等，習慣
> 上都是作為單數。

3.12 工人們能在三個半月內造好我們的新房子。

✔ The workers can complete our new house in three and <u>a half</u> months.

✘ The workers can complete our new house in three and <u>half a</u> month.

> "半個月"、"半年"、"半小時" 用 half a month, half a year, half an hour。一個半以上的"半"都用 ... and a half，例如：two and a half years（兩年半）、three and a half weeks（三個半星期）、four days and a half（四天半）。表示一個半以上的具體東西時也如此：one pound and a half, two tons and a half, three apples and a half 等等。

3.13 他們決定買一輛新車。

✔ They have made up their <u>minds</u> to buy a new car.

✘ They have made up their <u>mind</u> to buy a new car.

> make up their (/ our) minds 中，用 minds 比用 mind 普遍。

3.14 人們一致稱頌他。

✔ <u>People</u> praised him unanimously.

✘ <u>Peoples</u> praised him unanimously.

> people 作"人們"（= men and women）解時，是單數形式，作複數用。
> peoples 是"多個民族"、"各國人民"，不是"多數人"，如 the peoples of Asia（亞洲各民族、亞洲人民）。

3.15 她為他做了一條新褲子。

✔ She made him a new <u>pair of</u> trousers.

✘ She made him a new trousers.

scissors 和 trousers 等名詞常用複數形式。"一把剪刀"或"一條褲子"常為 a pair of scissors 或 a pair of trousers，間或也有人說 a scissors, a trousers，但以不用為宜。

3.16 我們提前兩年完成了第二個五年計劃的主要目標。

✔ We fulfilled the major objectives of the Second Five-<u>Year</u> Plan two years ahead of schedule.

✘ We fulfilled the major objectives of the Second Five-<u>Years</u> Plan two years ahead of schedule.

five-year 作為一個複合形容詞，year 不用複數。又如 a twelve-year-old boy, a five-dollar note, a one-hundred-meter race 等，同此。

3.17 這幅水彩畫比那幅油畫更吸引觀眾。

✔ This painting in watercolours is more appealing to visitors than that one in <u>oils</u> (oil colours).

✘ This painting in watercolours is more appealing to visitors than that one in <u>oil</u>.

"水彩畫顏料"和"油畫顏料"都該用複數。

ii.　Pronouns 代名詞

3.18 我和他相識已經九個月了。

✔ <u>He and I</u> have known each other for nine months.

✘ <u>I and he</u> have known each other for nine months.

單數的不同人稱的代名詞連用，其次序一般是 you and I; you and he; he and I; she and I。複數人稱代名詞的次序是 we and you; you and they; we, you, and they。

3.19 我自己不願意去那家公司工作。

✔ <u>I myself</u> am unwilling to work in that company.

✘ <u>Myself</u> am unwilling to work in that company.

> myself, yourself, himself, herself, itself, ourselves, yourselves, themselves, oneself 等反身代名詞可用來加強語氣，但必須跟在其所加強的人之後，不能單獨出現當作代名詞用。
>
> I <u>myself</u> went there.
>
> I'll do it <u>myself</u>.
>
> He did it <u>himself</u>.
>
> 也可以用作受詞或主詞補語。但該句的主詞必須與此反身代名詞所指的為同一人，如：
>
> She hurt <u>herself</u>.
>
> （她受傷了。／她傷到自己。／她傷害自己。）
>
> You aren't quite <u>yourself</u> today.
>
> （你今天有點兒異樣。）

3.20 沒有人知道這件事情。

✔ <u>Nobody</u> knows about this.

✘ <u>No body</u> knows about this.

> nobody 不可寫作 no body；同樣 anybody, somebody, everybody 都不可以分開來寫。說 "沒有人"，用 no one 或 none 都可以。

3.21 我會把自己的書送給他。

✔ I will give <u>my own</u> book to him.

✘ I will give <u>myself</u> book to him.

> myself 等複合人稱代名詞不能作限定詞用，因為它不能作 "自己的" 解，只有 "我自己，我親自" 的意義。

3.22 他左手拿着一把槍。

✔ He held a gun in <u>his</u> left hand.

✘ He held a gun in left hand.

中文表示所有格的人稱代名詞往往在句中省略，但在英語裏一般不可省略。試看下列句子：

他頭上戴着一頂帽子。He had a cap on <u>his</u> head.

她用手遮住了眼睛。She covered her eyes with <u>her</u> hands.

下課後我們複習功課。After class we review <u>our</u> lessons.

3.23 他不是我們的同學。

✔ He is not <u>our</u> classmate.

✔ He is not <u>one of our</u> classmates.

✘ He is not <u>an our</u> classmate.

沒有 * an our classmate 這樣的說法，可以說 He is <u>one of</u> our classmates. 或 He is a classmate of ours. 。如果說 He is <u>no</u> classmate of ours. 則有 "我們沒有這樣的同學" 的貶意。

3.24 他是她的一個老朋友。

✔ He is an old friend of <u>hers</u>.

✘ He is an old friend of <u>she</u>.

an old friend of she 不符合習慣，應改作 an old friend of hers。He is <u>a friend of my father</u>. 雖不及 He is <u>a friend of my father's</u>. 普遍，但並不算錯誤。

3.25 那時我們三姐妹正在湖邊。

✔ <u>My two</u> sisters <u>and I</u> were at the lakeside then.

✘ <u>Three of our</u> sisters were at the lakeside then.

three of our sisters 是指 "我們姐妹中的三人"（不指三姐妹）。My two sisters and I 是我們姐妹三人。

3.26 不要告訴別人，這事只能你我知道。

✔ Don't tell anyone else. It is a matter strictly between you and <u>me</u>.

口語：Don't tell anyone else. It is a matter strictly between you and I.

> 在介詞 between 後面要用受詞。雖然在口語中也會出現 between you and I，但不宜仿效。

3.27 第一個發現這個秘密的是我。

✔ It was I that first discovered the secret.

口語：It was me that first discovered the secret.

> I 是主詞補語，它的格應和主詞相同，最好使用主格；又如 It's she reading aloud in the room.。以下三句雖不合規則，但在口語裏很普遍：
>   It's me!
>   That's him!
>   I wouldn't do that if I were her.

3.28 我比他年齡小。

✔ I am younger than he.

口語：I am younger than him.

> 在 than 和 as 後面的代名詞，用主格或用受格，決定於這個代名詞在從屬句中的作用。這句若不省略，應該是 I am younger than he is (young).。但在口語裏，I am younger than him. 也常聽到。

3.29 拿她和他相比，我比較喜歡她。

✔ I like her better than him.

✘ I like her better than he.

> 這句若不省略，應為 I like her better than I like him.。為了避免誤解，可以不用省略結構，或改作 I like her better than I do him.。

3.30 我比她更喜歡他。

✔ I like him better than she does (=better than she likes him).

✘ I like him better than her.

> 這裏 she 是 like 的主詞，應該用主格。

3.31 她和他一樣高。

✔ She is as tall as <u>he</u>.

✘ She is as tall as <u>him</u>.

> 按傳統文法，第一個 as 是副詞，第二個 as 是連接詞，所連接的句子是 She is as tall 和 he is tall，所以 he 應用主格。在現代英語裏，第二個句子並不算錯，但在正式的寫作裏還是用主格為宜。

3.32 我一點都不像她。

✔ I am not at all like <u>her</u>.

✘ I am not at all like <u>she</u>.

> like 作 "像" 解，是介詞，後面的代名詞應該用受格。

3.33 像他這樣的孩子不應任由他在外面隨便玩樂。

✔ Such a boy as <u>he</u> should not be allowed to run loose.

✘ Such a boy as <u>him</u> should not be allowed to run loose.

> as 後面代名詞的格應與 such a boy 保持一致。boy 為主格，因此應用 he，不能用 him。現更普遍的用法是 Such a boy as that...，以 that 代替代名詞 he 或 she，這樣的句子暗示此 boy 不是好孩子。

3.34 你想誰是學校最好的學生？

✔ <u>Who</u> do you think is the best student in the school?

✘ <u>Whom</u> do you think is the best student in the school?

> 這裏 do you think 可以視為插入語。"誰" 不是 do you think 的受詞而是 is the best student... 的主詞，所以應用主格 who。

3.35 我們和他們有同樣的問題。

✔ We had the <u>same</u> problem <u>as they</u> (had).

✔ Our problem was <u>the same as</u> theirs (was).

✘ We had the <u>same</u> problem <u>as theirs</u>.

> 在誤句中，主句的主詞是 we，而從屬句的主詞卻是 theirs（＝ their problem），所比較的事物不一致。如主句中用 we 作主詞，從屬句中主詞即須改為 they。如保留從屬句中的主詞 theirs，則主句的主詞要改為 our problem，句子其他部分也須作相應的改變。

3.36 樹上的葉子都落光了。

✔ The tree has shed <u>its</u> leaves.

✘ The tree has shed <u>it's</u> leaves.

> it 的所有格是 its；it's 是 it is 的縮寫形式，兩者絕不可相混。

3.37 一個人如果甚麼事都想做，必致一事無成。

✔ Nothing can be accomplished if one attempts to do <u>everything</u>.

✘ Nothing can be accomplished if one attempts to do <u>anything</u>.

> anything 一般用在疑問句或否定句中，例如：Is there anything in the box?。誤句從屬句 "if..." 中沒有否定的涵義，不可用 anything，應該用 everything。為了加強語氣，有 anything and everything 一語，意為 "任何一切事物"，因此原句也可以改作 Nothing <u>can be accomplished</u> if one attempts to do anything and everything。

3.38 有人來找過我嗎？沒有。

✔ Did any one come looking for me? <u>No</u>. / No one came.

✘ Did any one come looking for me? <u>None</u>.

> none 與 no one 雖然都作 "沒有人" 解，但略有區別，none 往往有固定範圍，如 none of them, none of the people，而 no one 沒有這種限制。試比較下列的句子：
>
> 學生中有人做好功課嗎？沒有。
> Did any of the students finish their homework? <u>None</u> of them did.
> 有人能解答這個問題嗎？沒有。
> Is there anyone who can solve this problem correctly? <u>No</u>. / No one can.

3.39 他說他寫過信給她，但是她沒有收到。

✔ He said he had written (to) her, but she never received <u>his</u> <u>letter</u>.

✘ He said he had written (to) her, but she never received <u>it</u>.

> 誤句中的 it 是代名詞，但它所代表的詞在句子中並未出現，因此不能用。美語中常將上例中之 "to" 字省略。

3.40 他一直在寫，那本書明天就要寫好了。

✔ He has been writing. <u>The book</u> will be finished tomorrow.

✘ He has been writing. <u>It</u> will be finished tomorrow.

> 參見例 3.39。

3.41 普魯斯特在他的作品中表現了對生命的熱愛。

✔ <u>In his works Proust</u> expressed his ardent love for life.

✘ <u>In Proust's works he</u> expressed his ardent love for life.

> 一般來說，代名詞應出現在所代名詞之後，但有例外。像這裏應以 Proust 作句子的主詞，在主詞出現之前用人稱代名詞所有格來修飾 works。類似的句子如：
>
> 狄更斯在作品中揭露了英國社會的醜惡。
> In <u>his</u> works Dickens exposed the evils of English society.
> 黃自在歌曲中激發了人民的愛國熱情。
> In <u>his</u> songs Huang Tze arouses the patriotic feelings of the people.
> 詩人在詩篇中描述了人民在壓迫者鐵蹄下的悲慘生活。
> In <u>his</u> poem the poet describes the miserable life the people had under the iron heel of the oppressor.

3.42 這就是他住的地方。

✔ He lives <u>here</u>.

✔ <u>This is</u> (the place) <u>where</u> he lived.

✘ Here is <u>where</u> he lived.（指他住的 house, district 等。）

✘ Here is <u>which</u> he lived.

關係詞 where 常與表示場所的先行詞，如 the place, the village 等連用；請看以下例句：

    This is (the place) <u>where</u> he was born.

    Show me the place <u>where</u> Dr. Sun Yat-sen lived.

表示地方、時間、原因的關係詞之前的先行詞如 the place、the time、the reason 均可省略，因省略後意義仍然清楚：

    Show me (the place) <u>where</u> Dr. Sun Yat-sen lived.

    That is (the period) <u>when</u> he lived there.

    That is (the reason) <u>why</u> he spoke.

Here 放在句首的情形，往往用在引起對方注意的招呼中，如：

    <u>Here</u> comes the bus.

    <u>Here</u> he comes.

    <u>Here</u> is the book for you.

3.43 你看過我祖父母住的房子嗎？

✔ Did you see the house our grandparents lived <u>in</u>?

✘ Did you see the house <u>in which</u> our grandparents lived?

✔ Did you see the house <u>where</u> our grandparents lived?

✘ Did you see the house <u>which</u> our grandparents lived?

關係代名詞 which 和 that 是用來代替附屬子句 our grandparents lived in the house 中的 the house，所以介詞 in 不能省略。in 也可放在 which 之前，但較呆板。

3.44 他們被迫到南方勞動，那裏需要可供剝削的人力。

✔ They were forced to labour in the South <u>which needed</u> an exploitable population.

✔ They were forced to labour in the South <u>where</u> an exploitable population <u>was needed</u>.

✘ They were forced to labour in the South where needed an exploitable population.

関係副詞 where 不能作從屬句中的主詞，因此必須改用関係代名詞 which 作為從屬句中的主詞，但是也可以保留関係副詞 where，而改變從屬句的結構，把原來動詞 needed 的受詞改為主詞，並改變動詞的語態。

3.45 這地方他上個月參觀過。

✔ This is the place <u>that</u> he visited last month.

✘ This is the place <u>where</u> he visited last month.

関係副詞 where 往往用來引導從屬句，修飾主句中表示地方的名詞，但不能機械地搬用，還應視具體情況而定。這裏從屬句中的動詞 visited 是及物動詞，就須用関係代名詞 that 來連接兩個子句，並作 visited 的受詞，意即 visited the place。試與下列句子比較：This is the place <u>where</u> (/ <u>in which</u>) he once lived.。

3.46 你看到他親自建造的那棟房子嗎？

✔ Did you see the house <u>that</u> he built himself?

✘ Did you see the house <u>where</u> he built himself?

參見例 3.45。

3.47 把錢留在你發現的地方。

✔ Leave the money <u>where</u> you found it.

✔ Leave the money <u>at the place where</u> you found it.

✘ Leave the money <u>at where</u> you found it.

Where you found it 可當副詞子句或形容詞子句。

當副詞子句時不能有介詞在其前。

當形容詞子句用時則是修飾其前的名詞 the place。

名詞 the place 之前應有介詞以構成一個表示地方的介詞短語。

3.48 這是我要講的話。（我講完了。）

✔ <u>This is what</u> I want to say.

✔ That's all I wanted to say.

✘ This is all what I want to say.

> 正句一用於講話之前或之後，正句二用在結束講話時。關係代名詞 what
> ＝ that which, any which, those which，有雙重作用。這裏 what 既起
> 連接兩個子句的作用，而本身又是從屬句中的受詞，所以 all 是多餘的，
> 也可以保留 all，省略關係代名詞 what。從語意上看，what 子句本身
> 已隱含 "所" 及 "所有" 的意思，所以 all what 中的 all 是多餘的。

3.49　我只知道他不久就要離開我們了。

✔ All (that) I know is that he'll soon leave us.

✔ What I know is that he'll soon leave us.

✘ All what I know is that he'll soon leave us.

> 參見例 3.48。

3.50　他們正在交談。

✔ They are talking to / with each other.

✘ They are talking each other.

> each other 是複合代名詞，不是副詞，其用法舉例如下：
>
> > Do they know each other?
> > They changed places with each other.
> > They asked each other many questions.
>
> 注意：(1) each other 和 one another 在現代英語裏用法相同，沒有區
> 別的必要；(2) each other 不可用作主詞。

3.51　他咳嗽得很厲害，所以沒有來。

✔ He had a bad cough. That's why he didn't come.

✔ He has a bad cough. That is why he can't come.

✘ He had a bad cough. It / This is why he didn't come.

> 指前面講到或感覺上比較遠的事物，通常用 that / those；指下面將要講
> 到或感覺上比較貼近的事物，通常用 this / these。例如：

> That's all.
> What I'd say is this: What's done is done.

3.52 他往常愉快的心情不見了，讓我很困惑。

✔ He lost his usual cheerfulness. That puzzled me.

✘ He lost his usual cheerfulness. It puzzled me.

> 參見例 3.51。

iii.　Articles 冠詞

3.53 斧頭是有用的工具。

✔ An axe is a useful tool.

✘ An axe is an useful tool.

> a 用在以子音開頭的詞的前面，如 a student、a university、a one-sided view、a European 等。An 用在以母音開頭的詞的前面，如 an apple, an interesting story、an hour 等。這裏所説的子音和母音指音 (sound) 而言，不指字母 (letter)。

3.54 王清能設計軟件，以小學生來説是很了不起。

✔ Wang Ching can create software programs, which is amazing for a primary school student.

✘ Wang Ching can create software programs. This is amazing for the primary school students.

> 定冠詞 the 表示特指事物，這裏用不定冠詞 a 以泛指初中學生。中文表達通稱不需冠詞，所以一般學生用英文表達類似情況經常忘了要加冠詞。

3.55 他一向都是積極參與學校的活動。

✔ He always takes an active part in school activities.

✘ He always takes active part in school activities.

> 動詞詞組 to take part in 作 "參加" 解,若為 "積極參加",該用 take an active part in,這是習慣用法。也不可說 *take part in school activities actively。

3.56 如果你對我說謊,你會後悔的。

✔ If you ever lie to me, you'll regret it.

✔ Don't ever lie to me or you'll regret it.

✘ If you ever tell lie to me, you'll regret it.

> "說謊" 平常用動詞 lie,也可以說 to tell a lie 或 tell lies。類似的有 to take a walk, to have a look, to make a fuss (小題大做) 等,但不能說 *to have looks, to make fusses。

3.57 她上研究所了。

✔ She has started graduate school.

✘ She has started the graduate school.

> 與 start school 一樣,"上研究所讀書" 是 start graduate school,不需加冠詞。但若指有事到某研究所去時,則可加 the。

3.58 在美國南方,種族歧視比北方更為顯著。

✔ Racial discrimination in the South of the U.S.A. is more marked than in the North.

✔ Racial discrimination is more marked in the southern part of the U.S.A. than in the North.

✘ In south in the U. S. A. racial discrimination is more marked than in north.

> east、west、north、south 指一國的區域時,第一個字母須大寫,前面加 the,如上例。當指方位時,就不必大寫。例如:
>
> The sun rises in the east.
>
> 至於 The swallows fly south. 和 Our dormitory faces east. 中的 south、east 是副詞,所以沒有冠詞。

3.59 "為民眾服務"成為歷來最流行的口號。

✔ To serve <u>the</u> people became one of the most popular slogans of all times.

✘ To serve people became one of the most popular slogans of all times.

> people 不加定冠詞 the 時，作 "人們" 解，the people 指 "人民"。

3.60 葛斯勒兩兄弟是兩個勤奮的鞋匠。

✔ <u>The</u> Gessler brothers were two diligent cobblers.

✘ Gessler brothers were two diligent cobblers.

> 某氏兄弟、姊妹，某一家人的總稱在姓氏前都要加定冠詞，如 the Smith sisters, the Johnsons。

3.61 德國人是勤勞的民族。

✔ <u>The</u> German people are industrious.

✘ German people are industrious.

> 在表示某國人民的詞前面要加定冠詞，如 the Korean people, the Japanese people, the American people 等。

3.62 我一點也不知道她為甚麼這樣難過。

✔ I have not <u>the</u> slightest idea why she is so upset.

✘ I have not slightest idea why she is so upset.

> 形容詞最高級前面照例須用定冠詞。

3.63 大多數學生考完了試。

✔ Most of <u>the</u> students have finished the exam.

✘ Most of students have finished the exam.

> 這裏的 students 前面，必須加定冠詞，表示限定在這一範圍內的學

生們。few of students, all of questions, many of teachers 等都應改作 few of the students, all of the question, many of the teachers。但是 thousands of apples 中沒有 the，這裏 thousands of 相當於一個形容詞。再比較 most students, few students, all the questions, many teachers of the school。

3.64 尼克遜政府窮於應付人民愈來愈強烈的不滿。

✔ **The** Nixon administration had difficulty dealing with the growing dissatisfaction of the people.

✘ Nixon administration had difficulty dealing with the growing dissatisfaction of the people.

人名作形容詞用時，必須用定冠詞，如 the Shakespeare plays（莎士比亞的劇本）、the Macmillan cabinet（麥克米倫內閣）、the Kennedy administration（甘迺迪政府）等。

3.65 我們將在課堂上聽寫。

✔ We are going to have dictation in class.

✘ We are going to have dictation in **the** class.

in class, in school, at home, go to bed, in prison（在獄中）等慣用語中都不需冠詞，但 in the office 要加冠詞。

3.66 我們吃過午飯就開始。

✔ We will start it after lunch.

✘ We will start it after **the** lunch.

dinner, breakfast, lunch, supper, tea 等作為一般或抽象的餐名時，前面不用冠詞。例如：

Call me when <u>dinner</u> is ready.

after（或 before, to, at）dinner（或 breakfast, lunch, etc.）等詞組裏也沒有 the。當它們指確定的或所吃的東西時，前面有冠詞：

The <u>dinner</u> was a great success.

We had a good <u>dinner</u>.

3.67 昨天我買了一本《諾頓英國文學選集》第二冊。

✔ Yesterday I purchased a copy of *Norton Anthology of English Literature*, <u>Vol. 2.</u>

✘ Yesterday I purchased a copy of *Norton Anthology of English Literature*, <u>the Volume two.</u>

> 序數詞前面一般有 the，例如：the second floor, the sixth lesson, the Second World War，但我們説 Number One, Book Two, Volume Four, Lesson Three (＝ the first one, the second book, the fourth volume, the third lesson), World War II (＝ the Second World War)。

3.68 他們不再相信實用主義。

✔ They no longer believe in pragmatism.

✘ They no longer believe in <u>the</u> pragmatism.

> pragmatism、naturalism 等以 -ism 結尾的抽象名詞前不加冠詞。

3.69 恐怖主義是愛好和平者的公敵。

✔ Terrorism is the common enemy of all people who love peace.

✘ <u>The</u> Terrorism is the public enemy of all people who love peace.

> 參見例 3.68。

3.70 王博士報告有關理論物理的最新發展。

✔ Dr. Wang gave a lecture on the latest developments in theoretical physics.

✘ Dr. Wang gave a lecture on the latest developments in <u>the</u> theoretical physics.

> "理論物理" 作為一種科目，不須加定冠詞。其他如 political science, Chinese literature, English history 等也是如此。

3.71 南方人喜歡吃米，不太吃饅頭。

✔ The southerners prefer rice to steamed bread.

✘ The southerners prefer <u>the</u> rice to the steamed bread.

> rice, flour 等物質名稱前面不加冠詞。

3.72 他因該戰役的功績晉升為上校。

✔ He was promoted <u>to the rank of</u> colonel because of his meritorious service in the battle.

✘ He was promoted the colonel because of his meritorious service in the battle.

> 職務的名稱前面不必用冠詞。例如：
> He served as <u>second mate</u> on the ship.（他在船上當二副。）
> He has been commissioned as <u>lieutenant</u>.（他最近獲任命為中尉。）

iv. Verbs 動詞

1) Verbs easily misused 容易用錯的動詞

3.73 她把畫掛在她書房牆上。

✔ She <u>hung</u> the picture on her study wall.

✘ She <u>hanged</u> the picture on her study wall.

> hanged 是 hang（吊死，絞死）的過去式。hang 作 "掛" 解時的過去式是 hung，過去分詞也是 hung。

3.74 他失去平衡，跌倒在地上。

✔ He lost his balance and <u>fell</u> down.

✘ He lost his balance and <u>felled</u> down.

> felled 是動詞 fell 的過去式，作 "砍倒" 解，是及物動詞。這裏 "跌倒" 應是 fall，它的過去式是 fell，過去分詞是 fallen。

3.75 我剛才把這個照相機放在桌上。

✓ I laid the camera on the table a moment ago.

✗ I lay the camera on the table a moment ago.

> 從這句中文中可以看出動詞須用過去式,但 lay 是 lie 的過去式,作 "躺"
> 解,是不及物動詞。這裏應用動詞 lay,它的過去式和過去分詞都是
> laid。"將……放、置":lay, laid, laid(及物),"躺、臥、橫":lie, lay,
> lain(不及物)。注意:兩個形同義不同的 lay,不要用錯。

2) Tenses 時態

3.76 他去過韓國。

✓ He has been to Korea.

✓ He visited Korea some time ago.

✗ He has gone to Korea.

> He has gone to Korea. 是 "他已經到韓國去了",指目前人已在韓國或
> 在赴韓國的途中。表示 "過去曾去過某處",應用 have / has been,或
> 用動詞的過去式和表示過去時間的副詞來表達。

3.77 王先生來看過她,還留了一個包裹。

✓ Mr. Wang came to see her and he left a package.

✓ Mr. Wang has been here to see her and he left a package.

✗ Mr. Wang has come to see her and he has left a package.

> 現在完成時態指現在,而過去一般時態指過去;現在完成時態說明動
> 作的結果,而過去一般時態,除了動詞 to be 以外,都說明動作。Mr.
> Wang has come. 是 "王先生現在已經來了";Mr. Wang came. 才是 "王
> 先生來過",說明一個動作。has left a package 所表示的概念與 has
> come to see you 相同,如果說 Mr. Wang has come to see you. He is
> now waiting downstairs. 就沒有毛病。

3.78 上個禮拜天我去買東西。

✓ I went shopping last Sunday.

✘ I have gone shopping last Sunday.

> 參見例 3.77。

3.79 他離開倫敦已很久了。

✔ He has been <u>away from</u> London for quite a long time.

✔ It is quite some time <u>since</u> he left London.

✘ He has <u>left</u> London for a long time.

> to leave 和 die, graduate, get up, retire 等動詞一樣，是所謂的 point-of-time verb（或稱 terminative verb），是表達一霎時發生的動作，動作之發生並無延續狀態，因此不能像 period-of-time verb（或稱 durative verb）那樣可用 have + p.p. + for a long time（或 over two years 等）的形式來表達延續時間的概念，所以本句必須用 leave 的過去式，或以同義的 durative verb 來替換 leave。中文裏沒有這種觀念，因此即使英文程度不錯的人也常常弄錯。茲再舉數例：
>
> 我已經醒來兩小時了。
> I <u>have been up</u> two hours.（而不是 *I have waken two hours. 或 *I have got up two hours.）
> 他已經退休三年多了。
> He <u>has been retired</u> over three years.（不是 *He has retired over three years.）
> 我大學畢業已經五年了。
> I <u>have been out of</u> college five years.（不是 *I have graduated from college five years.）
>
> 以上所述是極重要的英文文法觀念，可惜坊間文法書中極少論及，請讀者特別留意。

3.80 我來非洲已經五個月了。

✔ I have <u>been</u> in Africa for five months.

✔ I have <u>lived</u> in Africa for five months.

✔ I <u>came</u> to Africa five months <u>ago</u>.

✔ It is five months <u>since</u> I came to Africa.

✘ I <u>have come</u> to Africa five months.

✘ I <u>come</u> to Africa five months.

> 參見例 3.79。第四個句子也可作 It has been....。

3.81 他的大哥已經過世四年了。

✔ His elder brother <u>has been dead</u> four years.

✔ His elder brother <u>died</u> four years <u>ago</u>.

✔ It has been four years <u>since</u> his elder brother <u>died</u>.

✘ His elder brother <u>has died</u> four years.

> 參見例 3.79。

3.82 王太太找到了她失散十七年的兒子。

✔ Mrs. Wang has found the son she lost seventeen years <u>ago</u>.

✔ Mrs. Wang found her son, who <u>had been</u> lost for seventeen years.

✘ Mrs. Wang has found the son she <u>has</u> lost for seventeen years.

> 參見例 3.79。

3.83 你多久沒見過你父母了？

✔ How long has it been <u>since</u> you saw your parents last?

✘ How long <u>haven't</u> you seen your parents?

> 參見例 3.79。正句也可把 last 移到 saw 之前。

3.84 三小時前我已經把公寓油漆好了。

✔ I <u>finished painting</u> the apartment three hours ago.

✘ I <u>have finished painting</u> the apartment three hours ago.

> 現在完成時態 have finished 指現在，但 three hours ago 指過去，顯然
> 有矛盾。不少學生常犯這樣的錯誤，必須注意用了 ago，動詞就必須用
> 過去一般時態。

3.85 上星期我們參觀過王氏化學工廠。

✔ Last week we <u>visited</u> Wang's Chemical Works.

✘ Last week we <u>had visited</u> Wang's Chemical Works.

參見例 3.87。

3.86 王定的弟弟在第一次世界大戰中負傷過好幾次。

✔ Wang Ding's brother <u>was</u> wounded several times during the First World War.

✘ Wang Ding's brother <u>had been</u> wounded several times during the First World War.

參見例 3.87。

3.87 他在暑假中讀完了五本小説。

✔ He <u>finished reading</u> five novels during the summer break.

✘ He <u>had finished reading</u> five novels during the summer break.

例句 3.85 到 3.87 都屬於過去時態的範疇，但不能因為在中文中出現了 "曾"、"過"、"了" 等，就認為在英語中該用過去完成時態。過去完成時態表示在過去某一特定時刻已完成的動作，或表示在過去某項動作之前已經完成的動作，而不能用來表示過去曾做過的動作。例如：

He <u>had finished</u> his work <u>at six yesterday evening</u>.

He <u>had finished</u> his work when I called on him <u>at six yesterday evening</u>.

3.88 他將在下個月來這裏。

✔ He is <u>coming</u> here next month.

✘ He is <u>going to come</u> here next month.

to be going to 常和動詞原形連用，表示未來的動作。例如：The paper says it is going to rain. ，但和 come 一起用的時候比較少見。go, come, stay, leave, start 等動詞，往往用現在進行時態表示未來的動作。例如：

> He is not going to tonight's meeting, is he?
> He is staying with the Smiths for two days.
> Mr. Li is leaving for Bombay in a week or two.
> The movie is starting in ten minutes.

3.89 明天如果天晴，我們要去郊遊。

✔ We will go for an outing if it is nice out tomorrow.

✘ We will go for an outing if it will be nice out tomorrow.

> 用 if 引導的、表示未來的條件從屬句，通常用一般現在時態，不用將來時態，而主句則通常用將來時態。觀察下列各句（第三句是例外）：
>
> I will let you know if the question is settled by then.
> If you go there at five they will be waiting for you.
> If he does not return tomorrow, send him a telegram.
> If it rains, I will stay at home.

3.90 我離開香港前會來看你的。

✔ I will come to see you before I leave Hong Kong.

✘ I will come to see you before I will leave Hong Kong.

> 表示未來的時間副詞從屬句，通常用一般現在時態，但用 when 引導的名詞從屬句，如表示未來，則必須用將來時態，試觀察下列各句：
>
> I will have finished my work by the time he returns.
> As soon as he comes we will start working.
> I don't know when he will come; but when he comes I will speak to him.

3) Agreement of tenses 時態呼應

3.91 那傢伙很狡猾、小氣，他給農場的僱工吃得很少。

✔ That guy was very sly and stingy. He gave the farmhands very little to eat.

✘ That guy was very sly and stingy. He gives the farmhands very little to eat.

> 兩個獨立句子的動詞表示的動作雖有先後，但都屬過去的範疇，動詞該用過去時態。

3.92 他打開門，拔腳就逃。

✔　He opened the door and <u>ran</u> off.

✘　He opened the door and <u>runs</u> off.

> 在同一句中，兩個動詞表示的動作雖有先後，但都屬過去的範疇，動詞該用過去時態。參見例 3.91。

3.93 他昨天對我說，他在暑假期間要到泰國去。

✔　Yesterday he told me that he <u>was</u> going to Thailand for the summer vacation.

✘　Yesterday he told me that he <u>is</u> going to Thailand for the summer vacation.

> 間接引語的時態受主句時態的制約，主句的時態是過去式，間接引語的時態也應該用過去式，但表示習慣的動作、常例或一般真理時，間接引語的時態不受主句時態的制約。例如：
> When I was a boy, my teacher told me that the earth <u>is</u> round.
> He told me that he <u>goes</u> there every winter.

3.94 他說晚上八時之前本來可以把功課做好。

✔　He said that he <u>would</u> have finished his homework by eight in the evening.

✘　He said that he <u>will</u> have finished his homework by eight in the evening.

> 參見例 3.93。

3.95 他說他從來沒有到過泰國。

✔　He said that he <u>had</u> never been to Thailand.

✘　He said that he <u>has</u> never been to Thailand.

參見例 3.93。

3.96　我說我還沒把包裹寄出。

✔　I said I <u>hadn't</u> mailed the parcel yet.

✘　I said I <u>haven't</u> mailed the parcel yet.

參見例 3.93。

3.97　老師指出你報告中的錯誤後，你要怎麼辦呢？

✔　What will you do after the teacher <u>points</u> (/ has pointed) out the mistakes in your report?

✘　What will you do after the teacher <u>pointed</u> out the mistakes in your report?

某些從屬句（特別是受詞從屬句）的動詞時態，常受主句裏動詞時態的制約。關於受詞從屬句的時態連續已見上例。

after 子句以及有關時間的副詞子句多以現在式取代未來式，以現在完成式取代未來完成式。

3.98　這是你剛才要找的人嗎？

✔　<u>Is</u> this the man (whom) you were looking for a moment ago?

✘　<u>Was</u> this the man (whom) you were looking for a moment ago?

修飾主句的形容詞子句的時態不受時態連續限制，應按具體需要而定。
試觀察下列句子中主要子句及從屬子句的時態：

The girl who <u>is sitting</u> behind you <u>will play</u> the piano.

The girl (who is) sitting over there <u>was</u> my student.

The boy (whom) you <u>met</u> in the gym the other day <u>is</u> the best student in my class.

The boy (whom) you <u>saw</u> the other day <u>is running</u> towards us.

3.99　站在門口的那個女孩在去年的馬拉松比賽中得了第一名。

✔　The girl who <u>is</u> standing at the doorway came in first in last year's marathon.

✘　The girl who <u>was</u> standing at the doorway came in first in last year's marathon.

參見例 3.98。

3.100　這書如果圖書館買六本，那就足夠流通了。

✔　If the library buys six copies of this title, there <u>will</u> be enough to go around.

✘　If the library buys six copies of this title, there <u>would</u> be enough to go round.

這句表示將來可能發生的情況，一般應用將來時態，在條件子句中可用一般現在時態代替將來時態。

4)　Aspects misused 語態的誤用

3.101　事故是昨天下午發生的。

✔　The accident <u>happened</u> yesterday afternoon.

✘　The accident <u>was happened</u> yesterday afternoon.

參見下例 3.106。

3.102　抗日戰爭在 1937 年爆發。

✔　The War of Resistance against Japan <u>broke out</u> in 1937.

✘　The War of Resistance against Japan <u>was broken out</u> in 1937.

參見下例 3.106。

3.103　我們的故鄉發生了巨大的變化。

✔　A great change <u>has</u> taken place in our home town.

✘　A great change <u>was</u> taken place in our home town.

參見下例 3.106。

3.104 在維多利亞時代，民主只是有錢人的特權。

✔ In the Victorian Age democratic privileges <u>belonged to</u> the rich only.

✘ In the Victorian Age democratic privileges <u>was belonged to</u> the rich only.

參見下例 3.106。

3.105 他們逐漸消失在黑暗中。

✔ They gradually disappeared in the darkness.

✘ They <u>were</u> gradually disappeared in the darkness.

參見下例 3.106。

3.106 他雖然一句話也沒説，可是心裏感覺到自己是失敗了。

✔ Though he didn't say a word, in his heart he felt he <u>had</u> failed.

✘ Though he didn't say a word, in his heart he felt he <u>was</u> failed.

例句 3.101 到 3.106 中的動詞 happen, belong, disappear, fail 都是不及物動詞，不可能有被動語態。詞組 to break out, to take place 也是如此。

3.107 我們雖然遭受嚴重的天然災害，但一定能克服困難。

✔ Though we <u>suffer from</u> serious natural disasters, we are sure to overcome all difficulties.

✘ Though we <u>are suffered from</u> serious natural disasters, we are sure to overcome all difficulties.

參見下面例 3.109。

3.108　每一輛車在出廠之前必須經過嚴格的檢驗。

✔　Every car must <u>pass</u> a strict test before it leaves the factory.

✘　Every car must <u>be passed</u> a strict test before it leaves the factory.

> 參見下面例 3.109。

3.109　他在幼年時代經歷了許多苦難。

✔　He <u>underwent</u> many hardships during his childhood.

✘　He <u>was undergone</u> many hardships during his childhood.

> 例句 3.107 到 3.109 出現的 "遭受"、"經過"、"經歷" 在中文中有被動意思，但在英語中 suffer, pass, undergo 應用主動語態。

3.110　我是 1991 年受傷的。

✔　I <u>was wounded</u> in 1991.

✘　I <u>wounded</u> in 1991.

> 參見下面例 3.114。

3.111　全國各地成立了許多閱讀組織。

✔　Many reading groups have <u>been established</u> all over the country.

✘　Many reading groups have <u>established</u> all over the country.

> 參見下面例 3.114。

3.112　這些目標一定可以超越的。

✔　These targets are bound to <u>be surpassed</u>.

✘　These targets are bound to <u>surpass</u>.

> 參見下面例 3.114。

3.113 他一點也不驚訝。

✔ He was not at all surprised.

✘ He did not surprise at all.

> 參見下面例 3.114。

3.114 自 2018 年起那國家已經擺脫了口蹄疫。

✔ That country has been free from foot-and-mouth disease since 2018.

✘ That country has freed foot-and-mouth disease since 2018.

> 例句 3.110 到 3.114 中的 "受傷"、"成立"、"超越"、"驚訝" 及 "擺脫了" 等在中文原句中好像沒有被動語態，學生受了中文影響，在用英語表達時也用主動語態，這是錯誤的。另參見例 3.79。

5） Auxiliary verbs 助動詞

3.115 這一定不是真的。

✔ This cannot be true.

✘ This must not be true.

> ⑴ must 可以用來表示 "命令"、"義務"。例如：
>
> You must do it at once.
> We must go to school in the morning.
>
> 其否定語是 must not (= mustn't)，表示 "絕對不可"，"一定不可"。例如：
>
> You mustn't play soccer in the street.
> You mustn't spit on the floor.
>
> ⑵ 對於未知的事情有所推測，肯定用 must，否定用 cannot。例如：
>
> That must be a mistake.
> No, it cannot be a mistake.
> You must be very tired; you have worked for quite a long time.
> You cannot be tired; you have only just begun to work.
>
> 必須注意，must 用於第二義時往往與 be 結合。

3.116　他明天必須把報告交來。

✔　He <u>must</u> hand in his report tomorrow.

✔　He <u>has to</u> hand in his report tomorrow.

✘　He <u>need</u> hand in his report tomorrow.

> need 作助動詞用時，只能用於疑問句和否定句中，沒有時式的變化，第三人稱單數不加 s，後面接沒有 to 的否定式，過去式與現在式形式上相同。例如：
>
> <u>Need</u> he hand in his report tomorrow?
> No, he <u>need</u> not.
> <u>Need</u> he go to the farm tomorrow?
> No, he <u>needn't</u>.

3.117　昨天他必須上市場去。

✔　He <u>had</u> to go to the market yesterday.

✘　He <u>needed</u> to go to the market yesterday.

✘　He <u>need</u> go to the market yesterday.

> need 作普通動詞用時，有時式、人稱、數的變化，可以和有 to 的不定式用於肯定句中，但用 must 或 have to 較為普遍，上列第二句不及第一句普遍。又如：He must（很少用 needs to）start early.。

3.118　今天用不着把報告交來。

✔　You <u>don't have to</u> hand in your report today.

✘　You <u>must not</u> hand in your report today.

> must not 是 "絕對不可"、"一定不可" 已見上述。"用不着"、"無庸"、"無須" 應用 don't have to 或 don't need to（＝ needn't）表達。試比較：You <u>mustn't</u> miss the lesson, though we <u>needn't</u> have it on Thursday.（你們絕對不能缺課，雖然我們不一定會在星期四上課。）

3.119　只要我們堅持做下去，最後一定會成功。

✔　We will <u>surely</u> succeed in the end so long as we keep on working.

✔ We are <u>sure to</u> succeed in the end so long as we keep on working.

✘ We <u>must</u> succeed in the end so long as we keep on working.

不少學生受到中文思維的影響，看到"一定"、"必然"往往用 must 來表達。must 表示"命令"、"義務"、"責任"，或用以推測未知的事情，已如上述。上面的句子表示將來肯定會有某種結果，就不可用 must，應用 will。觀察下列句子：

只要我們大家全力以赴，必然會克服困難的。

    ✔ If only we try with all our might, we will overcome the difficulties.

    ✘ If only we try with all our might, the difficulties must be overcome.

不管是甚麼困難，我們一定會達成目標。

    ✔ Whatever the difficulties, we will surely achieve our end.

    ✘ Whatever the difficulties, we must achieve our end.

---

6) The to-infinitives 不定詞

3.120 暴君迫使他們從早工作到晚。

✔ The tyrant made them <u>work</u> from dawn till dusk.

✘ The tyrant made them <u>to work</u> from dawn till dusk.

---

feel, hear, see, let, make, have, watch 等動詞後面複合受詞中的不定詞符號 to，照例必須省去。

3.121 我們分三個小組來討論吧！

✔ Let us <u>split up</u> into three groups to discuss it.

✘ Let us <u>to split up</u> into three groups to discuss it.

參見例 3.120。

3.122 我會叫他把這些句子抄好。

✔ I'll have him <u>copy</u> these sentences.

✘　I'll have him <u>to copy</u> these sentences.

> 參見例 3.120。

3.123　你最好立刻就去。

✔　You had better <u>go</u> there right now.

✘　You had better <u>to go</u> there right now.

> had better, had best, would rather, cannot but 等慣用語，後面跟原形動詞，不用 to。

3.124　我到學校時忘了鎖腳踏車。

✔　I forgot <u>to lock</u> my bike when I came to school.

✘　I forgot <u>locking</u> my bike when I came to school.

> forget 後面跟動名詞或跟不定詞表示兩種不同的概念：跟動名詞作 "忘記曾經……" 解，跟不定詞作 "忘記而不曾……" 解。錯句的意義是 "我到學校時曾把腳踏車鎖好，這件事我後來忘記了"，顯然與中文原意不合。"應做某事而忘了去做" 應用 forget 接不定詞。試比較下列句子：
>
> He <u>forgot giving</u> her the letter.（他忘了曾經把信交給她這件事。）
> He <u>forgot to give</u> her the letter.（他忘了把信交給她。）

3.125　我得記住明天要把作文寫好。

✔　I must remember <u>to finish</u> my composition tomorrow.

✘　I must remember <u>finishing</u> my composition tomorrow.

> remember 後面跟動名詞或不定詞表示兩種不同的概念，與 forget 相類似，參見例 3.124。試比較下列句子：
>
> I <u>remember meeting</u> him somewhere.（我記得曾經在某處碰見過他。）
> I <u>must remember to meet</u> him at the station at six this evening.
> （我必須記住今晚六時要去車站接他。）
> He <u>remembered turning off</u> the light when he left the room.
> （他記得離開房間時曾先把燈關了。）
> <u>Remember to turn off</u> the light when you leave the room.

（記住離開房間時要把燈關了。）

3.126 他提醒她做好她份內的事。

✔ He reminded her <u>to do</u> her job.

✘ He reminded her <u>of doing</u> her job.

> remind...of... 後面跟動名詞，表示 "提醒某人已經做過某事"。若是 "提醒某人應做某事"，應用 remind...to do...。試比較下列句子：
>
> He <u>reminded me of</u> my attending the lecture last Friday.
> （他讓我想起我上星期五去聽過那次演講。）
> He <u>reminded me to attend</u> the lecture this afternoon.
> （他提醒我下午要去聽演講。）

3.127 他開始學法語。

✔ He <u>is beginning to study</u> French.

✔ He <u>has begun to study</u> French.

✘ He <u>is beginning studying</u> French.

> begin 可以接不定詞也可以接動名詞，He began to study French. ＝ He began studying French.。但在 is beginning, was beginning 等後面常接不定詞，也許是為了避免 -ing 的重複。

3.128 告訴他不要做這件事。

✔ Tell him <u>not to</u> do it.

✘ Tell him <u>don't</u> do it.

> "告訴他……" 整句是祈使句，但 "不要做這件事" 在這裏不是直接引語，不能視作祈使句，因此不能用 "don't ＋ 原形動詞" 這一結構。

3.129 新生一下車，我們就趕上去幫他們提行李。

✔ As soon as the new students got off the bus, we hurried over <u>to help carry</u> their bags.

✘ As soon as the new students got off the bus, we hurried over,

<u>carrying</u> their bags.

> 用現在分詞描述情況，它所表示的動作往往與句中謂語動詞所表示的動作同時進行。carrying 顯然不是與 hurried 同時進行，應改用不定詞 to help carry... 表示 "趕去" 的目的，否則便是 "手裏拿了行李奔過去"，不是 "奔過去拿行李" 了。

3.130　他趕上去扶她起來。

✔ He rushed over <u>to help</u> her up.

✔ He rushed over <u>and helped</u> her up.

✘ He rushed over, <u>helping</u> her up.

> 參見例 3.129。

7）　Participles 分詞

3.131　展出的是幾幅齊白石的名畫。

✔ There are some masterpieces <u>painted</u> by Chi Pai-shih on exhibition.

✘ There are some masterpieces <u>painting</u> by Chi Pai-shih on exhibition.

> 現在分詞 painting 表明主動的或未完成的動作，這裏的必須改用過去分詞。現代英語裏，正句裏的 painted 一字，往往亦略去。

3.132　書前面有簡短的序言。

✔ There is a short foreword <u>preceding</u> the book.

✘ There is a short foreword <u>preceded</u> the book.

> precede 作 "在……之前" 解。a short foreword 是放在述詞後的主詞，應用現在分詞 preceding 表明主動的動作，句義與 There is a short foreword which <u>precedes</u> the book. 相同。

3.133 昨天發生的事故有誰在裏面，你知道嗎？

✔　Do you know anyone who was in the accident that happened yesterday?

✘　Do you know anyone who was in the accident happened yesterday?

> 錯句中的 happened 是過去分詞，一般而言，過去分詞形式有被動的意義，但 happen 是不及物動詞，不能用作被動形式。若用現在分詞 happening 則表示未完成的動作，與中文原意不合，因此，改用形容詞子句表達。下列例句也犯了同樣的錯誤。
>
> 我上個月發表的有關創造力的文章，你讀了沒有？
>
> ✔　Have you read my article about creativity that appeared in last month's journal?
>
> ✘　Have you read my article about creativity appearing in last month's journal?
>
> ✘　Have you read my article about creativity appeared in last month's journal?

3.134 我覺得這本書非常無聊。

✔　I find this book boring.

✘　I find this book bored.

> 參見例 3.136。此外，請比較：You are boring. I am bored.。

3.135 這突如其來的消息令人覺得有趣。

✔　This sudden news is really interesting.

✘　This sudden news is really interested.

> 參見接下來的例 3.136。另請比較：This book is interesting. I'm interested in it.。

3.136 他的突然失蹤令人驚慌。

✔　His sudden disappearance is alarming.

✗ His sudden disappearance is <u>alarmed</u>.

例句 3.134 到 3.136 中的過去分詞都有被動的意義，但句子中需要的是主動引起別人某種情感的語詞，應用現在分詞。屬於相同性質容易被誤用的有 disgusting, disgusted; amazing, amazed; amusing, amused; confusing, confused; astonishing, astonished; astounding, astounded; disappointing, disappointed; discouraging, discouraged 等。

3.137　她看起來很失望。

✓ She looks <u>disappointed</u>.

✗ She looks <u>disappointing</u>.

參見下面例 3.138。

3.138　他的話使我不安。

✓ His remark <u>disturbed</u> me.

✓ His remark <u>made</u> me <u>disturbed</u>.

✗ His remark <u>made</u> me <u>disturbing</u>.

例句 3.137、3.138 的情況，同例句 3.134、3.135、3.136 剛好相反。凡是由於某種外來的因素而產生某種情緒，都用過去分詞；這些分詞實際上已有一般形容詞的性質，不一定強調它的被動意義。

3.139　對不起，讓你久等了。

✓ I am sorry <u>to have kept</u> you <u>waiting</u>.

✓ I am sorry <u>I kept</u> you <u>waiting</u>.

✗ I am sorry <u>to have kept</u> you <u>to wait</u>.

keep 後面接名詞（或代名詞）+ 分詞構成的複合受詞，而不接名詞（或代名詞）+ 不定詞構成的複合受詞。

3.140　他收拾好行裝，急忙趕向車站。

✓ <u>Having packed</u> his things, he hurried to the train station.

✔ After getting his things together, he hurried to the train station.

✘ Getting his things together, he hurried to the station.

> 現在分詞所表示的動作往往與句中述部動詞所表示的動作同時進行。上面句子中 "收拾……" 的動作不可能與 "趕向……" 同時發生，兩個動作必須有先後，才合乎邏輯，因此錯句的現在分詞要改為完成分詞或改為介詞 after 後面跟動名詞。請注意以下的例外：
>
> Entering the room, he was greeted by the ambassador.
> Arriving at the station, we learned that the train had already gone.
> Hearing footsteps, we stopped talking.
>
> 上面三句中的現在分詞可以代替完成分詞，表示述部動詞的動作緊接着分詞的動作。

3.141 聽到這不幸的消息，他眼淚盈眶。

✔ Hearing the bad news, he could not help bursting into tears.

✔ When he heard the bad news, tears gushed from his eyes.

✘ Hearing the bad news, tears gushed from his eyes.

> 從結構上來看，錯句裏的 hearing the bad news 是歸屬於 tears 的，但在邏輯上連接不起來，因 tears 不是分詞短語的行為主體，語法上稱之為 "不連結的分詞短語"（dangling phrase）。雖然名作家的作品中偶有類似的句子，但初學英語者應按照正規，避免不合邏輯的表達方式。有些分詞，已成為獨立成分，不能與不連接分詞相提並論。例如：
>
> Generally speaking, this novel is not interesting.
> Judging by his appearance, he can't be more than twenty.

3.142 看到他來，她臉色慘白。

✔ Seeing him coming over, she paled / turned pale.

✔ When she saw him coming over, her face turned pale.

✘ Seeing him coming over, her face turned pale.

> 參見例 3.141。

8)　　Gerunds 動名詞

3.143　他停止與室友談話。

✔　He stopped <u>talking</u> with his roommates.

✘　He stopped <u>to talk</u> with his roommates.

> 動詞 stop 後面接不定詞或後面接動名詞表示完全不同的概念。前者作 "把旁的事停下來而從事……"，後者作 "停止……" 解，"He stopped to talk with his friends." 是 "他停下來同朋友談談" 之意。

3.144　王先生花了兩天整理房子。

✔　Mr. Wang spent two days <u>cleaning</u> his house.

✘　Mr. Wang spent two days <u>to clean</u> his house.

> 動詞 spend 如用以指花費時間，後面必須用動名詞，但 He spent two thousand dollars to furnish his house. 則可用不定詞。

3.145　他已習慣長時間工作了。

✔　He is used to <u>working</u> long hours.

✘　He is used to <u>work</u> long hours.

> to be used to 是指主詞對某項事物的適應性，它不同於 used to（參見例 4.47）。這裏 used 後面的 to 是介詞，後面跟名詞或動名詞。例如：
>
> He <u>is used to</u> hard work.
> I <u>am used to</u> reading aloud.

3.146　他堅持親自做這件事。

✔　He insisted <u>on doing</u> it himself.

✘　He insisted <u>to do</u> it himself.

> insist 後面必須用介詞 on 或 upon，其後接動名詞或名詞，如 to insist on one's innocence。insist 後面也可用 that 引導的名詞從屬句，如 to insist that one is innocent。

3.147 他成功獲得了第一獎。

✔ He succeeded in winning first prize.

✘ He succeeded to win first prize.

> succeed 後面不能跟不定詞,必須用介詞 in,後面接名詞或動名詞。

3.148 這輛摩托車需要修理了。

✔ This motorcycle needs (/ wants) repairing.

✔ This motorcycle needs to be repaired.

✘ This motorcycle needs being repaired.

> "需要修理"雖然有被動的意味,但英語中接在 need、want 等後面的動名詞等於被動語態的不定詞。例如:
>
> Your boots need mending (= need to be mended).
> Your work needs correcting (= needs to be corrected).

3.149 這本書不值得一讀。

✔ This book is not worth reading.

✘ This book is not worth being read.

> 參見例 4.148。

3.150 到達英國時,一幅美麗的景色呈現在我們眼前。

✔ On arriving in England, we saw a beautiful scene.

✔ When we arrived England, a beautiful scene presented itself before our eyes.

✘ On arriving England, a beautiful scene presented itself before our eyes.

> 錯句中動名詞短語 On arriving in England,按結構隸屬 a beautiful scene。但 a beautiful scene 不是動名詞短語的行為主體,必須把動名詞短語的行為主體在句子中表達出來。以下錯句也有同樣的情形:聽到這一消息,他面露喜色。

> ✔ <u>On hearing</u> the news, he beamed with delight.
> ✔ <u>When the news reached</u> his ears, a joyful expression spread over his face.
> ✘ <u>On hearing</u> the news, a joyful expression broke out on his face.

v.　Adjectives and adverbs 形容詞和副詞

1)　Adjectives easily misused 容易用錯的形容詞

3.151　我們必須盡可能生產更多優良的絲布。

✔ We must produce as <u>much</u> fine silk <u>cloth</u> as possible.

✘ We must produce as <u>many</u> fine silk <u>cloths</u> as possible.

> many 用於可數名詞前面，much 用於不可數名詞前面。cloth 作 "布料" 解，是不可數名詞，沒有複數；作 "一塊布"、"桌布" 解，才是可數名詞，複數是 cloths。

3.152　抱歉得很，我法語懂得很少。

✔ I am sorry I know <u>so</u> little French (= very little French).

✘ I am sorry I know <u>a</u> little French.

> a little 作 "有一些"、"雖少還有" 解。例如：I have a little money with me. It might be enough for a pair of shoes。（我身邊帶着一點錢，也許夠買一雙鞋。）little 是 "很少"、"幾乎沒有" 之意。錯句前後矛盾，改正後才合乎情理。如説 "I am glad I know a little French." 也合乎情理。

3.153　在台北，她的朋友很少。

✔ She has <u>few</u> friends in Taipei.

✘ She has <u>a few</u> friends in Taipei.

> a few 與 few 的區別和 a little 與 little 的區別類似，參見例 3.152。錯句中的 a few，應作 "有一些" 解。

3.154 我有些事要做。

✔ I have a few things to do.

✘ I have few things to do.

> 參見例 3.153。

3.155 他們幾乎沒有時間把工作做完。

✔ They have little time to finish their work.

✘ They have few time to finish their work.

> few 和 a few 用在可數名詞前面；little 和 a little 用在不可數名詞前面。

3.156 我們必須盡可能少犯錯誤。

✔ We must make as few errors as possible.

✘ We must make as fewer errors as possible.

> 在連接詞 as... as 和 so... as 間，只可用形容詞或副詞的原級。例如：
>
> He is as hardworking as his sister.
> We must work as hard as possible.
> You do not study so well as the others.

3.157 為了節約，盡可能少花錢。

✔ Use as little money as possible to economize.

✘ Use as less money as possible to economize.

> 參見例 3.156。

3.158 她燒菜可以媲美我們任何一個。

✔ She is as good a cook as any of us.

✘ She is as a good cook as any of us.

> 誤句第一個 as 是副詞，不能修飾名詞，因此要把 good 提前。其他例句如：

> He is as <u>poor</u> a listener as she.
> The old woman has as <u>good</u> a memory as any youngster.

3.159 他工作和他弟弟一樣努力，但比不上他姊姊。

✔ He works as hard as his younger brother, but <u>not as</u> hard as his elder sister.

✘ He works as hard as his younger brother, but <u>does not work</u> hard as his elder sister.

> 把兩個相同的人或事物比較時，必須用 as...as 或 not so / as...as。誤句後半句中少了 so / as，就不能表示比較的意義，類似的例子有：
>
> He is <u>as</u> smart <u>as</u> his brother.
> He is not <u>so / as</u> smart <u>as</u> his brother.
> He walks <u>as</u> slow <u>as</u> his mother.
> He does not walk <u>so / as</u> slow <u>as</u> his mother.

3.160 這個新電腦的資料儲存量是舊的一百倍。

✔ This new computer stores 100 times <u>as much information</u> as the old one.

✘ This new computer stores 100 times <u>information as much</u> as the old one.

> 用 as...as 表示某物是另一物的幾倍，應特別注意詞序。例如：
> This river is three times <u>as</u> long <u>as</u> that one.
> She is twice <u>as</u> old <u>as</u> her brother.

3.161 這頓晚飯即使不比你昨天做的更好，至少也是一樣好。

✔ This dinner is as delicious <u>as</u> the one you made us yesterday, if (it is) not more so (than the one you made us yesterday).

✘ This dinner is as delicious, if not more so, <u>than</u> the one you made us yesterday.

> 兩物進行比較時，不要把 as 與 than 混淆，在增添修飾語之前，應把要

> 比較的東西全部講清楚，而增添語中重複的詞組則不妨省略。

3.162 她比你聰明，但是學識不如你豐富。

✔ She is brighter <u>than</u> you, but not so well read (as you).

✘ She is brighter, but not so well read <u>as</u> you.

> 參見例 3.161。

2） Adjectives and other parts of speech easily confused 形容詞和其他詞類的混淆

3.163 我沒有姊妹。

✔ I <u>have no</u> sister(s).

✔ I <u>haven't</u> got any sisters.

✘ I <u>have not</u> sister.

> 此處 no 是形容詞，加在名詞前作修飾用，等於 not any，not 是副詞，不能直接修飾名詞。又如：* In dictatorial countries people have no any freedom. 句中應把 any 刪去，或把 no 改為 not。

3.164 不要怕他。

✔ Don't <u>be afraid of</u> him.

✔ Don't <u>fear</u> him.

✘ Don't <u>afraid of</u> him.

> afraid 是形容詞，在句中作補語用，必須加 be 動詞。

3.165 他準備好了嗎？

✔ <u>Has</u> he <u>got</u> everything <u>ready</u>?

✔ <u>Is</u> he ready?

✘ <u>Has</u> he <u>ready</u>?

> ready 是形容詞，在句中作補語，前面必須加上連繫動詞。

3.166 我們必須在兩點鐘前把一切準備好。

✔ We must <u>get everything ready</u> by two.

✔ We must <u>be ready</u> by two.

✘ We must <u>be ready everything</u> by two.

> ready 是形容詞,後面不能加受詞;to get...ready 是把(某事、某物)準備好。

3.167 這顆鑽石值二十萬元。

✔ This diamond <u>is worth</u> 200,000 dollars.

✘ This diamond <u>worths</u> 200,000 dollars.

> worth 是形容詞,不能作動詞用。

3.168 喬治氣得發抖。

✔ George trembled with <u>anger</u>.

✘ George trembled with <u>angry</u>.

> 介詞 with 後面應用名詞作介詞受詞;angry 是形容詞,anger 是名詞。

3.169 他態度太謙遜。

✔ He is over <u>modest</u>.

✘ He is over <u>modesty</u>.

> modesty 是名詞,modest 是形容詞,描寫或修飾主詞,應以形容詞作補語。

3.170 我印象非常深刻。

✔ I am <u>very</u> impressed.

✘ I am <u>very much</u> impressed.

> very much 修飾動詞,very 修飾副詞或形容詞,所以這句應用 very。
> 試比較:

> I am <u>very</u> fond of dancing.
> I like dancing <u>very</u> much.

3.171 她看起來很高興。

✔ She looks very <u>happy</u>.

✗ She looks very <u>happily</u>.

> be, look, smell, taste 等詞用作連繫動詞時，後面只能接形容詞、代名詞作補語。比較：
>
> He <u>looks</u> greedy.
>
> He <u>looked</u> greedily at the money.（此句中 looked 為一般動詞，意為 "看着"，不作連繫動詞用。）
>
> 下列句子中的錯誤屬同類性質：
>
> ✔ The table feels <u>smooth</u>.
> ✗ The table feels <u>smoothly</u>.
> ✔ The television has been wiped <u>clean</u>.
> ✗ The television has been wiped <u>cleanly</u>.

3.172 如果你不能保持安靜，請你離開。

✔ If you can't keep <u>quiet</u>, please leave.

✗ If you can't keep <u>quietly</u>, please leave.

> 這裏 keep 表示狀態，作連繫動詞，後面應用形容詞 quiet，不用副詞 quietly。其他的例子如下：
>
> My mother doesn't like to sit <u>idle</u>.
>
> The child sat <u>still</u> for quite a long while.
>
> Completely taken aback, he stood <u>mute</u>.
>
> In the evening he came home <u>tired</u>.

3) Adverbs easily misused 容易用錯的副詞

3.173 他沒有看過那部電影，我也沒有看過。

✔ He hasn't seen the movie. I haven't seen it <u>either</u>.

✗ He hasn't seen the movie. I haven't seen it <u>too</u>.

too 表示 "也"，在肯定句中與 also 同義而更口語化。too 一般放在句末，或作為插入語放在句中。also 通常靠近動詞，不放在句末。例如：

> He likes chocolate; I <u>also</u> like it.
>
> He likes chocolate; I like it <u>too</u>.

表示 "也不"，不可以在否定語的後面用 too，應用 either 或用 nor 表示否定。但口語裏有時為了強調也把 also 放在否定語的前面。例如：

> He doesn't like *Gone With the Wind;* I don't like it <u>either</u>.
>
> He doesn't like *Gone With the Wind;* I <u>also</u> don't like it.
>
> He doesn't know her telephone number; <u>nor</u> do I.

3.174 他不難過，我也不難過。

✔ He was not upset. <u>Neither</u> / <u>Nor</u> was I.

✘ He was not upset. <u>So</u> was I.

承接前句述詞的動作，因而構成新的句子時，新句子的詞序是：動詞在前，主詞在後。但應注意：肯定時用副詞 so，否定時用 neither 或 nor。例如：

> He likes to play the guitar, and <u>so</u> do I.
>
> He has been to France, and <u>so</u> has she.
>
> He doesn't like playing tennis; <u>neither / nor</u> do we.
>
> He wouldn't go to church; <u>neither / nor</u> would you.
>
> He can't whistle; <u>neither / nor</u> can you.

3.175 連小學生都不會相信這樣的謊言。

✔ <u>Not even</u> schoolchildren will believe such a lie.

✔ <u>Even</u> schoolchildren will <u>not</u> believe such a lie.

✘ <u>Even no</u> schoolchildren will believe such a lie.

"連……也不……" 用 not even... 或 even...not... ，而不可用 even no... 。

3.176 他還沒有來。

✔ He has <u>not</u> arrived <u>yet</u>.

✘ He has <u>still not</u> arrived.

在一般否定句中表示 "還"、"尚"、"至今還" 應用 yet，不用 still，比較：

He is <u>still</u> here. (現尚在此)
He is not here <u>yet</u>. (尚未來此)

在肯定句中兩者可以通用。例如：

There is yet (=still) time.

3.177 他們剛到達。

✔ They came <u>just now</u>.
✔ They <u>have just</u> come.
✘ They <u>just</u> came.

just 作 "剛才"、"方才" 解，一般與完成時態連用。第三個例句有人認為不對，不過在現代英語裏，這並不算錯。just now 作 "片刻之前" (＝ not long ago)，與過去一般時態連用；作 at this moment 解，與現在一般時態連用。例如：He is rather busy <u>just now</u>. 。

3.178 我記得上個月見過他。

✔ I remember that I <u>met</u> him last month.
✘ I remember that I <u>ever met</u> him last month.

ever 表示 "曾經"，但不能用在肯定直述句中，只用在疑問句、否定句中，或與最高級連用，強調語氣。例如：

Have you <u>ever</u> been to Keelung?
Nothing <u>ever</u> happens in this sleepy town.
This is the worst book I have <u>ever</u> read.

3.179 他有點不好意思，所以低下了頭。

✔ He was <u>a little</u> ashamed and hung his head.
✘ He was <u>little</u> ashamed and hung his head.

little 和 a little 這裏作副詞。其區別與作形容詞相同，參見例 3.153。

3.180 他母親去世已久。

✔ His mother has been <u>dead for many years</u>.

✔ His mother <u>died long ago</u>.

✘ His mother has been <u>dead long ago</u>.

> ago 表示從現在算起若干時間以前,而不是指從過去某一時刻到現在的一段時間。例如:an hour ago, a few years ago, long ago 等。凡有 ago 的時間副詞只能與過去時態連用。

3.181 我三天前就把那本書借給他了。

✔ I lent him the book three days <u>ago</u>.

✘ I lent him the book three days <u>before</u>.

> 從現在起若干時間以前,"該用 ago。只説"以前",也可用 before。例如:
>
> I have never seen it <u>before</u>.
> I never saw it <u>before</u>.

3.182 她是兩小時以前離開的。

✔ She left here two hours <u>ago</u>.

✘ She left here <u>before</u> two hours.

> before 作介詞,與表示一個時刻、日期或年代的詞或詞組連用。例如:before 5 o'clock, the day before yesterday, before 1949,而不能與表示一段時間的詞連用。

3.183 我很愛我的父親。

✔ I love my father <u>dearly</u>.

✔ I love my father <u>very much</u>.

✘ I <u>very</u> love my father.

> very 不能直接修飾動詞,用以修飾動詞表示程度的副詞是 very much。

4） Adjectives mistaken for adverbs 形容詞誤用為副詞

3.184 因為食物不夠，我格外感到飢餓。

✔ I felt all the more hungry, for there was <u>not</u> enough food.

✘ I felt all the more hungry, for there was <u>no</u> enough food.

> 可以説 no good food, no suitable clothes，因為這裏 no 修飾 food, clothes（＝ no food that is good, no clothes that are suitable）。 本句應該用 not enough food，因這裏 not 修飾形容詞 enough。同樣，*There is no much time left. 應改為 There is not much time left.。

3.185 你不能指望我在一小時內做這麼多工作。

✔ You cannot expect me to do <u>so</u> many things in only one hour.

✘ You cannot expect me to do <u>such</u> many things in only one hour.

> such 作 "這樣的" 解時，是形容詞，修飾名詞。例如：such a book, such things。表示 "這麼多"、"那麼久" 等應用副詞 so 來修飾形容詞。例如：so many things, so much food, so quickly, so long 等。

3.186 她氣得説不出話來。

✔ She was <u>so</u> angry that she could hardly speak.

✘ She was <u>such</u> angry that she could hardly speak.

> 參見例 3.185。

3.187 這裙子好舊呀！

✔ <u>What</u> an old dress (it is)!

✔ <u>How old</u> the dress is!

✘ <u>How</u> an old dress it is!

> how, what 同樣可以引導出感歎句，但 how 修飾所要強調的形容詞或副詞。若修飾所要強調的名詞，該用 what。

3.188 他法文看得很快。

✔ He reads French <u>very well</u>.

✔ He is <u>good at</u> reading French.

✘ He reads French <u>very good</u>.

> good 是形容詞，不能修飾動詞 reads，應用副詞 well。

3.189 我們看見一個人站在河邊。

✔ We saw a man standing <u>by</u> the river.

✔ We saw a man standing <u>near</u> the river.

✘ We saw a man standing <u>nearby</u> the river.

> nearby 嚴格地來説只能作形容詞或副詞，不能當介詞用。例如：
>
> The peasants live in the village <u>nearby</u>.
> The children are playing <u>nearby</u>.

5） Comparatives and gradability 比較級和等級

3.190 這兩本書哪一本有意思？

✔ Which of the two books is <u>more</u> interesting?

✘ Which of the two books is <u>the most</u> interesting?

> 兩人或兩物相比，在文字中一般應該用比較級。

3.191 她德語説得和她老師一樣流利。

✔ <u>Her</u> German is as fluent as her <u>teacher's</u>.

✔ <u>She speaks</u> German as fluently as her teacher (does).

✘ <u>Her</u> German is as fluent as her <u>teacher</u>.

> 這裏所比的是 "她的德語" 和 "她老師的德語"，而不是把她的德語和她的老師這個人相比，所以必須説 her teacher's，即 her teacher's German。或把 "她説德語" 和 "她老師説德語" 比較。

3.192 華北人與華南人不同。

✔ The people of North China are different from <u>those of</u> South China.

✘ The people of North China are different from South China.

所不同者是華北人和華南人，而不是華北的人和華南這一地區本身，所以應加 those of，those 代替 the people，以免重複。

3.193 他的新小說和上一本風格不同。

✔ <u>The style of</u> his new novel is different from <u>that of</u> his last one.

✔ His new novel is different from his last one <u>in style</u>.

✘ <u>The style of</u> his new novel is different from his last novel.

正句第一句比較新小說的 style 和舊小說的 style，所以必須用 that of。第二句說明在 style 方面新舊小說不同，所比的是新舊小說。

3.194 有些病人覺得上午比下午好些。

✔ Some patients usually feel better in the morning than <u>in</u> the afternoon.

✘ Some patients usually feel better in the morning than the afternoon.

這裏所比較的是 patients feel in the morning 和 patients feel in the afternoon，而不是比較 patients 和 the afternoon，所以介詞 in 不可省略。

3.195 瑪麗是姊妹中最漂亮的。

✔ Mary is prettier <u>than any of her sisters</u>.

✔ Mary is the prettiest <u>of all the daughters</u> in the family.

✘ Mary is the prettiest <u>of all her sisters</u>.

all her sisters 不包括 Mary 本人在內。這裏應該是 " 所有女孩子中 "，所以用 of all the daughters。

vi.　Prepositions 介詞

1）　Prepositions misused 不該用而用

3.196　他們昨晨七時到那裏。

✔　They got there at seven yesterday morning.

✘　They got <u>to</u> there at seven yesterday morning.

> there 是副詞，通常前面不該有介詞，也不可用 I come to here，應説
> I come here。但 from here / there, near here / there, over there, up
> here / there 等都可以用。例如：
>
>> Let's go <u>up there</u>.
>> Do you see that man <u>over there</u>?
>> I can't see it <u>from here</u>.

3.197　他有時候週末回家。

✔　Sometimes he goes home on the weekend.

✘　Sometimes he goes <u>to</u> home on the weekend.

> home 用作副詞時，前面不加 to，例如：come home、go home、
> Is he home yet?（他到家了嗎？）、I saw him on his way home.、He
> arrived home. 等語裏都沒有 to 或 at。但是我們説 He is at home.、I
> went to his home.，這裏 home 用作名詞。

3.198　你每天幾點鐘上班？

✔　When do you go to work every day?

✘　When do you go to work <u>in</u> every day?

> every day 前面不用 in，也不用 on。this morning, this afternoon, this
> evening, next week, next month, next year 等前面也不用 in，但是 in
> the morning, in the afternoon, in the evening, in the night(at night), in
> the next week / month / year 等語中都用 in。

3.199 他們盡全力服務客戶。

✔ They are working hard to serve their clients.

✘ They are working hard to serve <u>for</u> their clients.

> serve 作及物動詞，意為 work for，不要再加 for；作不及物動詞時，意為 "作……用"。例如：
>
> This bundle of clothes serves very well <u>for / as</u> a pillow.
> （這包衣服大可作為枕頭之用。）

3.200 兩年前她和張先生結婚。

✔ She <u>married</u> Mr. Chang two years ago.

✔ She <u>and</u> Mr. Chang <u>married</u> two years ago.

✔ She <u>and</u> Mr. Chang <u>got married</u> two years ago.

✘ She <u>married with</u> Mr. Chang two years ago.

> marry 可作及物動詞用。在現代英語裏，marry 作不及物動詞用時，通常後接修飾語。例如：
>
> He <u>married</u> very young.
> He <u>didn't marry</u> until he was forty.
>
> 在大多數情況下，作及物動詞用。例如：
>
> He <u>is going to marry</u> Miss Lin.
> They <u>were / got married</u> soon after the Civil War.
>
> 但 to marry 或 to be married 都不可以接 with：
>
>   誤：She married with Mr. Chang.
>   誤：She was married with Mr. Chang.
>
> 比較下面的句子：
>
> She and Mr. Chang <u>got married</u>.（她和張先生結婚。）
> She <u>married (/ was married to)</u> Mr. Chang.（她嫁給張先生。）
> She <u>is married</u>.（她已結了婚。）
>
> 第三句裏的 married 相當於形容詞，作補語用。

3.201 你必須面對現實。

✔ You have got to face reality.

✘　You have got to face <u>to</u> reality.

> face 作 " 面向（reality, danger, difficulty, etc.）" 解時，後面不需加介詞 to。face (the) south, face to the south，則都可以説。

3.202　我們要開會，希望你參加。

✔　We are going to have a meeting. I hope you'll come and join us.

✘　We are going to have a meeting. I hope you'll come and join <u>with</u> us.

> 參加黨派、社會團體或參加到某些人中去用 join，不用 join with 或 join in，例如：join the party, join the army, join us（them, etc.）。參加某種活動，最好用 take part in，例如：I hope you'll <u>take part</u> in the party.。

3.203　他們每星期有幾次討論農業技術。

✔　They discussed farming technique several times a week.

✘　They discussed <u>about</u> farming techniques several times a week.

> discuss 作 talk about together 解，是及物動詞，後面不要再加 about。

3.204　無論甚麼事都逃不了他的眼睛。

✔　Nothing escapes <u>his attention</u>.

✔　Nothing escapes <u>him</u>.

✘　Nothing escapes <u>from his attention</u>.

> escape 借喻 " 不被注意 "、" 被忘掉 "，是及物動詞，直接跟 notice, attention, memory 等名詞，或人稱代名詞。例如：
>
> Her name <u>escapes</u> my memory.
> Her name <u>escapes</u> me.
>
> to escape one's lips 作 " 脱口而出 " 解，也不接介詞。但下列句子中 escape 用作不及物動詞，後面可以接介詞：

> The killer <u>escaped</u> through the back door.
> The prisoner <u>escaped</u> from the prison.

3.205 團結對抗共同敵人！

✔ Unite and <u>oppose</u> our common enemy!

✘ Unite and <u>oppose to</u> our common enemy!

> oppose 是及物動詞，後面不接 to，表示行動；to be opposed to 表示狀態，這裏的 opposed 用作形容詞。比較下面兩句：
> We <u>oppose</u> aggressive war.（表示行動）
> We <u>are opposed to</u> this plan.
> （表示思想上不贊成，但未必有具體行動）

2) Missing prepositions 該用而不用

3.206 我們很早到達電影院。

✔ We arrived very early <u>at</u> the theatre.

✘ We arrived very early the theatre.

> arrive 為不及物動詞，後面如果有受詞要用 at 或 in。例如：They <u>arrived in</u> Taipei yesterday。一般大地方，如國家、省、大城市等前面用 in，凡小城鎮、學校等前面用 at。

3.207 開車半小時以後，我們到達了海灘。

✔ After half an hour's drive, we got <u>to</u> the beach.

✘ After half an hour's drive, we got the beach.

> come, go, get（來、去、到達）某地時，在表示地點的名詞前面應該用 to，如 go to school, go to Taipei, come to Shanghai 等。如果這些動詞後面所跟的是 here, there, home 等副詞，則不用 to。參見例 3.196、3.197。

3.208 他一個星期以後回校。

✔ He will be back <u>at</u> school in a week.

✘　He will be back school in a week.

> to be back 一語裏的 back 是副詞，不是介詞，所以後面要用 at (school) 或 in (the institute)。
>
> 假如有幾天沒上學了，要回學校上課則可説：
>
> > I will be back to school in a week.

3.209　所有軍事單位都忙着準備接受檢查。

✔　All the army units are busy preparing <u>for</u> the inspection.

✘　All the army units are busy preparing the inspection.

> 軍事單位是為了接受檢查而準備，不是籌備檢查這個工作。這裏的 prepare 作不及物動詞用。又如：
>
> > We must <u>prepare for</u> the worst.（我們要做最壞的打算。）
>
> 下列句中的 prepare 則是作及物動詞，不可接 for：
>
> > The teacher <u>is preparing</u> his final examinations.
> > （老師在準備期末考題。）
> > My mother <u>is preparing</u> dinner.（母親在準備晚餐。）

3.210　你的朋友住在哪一個房間？

✔　<u>In which room</u> does your friend <u>live</u>?

✔　<u>Which room</u> does your friend <u>live in</u>?

✘　<u>Which room</u> does your friend <u>live</u>?

> 不説 to live a room，必須説 to live in a room。下列各句中的介詞都不可遺漏：
>
> > He asked John <u>with what</u> tools he had been working.
> > The man wants something <u>with which</u> to write.

3.211　我曾聽人談起他，但是我並不認識他。

✔　I have heard <u>of</u> him, but I have never met him.

✘　I have heard him, but I have never met him.

> "聽到別人提起某人或談論過某人"，用 hear of。若不用 of，意為 "聽到過某人講話、演奏、唱歌、唸書、走路、敲門" 等等。

3.212 誰敲門？

✔ Who is knocking <u>at</u> the door?

✘ Who is knocking the door?

> knock 為不及物動詞。通常説 to knock at / on the door。例如：
> Knock before you enter.=Knock at the door before you go in.
> Come in! Don't knock!=Don't knock at the door.

3.213 發明雷達具有非常重大的意義。

✔ The invention of radar was <u>of</u> great significance.

✘ The invention of radar was great significance.

> great significance 表示 "重大意義"、"意味深長"，不可作為形容詞來修飾主詞，須用 of great significance，of significance ＝ significant。因為 of ＋ 名詞＝形容詞，所以 of interest ＝ interesting，of importance ＝ important，of use ＝ useful。significance, use 等前面可以加 great, little, no 等以示程度，例如 of great use, of little use, of no use。但是格言 It is no use crying over spilt milk.（事已至此，徒悲無益）中就不用 It's of no use。其實現在口語上常用 It's no use to... 或 There is no use... 為句子開頭。

3.214 老師講話時他總是不聽。

✔ He never listens <u>to</u> the teacher when he is talking.

✘ He never listens the teacher when he is talking.

> listen 是不及物動詞，表示 "聽甚麼"，後面接 to。
> <u>Listen to</u> me.（聽我説。）
> <u>Listen to</u> the teacher.（聽老師的話。）
> <u>Listen to</u> the broadcast program.（聽廣播節目。）

3.215 本文告訴我們生態學家保護環境不受污染的熱忱。

✔ This article tells us <u>about </u>the enthusiasm of ecologists in protecting our environment from pollution.

✘ This article tells us the enthusiasm of ecologists in protecting our environment from pollution.

> 動詞 to tell 只有在 to tell him a story / the news 等句子中可以有間接、直接受詞。不可任意類推説 tell us the enthusiasm 或 tell you my life，必須説 tell us about... 或 tell us something about...。

3.216 她明天將談法國的情況。

✔ Tomorrow she will speak <u>on</u> the situation in France.

✘ Tomorrow she will speak the situation in France.

> speak 作 "談論" 解時，是不及物動詞，按照不同的意義，後面接 on, of 或 about。一般説 to speak on a subject (/ a point); to speak of / about a person or thing; to speak to / with a person。在下列句中，speak 當及物動詞用：
>
> His father <u>can speak</u> English, French, and German.
> He <u>is speaking</u> the truth.（他説的是真話。）

3.217 我們不應瞧不起比我們不幸的人。

✔ We should not look down <u>on / upon</u> those less fortunate than us.

✘ We should not look down those less fortunate than us.

> look down on 是慣用語，用 on 或 upon 均可，但決不可省去。

3.218 不要打擾我的工作。

✔ Don't interfere <u>with</u> my work.

✘ Don't interfere my work.

> interfere 是不及物動詞，後面接 with，表示 "打擾"、"妨礙"；接 in，表示 "干涉"，如 to interfere in the internal affairs of other countries（干涉他國內政）。

3.219　我們必須確定明天會中要討論的題目。

✔　We must decide <u>on</u> a topic to discuss at the meeting tomorrow.

✘　We must decide a topic to discuss at the meeting tomorrow.

> decide 作 "解決問題、爭論" 解時為及物動詞，不接介詞，如 to decide the question / the case。作 "決定……" 解時，後面接 on 或 upon，如 to decide on a plan / a topic / a difference；接不定詞或受詞子句時，則不用 on / upon，如：
>
> > I (have) <u>decided to</u> do my best.
> > We (have) <u>decided that</u> the meeting should be put off till next week.
>
> 接動名詞時必須用 on / upon。例如：
>
> > They <u>decided on</u> living in the countryside.（他們決定住在鄉下。）
>
> 在 I <u>haven't decided on / upon</u> when to start. 一語中的 on / upon 在口語裏往往省略。

3.220　美軍在樹林中搜捕游擊隊員，但沒有結果。

✔　The American army searched <u>for</u> the guerrillas in the forest in vain.

✘　The American army searched the guerrillas in the forest in vain.

> search 與 search for 表示不同的觀念。説 "搜查房間、人身、抽屜、口袋" 時，search 是及物動詞，因此説 to search the room / him / the drawer / his pocket。説 "搜捕、尋找某人" 時，search 是不及物動詞，後面應加介詞 for。

3.221　她甚至還自認為是個了不起的鋼琴家。

✔　She even went so far as to think <u>herself</u> a great pianist.

✔　She even went so far as to think <u>of</u> herself <u>as</u> a great pianist.

✘　She even went so far as to think <u>herself as</u> a great pianist.

> 認為某人或某事為何等樣人或何等樣事，可用 think＋受詞＋受詞補語，或 think of...as...，正句第一句比第二句普通些。用了 of，後面用 <u>as</u>；

沒有 of，就不可以用 as。又如：

> I <u>thought</u> him quite a louse.
> I <u>thought of</u> him as quite a louse.

3.222　你不應該打擾他的休閒。

✔　You should not intrude <u>upon</u> him during his time off.
✘　You should not intrude him <u>during</u> his time off.

> intrude 作 "闖進"、"打擾"、"侵入" 解時，是不及物動詞，後面跟 upon。

3.223　那個男孩子在玩陀螺。

✔　The boy is playing <u>with</u> his top.
✘　The boy is playing his top.

> 説 "打球"、"踢球"、"打牌"、"下棋"，用 play，不用 play with，如 play tennis / football / cards / chess。有時用 play at，如 play at chess。這裏 tennis、cards 等是指遊戲而言。玩某種東西應用 play with。例如：
>
> > The boy <u>is playing with</u> a stick.
> > The little girl likes <u>to play with</u> a doll.
>
> 這裏 a stick、a doll 表示玩具。

3.224　休息片刻後，他們繼續工作。

✔　After a brief break they went on <u>with</u> their work.
✘　After a brief break they went on their work.

> go on 是不及物動詞，on 是副詞，不是介詞。例如：
>
> > <u>Go on</u>, please.
> > He <u>went on</u> reading and never gave us so much as a nod.（他繼續看書，連頭都不向我們點一下。）（注意：這裏的 reading 是分詞，不是動名詞。）
>
> go on 後面接名詞，應加 with。例如：
>
> > They <u>went on</u> with their work / performance.

3.225 在美國黑人往往遭到歧視。

✔ In America black people are often discriminated <u>against</u>.

✘ In America black people are often discriminated.

> discriminate 作 "歧視"、"差別待遇" 解時，為不及物動詞，後面應跟介詞 against。作 "區別"、"識別" 解時，可當及物動詞用。例如：We must <u>discriminate</u> right <u>from</u> wrong. （我們必須分辨是非。）

3) Errors in using prepositions 誤用介詞

3.226 你在會上為甚麼一言不發？

✔ Why didn't you say anything <u>at</u> the meeting?

✘ Why didn't you say anything <u>on</u> the meeting?

> "在會上" 一般説 at the meeting，而不是 *on the meeting。

3.227 別為這些小事擔憂。

✔ Don't get upset <u>about</u> such trifles.

✘ Don't get upset <u>for</u> such trifles.

> "為某事擔憂（焦慮）" 應該用 get upset about / over, worry about, worry over；不可用 get upset for, worry for。

3.228 王先生不在家。

✔ Mr. Wang is not <u>at</u> home.

✘ Mr. Wang is not <u>in</u> home.

> "在家" 是 at home。在某人家，如 at my home, at your home 也都用 at。若指 "回家了"，則不用 at。例如：Mr. Wang is home. （王先生回來了。）

3.229 他很努力，結果在學習上有很大的進步。

✔ He worked hard. <u>As a result,</u> he made great progress in his studies.

✔ He worked hard <u>with the result that</u> he made great progress in his studies.

✘ He worked hard <u>with a result</u>, he made great progress in his studies.

> 作為一種結果，應説 as a result 或 with the result that。

3.230 這兩個字詞意義有甚麼區別？

✔ What is the difference <u>in</u> meaning between these two words?

✘ What is the difference <u>of</u> meaning of the two words?

> 兩者之間的區別，應説 the difference between these two 或 between A and B。兩者之間在某方面的區別，用 difference in, the difference in style / in character / in quality 等。

3.231 他們從烈士墓旁走過。

✔ They passed <u>by</u> the martyr's tomb.

✘ They passed <u>through</u> the martyr's tomb.

> "從……旁邊走過"該用 pass by。"從……（中間）穿過"用 pass through。例如：
>
> They must <u>pass through the forest</u> before dark.
> （他們必須在天黑以前穿過樹林。）

3.232 老師要我們把這一句用自己的話講出來。

✔ The teacher wanted us to rephrase the sentence <u>in</u> our own words.

✘ The teacher wanted us to rephrase the sentence <u>with</u> our own words.

> 表達"用"的概念時，一般用 with，只有在説話、表達、書寫、繪畫等少數場合用 in。例如：to express in English, to speak in a few words, to retell a story in one's own words, to paint in watercolours, to write in ink 等等。

3.233 你的錶幾點？

✔ What is the time <u>by</u> your watch?

✘ What is the time <u>of</u> your watch?

> 此處 by 是 "依照"、"根據" 的意思。直譯為："根據你的錶，現在幾點？"
> 所以該用 by，而不用 of。

3.234 我們將貫徹新的教育方針。

✔ We will <u>carry out</u> the new educational policy.

✔ We will <u>put</u> the new educational policy <u>into effect</u>.

✘ We will <u>carry on</u> the new educational policy into <u>effect</u>.

> "貫徹" 可用 to carry out, to carry through，或 to put...into effect。to carry on 是 "進行"、"繼續" 或 "經營"，如 to carry on the work / business 等。

3.235 我有你想的那麼笨嗎？

✔ Do you take me <u>for</u> a bigger fool than I am?

✘ Do you take me <u>as</u> a bigger fool than I am?

> 把某人（某物）誤認為某人（某物），應說 take...for... 或 mistake... for...。例如：
> I <u>mistook</u> him <u>for</u> his twin brother.
> He <u>took</u> wheat <u>for</u> leek when he first saw it.

3.236 他病了三天。

✔ He has been sick <u>for</u> three days.

✘ He has been sick <u>since</u> three days.

> 這裏現在完成時態 have / has been 表示從過去某一時日到現在的一段時間存在的行為或狀態，與它連用的時間副詞應為 "for + 若干時"，如 for a year, for three hours 等，意思是歷時多少。

3.237 他自從星期三以來都很忙。

✔ He has been busy <u>since</u> Wednesday.

✘ He has been busy <u>from</u> Wednesday.

> "自從……以來"，該用 since。說從某一天（某一時刻）到某一天（某一時刻）才用 from，如 from Monday till Friday。

3.238 在房間角落裏散放着一些零星物件。

✔ There were some odds and ends lying <u>in</u> the corner of the room.

✘ There were some odds and ends lying <u>at</u> the corner of the room.

> "在房間角落裏"該用介詞 in。例如：
>
> He stood <u>in the corner</u>.
> There is a lamp <u>in the corner</u> of the room.
>
> at the corner 指房子外部的拐角。例如：
>
> A little boy squatted <u>at the corner</u> of the hut.
> I'll be waiting for you <u>at the street corner</u> at three o'clock sharp.
> A tree stood <u>at the corner</u> of the wall.
>
> 此外，on the corner 則往往指物件表面的角。例如：
>
> The girl put the apple <u>on the corner</u> of the table.

3.239 我們反對干涉他國內政。

✔ We oppose interference <u>in</u> the internal affairs of other countries.

✘ We oppose interference <u>of</u> the internal affairs of other countries.

> interference 與 interfere 一樣，後面用 in 或 with。用 in 表示"干涉"，用 with 表示"妨礙"或"打擾"。參見例 3.218。

3.240 她丈夫死時，她的身體狀況已經很差了。

✔ When her husband died she was already <u>in</u> poor health.

✘ When her husband died she was already <u>of</u> poor health.

> "身體健康"應説 in good health，"身體不健康"説 in poor health, in delicate health 等。

3.241 他兩天後回來。

✔ He will return <u>in</u> two days.

✘ He will return <u>after</u> two days.

> 從現在開始，説在多少時間以後，應該用 in，不用 after，例如：
> He plans to finish the work <u>in three months</u>.
> I am sure we will hear from him <u>in a few days</u>.
> 如指"某個時刻或日期或事件以後"，可用 after。例如：
> I will be back <u>after four o'clock</u>. (或 after 4 August，或 after lunch)。

3.242 他要在那牆上開一扇門。

✔ He wants to put a door <u>in</u> that wall.

✘ He wants to put a door <u>on</u> that wall.

> 門不是掛在牆上，也不是靠在牆上，而是開在牆裏，應該用 in。比較下列各句：
> There is a painting <u>on the wall</u>.
> Why is that plank of wood leaning <u>against the wall</u>?
> The thief made a hole <u>in the wall</u>.

3.243 我是在昨天報上看到公寓的廣告。

✔ I saw the ad for the apartment <u>in</u> the paper yesterday.

✘ I saw the ad for the apartment <u>on</u> the paper yesterday.

> "登在報上"該用 in the paper / newspaper。寫在紙上則用 on paper，不加 the。

3.244 這幅畫上的樹跟我們園裏的那棵桃樹有些相像。

✔ The tree <u>in</u> this painting bears a slight resemblance to the peach tree in our yard.

✘　The tree <u>on</u> this painting bears a slight resemblance to the peach tree in our yard.

> "在畫上"應用 in the painting, in the picture。若是油畫也可說 on the canvas（按油畫必須畫在帆布上）。

3.245　用墨水寫。

✔　Write it <u>in</u> ink.

✘　Write it <u>with</u> ink.

> 說"用甚麼工具"，用 with。例如：
>
> Washington cut down the cherry tree with his new hatchet.
>
> 但說"用墨水"、"用各種顏色、油畫顏料等"，該用 in。例如：
>
> He painted <u>in oils</u>.
>
> She painted <u>in watercolours</u>.

3.246　村子裏有一條大街，幾條小巷。

✔　The village consists <u>of</u> a main street and several back lanes.

✘　The village consists <u>in</u> a main street and several back lanes.

> consist of 是"由……組成"，而 consist in 是"在於"、"就是"，比較下列句子：
>
> Our department <u>consists of</u> three sections.
>
> Success <u>consists in</u> perseverance.
>
> Happiness <u>consists in</u> doing one's duty.

3.247　我們的任何錯誤將來都可能帶來麻煩。

✔　Any mistakes on our part now may lead <u>to</u> problems later on.

✘　Any mistakes on our part now may lead <u>into</u> problems later on.

> 說"導致"、"引起"用 lead to，如 to lead to trouble, to lead to disaster, to lead to problems, to lead to something unpleasant 等。表示"向某物內部的動向"可用 into，如 go into a room, to come into a building, to get into trouble 等。

3.248 這本書是李先生寫的，不是張先生寫的。

✔ This book was written by Mr. Li, <u>not by</u> Mr. Chang.

✘ This book was written by Mr. Li <u>instead of</u> Mr. Chang.

> instead of 表示某事本應如此，或照常情、照一般推理應該如此而事實上卻相反，例如：
>
> 　　我本想買一本《哈姆雷特》，卻買了一本《李爾王》。
> 　　I intended to buy a *Hamlet*, but I bought a *King Lear* <u>instead</u>.
> 　　我去看王先生，王先生沒見到，倒遇到了李先生。
> 　　I met Li <u>instead of</u> Wang.
>
> 表示 "不是……而是" 時，則不可用 instead of，而用 not...but...。

3.249 我幫她在牆上貼海報。

✔ I helped her put some posters <u>on</u> the wall.

✘ I helped her put some posters <u>above</u> the wall.

> above 和 on 都作 "在……上面" 解，但 above 是一個東西在某個東西的上面，中間不接觸。例如：
>
> 　　The sun is high <u>above</u> me.
>
> on 是一在上一在下，兩者接觸的。例如：
>
> 　　I carry a pole <u>on</u> my left shoulder.

3.250 她因生病不能來。

✔ She cannot come <u>on account of</u> illness.

✔ She cannot come <u>because of</u> illness.

✘ She can not come <u>for</u> illness.

> 介詞 for 作 "原因"、"由於" 解，常與動詞 punish, excuse, criticize 等連用，或與形容詞 angry, famous 等連用。例如：
>
> 　　He <u>was criticized for</u> his neglect of duty.
> 　　Hualian <u>is famous for</u> its beautiful scenery.

3.251 他非常憎恨偽善者。

✔ He has a deep hatred <u>for</u> hypocrites.

✘ He has a deep hatred <u>to</u> hypocrites.

> 表示 "對某人懷着愛、恨" 等，常用 have a love for / of, have a hatred for / of。例如：
>
> We <u>have a love for / of</u> science.
> The working people <u>have a hatred for / of</u> all forms of exploitation.

3.252 問題的答案很簡單。

✔ The answer <u>to</u> this question is not difficult at all.

✘ The answer <u>of</u> this question is not difficult at all.

> 中文中的 "的" 在英語中不一定都用 of 來表示，有時須用 to。其他的例子如下：
>
> 我把房間的鑰匙弄丟了。
> I lost the key <u>to</u> the room.
> 中間矗立着烈士紀念碑。
> In the centre stands the monument <u>to</u> the martyrs.
> 腳踏實地是成功的鑰匙。
> Being practical has always been the key <u>to</u> success.
> 這部小説的續篇你看過沒有？
> Have you read the sequel <u>to</u> this novel?

3.253 他喜歡這家餐廳，不喜歡那家。

✔ He <u>prefers</u> this restaurant <u>to</u> that one.

✔ He <u>likes</u> this restaurant <u>more than</u> that one.

✘ He <u>prefers</u> this restaurant <u>than</u> that one.

> prefer 後若用名詞、代名詞或動名詞，應説 to prefer A to B。如 to prefer skiing to skating, to prefer this to that。

3.254 她一聽到這個消息，立刻痛哭起來。

✔ <u>On</u> hearing the news, she burst into tears.

✘ <u>After</u> hearing the news, she burst into tears.

> on 後面接動名詞有 "一⋯⋯就⋯⋯" 之意，即 immediately after 之意。
> 此處不宜用 after，因 after 不含 "其後立即" 之意。

3.255 他每年花不少錢在衣服上。

✔ He spends a lot of money <u>on</u> clothes every year.

✘ He spends a lot of money <u>for</u> clothes every year.

> "把錢花在⋯⋯上"，用 spend money on。説 spend money for... 極
> 少見。

3.256 他直接對主席負責。

✔ He is responsible directly <u>to</u> the chairman.

✘ He is responsible directly <u>for</u> the chairman.

> 説 "對人負責"，用 to be responsible to。例如：
>
> The government <u>is responsible to</u> the people.
>
> 説 "對事負責"，用 to be responsible for。例如：
>
> The government <u>is responsible for</u> the welfare of the people.
>
> 合併起來，可以説 The government is responsible to the people for
> their welfare.。

3.257 在補習老師幫助之下，露西考上好大學。

✔ <u>With</u> the help of a tutor, Lucie got into a good college.

✘ <u>Under</u> the help of a tutor, Lucie got into a good college.

> with 含有 "在⋯⋯幫助之下"、"有了⋯⋯"、"借⋯⋯" 之意。"在⋯⋯的
> 領導、統治、支配之下" 則用 under。例如：under the leadership of
> President Lee, under the control of the Ministry of Education 等。

3.258 我對她生起氣來了。

✔ I became angry <u>with</u> her.

✘ I became angry <u>to</u> her.

> 説 "對人生氣" 一般用 to be angry with someone。説 "對事生氣" 用 to

> be angry about / at something。例如：
>
> > Don't be angry <u>about / at</u> trifles.

3.259 對熟悉的朋友我們無需拘泥禮節。

✔ One needn't be overly formal <u>with</u> close friends.

✘ One needn't be overly formal <u>to</u> close friends.

> 與 formal 連用的介詞是 with。其他尚有 to be strict with, to be familiar with 等。

3.260 在不同氣候的國家，人們過着不同的生活。

✔ People living in countries <u>with</u> different climates lead different lives.

✘ People living in countries <u>of</u> different climates lead different lives.

> "不同氣候的國家"實際上是"有着不同氣候的國家"，應該用 countries with different climates。如用 of，則有"屬於不同氣候的……"之意，就不確切。

4) Prepositions and other parts of speech easily confused
介詞與其他詞類的混淆

3.261 暴君是注定要失敗的。

✔ Tyrants are bound to <u>fail</u>.

✘ Tyrants are bound to <u>failure</u>.

> to be bound to 中的 to 是不定詞符號，並非介詞。to be doomed to 中的 to 可作介詞，也可作不定詞符號。因此下列兩句都可以説：
>
> > Despots <u>are doomed to</u> failure.
> > Despots <u>are doomed to</u> fail.

3.262 他盼望去美國留學。

✔ He is looking forward to <u>going</u> to America to study.

✘ He is looking forward to <u>go</u> to America to study.

> to look forward to 裏的 to 是介詞，不是不定詞符號，後面應用名詞、代名詞或動名詞。

3.263 已經九點鐘了，我們必須靜下心做事。

✔ It's 9 o'clock now; we must <u>get down to</u> business.

✘ It's 9 o'clock now; we must <u>get down to do</u> business.

> to get down to 是慣用語，意思是 "靜下心來做……"，後面接名詞或動名詞。例如：
>
> When he first arrived in London, he <u>got down to</u> learning the English language.
>
> The holidays are over; we must <u>get down to</u> work again.
>
> （注意這裏 work 是名詞，不是動詞。）

3.264 我們上課時必須注意聽講。

✔ We should <u>pay</u> attention to <u>what</u> the teacher says in class.

✔ We should <u>be</u> very attentive in class.

✔ We should <u>listen</u> very attentively in class.

✘ We should <u>pay</u> attention to <u>listen</u> in class.

> to pay attention to 作 "注意" 解，後面接名詞或代名詞。

3.265 他反對讓她參加。

✔ He objected to <u>letting</u> her participate.

✘ He objected to <u>let</u> her participate.

> object 後面的 to 是介詞，後面應接名詞或動名詞。

3.266 我們把計劃作了一些修改，目的在於省時間。

✔ We made some changes in our plan with a view to <u>saving</u> time.

✘　We made some changes in our plan with a view to <u>save</u> time.

> 慣用語 with a view to 中的 to 是介詞，通常作 "為……"、"希望……"
> 解，後面一般接動名詞，間或接不定詞，但不合習慣。

3.267　我沒有能力獨立完成這項任務。

✔　I am <u>incapable of completing</u> this job by myself.

✔　I am unable to complete this job by myself.

✘　I am <u>incapable to complete</u> this job by myself.

> capable 和 incapable 後面接 of + 名詞或動名詞，不能接不定詞；able
> 和 unable 接不定詞。capable 指有特殊能力，有資格；able 指一般的
> 智力或體力。試比較：
>
> The baby <u>is able to</u> walk already.
> He <u>is capable of</u> giving brilliant lectures.
> He <u>was unable to</u> come, as he was too busy.
> She <u>seemed incapable of</u> undertaking such a task.

3.268　"你可以把我折磨死，但是你不能逼我承認。" 湯姆回
　　　答說。

✔　"You may torture me to <u>death</u>, but you can't force me to
　　confess," replied Tom.

✘　"You may torture me to <u>die</u>, but you can't force me to
　　confess." replied Tom.

> 這裏 to death 是介詞短語，用作副詞，表示折磨的過程。torture 後面
> 不可以接受詞 + 不定詞補語，但可以接受詞 + 目的副詞。可以說 The
> fascists <u>tortured</u> the patriot to make him talk. (……為了使他說話而折
> 磨……)，不可以說 *The fascists <u>tortured</u> the patriot to talk. 。

3.269　你必須遵照醫生的勸告。

✔　You must <u>follow</u> your physician's advice.

✔　You must <u>take</u> your physician's advice.

✘　You must <u>according to</u> your physician's advice.

according to 是複合介詞，不是動詞，作 "依據"、"依照" 解。例如：

> There will be heavy rains according to today's weather report.
> According to his experience, knowing a foreign language is useful when looking for a job.
> to act according to circumstances（隨機應變）

3.270 他走過橋，不久到了小屋前。

✔ He walked across (crossed) the bridge and soon came to a small house.

✘ He walked acrossed the bridge and soon came to a small house.

across 是介詞，如 to run across a street, to walk across the corridor, to swim across the river。cross 是動詞，如 The troops crossed the river.。

3.271 他因為之前沒有經驗而遭拒絕。

✔ He was rejected because he had no previous experience.

✘ Because of he had no previous experience, he was rejected.

because of 是複合詞，只能引導副詞短語，不能引導子句。because 是從屬連接詞，可以用來引導從屬子句。

3.272 全世界的人都反對污染。

✔ People everywhere are against pollution.

✘ People everywhere against pollution.

against 是介詞，不是動詞。against 在不同的上下文中有不同的意義。例如：

> The Polish workers are waging an unremitting struggle against their government.（波蘭工人正在和政府進行不懈的抗爭。）
> He leaned against the tree.（他倚樹而立。）
> It is not easy to swim against the current.（逆流游泳是不容易的。）

3.273 雖然遭到嚴重的天災，農民的收成還算可以。

✔ The farmers reaped fair harvests in spite of <u>having been</u> affected by serious natural calamities.

✘ The farmers reaped fair harvests in spite of <u>they had been</u> affected by serious natural calamities.

> 複合介詞 in spite of 後面接名詞或動詞短語，不可直接以從屬子句作為它的受詞。in spite of the fact that ＝ though。錯句也可以改作 The farmers reaped fair harvests in spite of the fact that (＝ though) they had been affected by serious natural calamities.。

3.274 在參訪該實驗室期間最使他感動的是研究人員的幹勁。

✔ <u>During his visit</u> to the lab, what impressed him most was the great enthusiasm of the researchers.

✔ <u>When he visited</u> the lab, what impressed him most was the great enthusiasm of the researchers.

✘ <u>During he visited</u> the factories in the suburbs, what impressed him most was the great enthusiasm of the researchers.

> during 是介詞，不能用來引導從屬句，必須把從屬句改為短語，或把 during 改去，用連接詞 when 引導從屬句。

vii.　Conjunctions 連接詞

3.275 從昨天下午到現在一直下雨，天還沒有放晴。

✔ It has been raining since yesterday afternoon <u>and it</u> hasn't cleared up yet.

✘ It has been raining since yesterday afternoon <u>but it</u> hasn't cleared up.

> 用 but 連接兩個子句時，上句和下句必須在意義上構成對比。如果意義趨向一致時，就該用 and。既然上句是 "從昨天下午到現在一直在下雨"，下句的 "還沒有放晴" 就與它趨向一致，不能用 but 構成對比。

3.276　他連聽都不聽她的，轉身就走了。

✔ He didn't even listen to her, <u>but</u> turned around and left.

✘ He didn't even listen to her, <u>and</u> turned around and left.

> 這句恰巧與例 3.275 相反，參見例 3.275。

3.277　音樂學校的學生不僅學音樂，也學其他科目。

✔ The music school students study <u>other</u> subjects <u>as well as</u> music.

✔ The music school students study <u>not only</u> music <u>but</u> some other subjects <u>too</u>.

✘ The music school students study music <u>as well</u> as some other subjects.

> 用 as well as 連接兩個類型相似的單詞或詞組時，在它前面的一個在意義上更為強調。音樂學校學生學音樂是理所當然，強調的是也學其他科目。X as well as Y（重點在 X）＝ not only Y but also X（不僅 Y 而且 X）。

3.278　不僅鄰國的人民，德國人民也同樣受到納粹黨徒的壓迫。

✔ The Nazis oppressed <u>German people as well</u> as the people in neighbouring countries.

✘ The Nazis oppressed the people in neighbouring countries <u>as well as the German people</u>.

> 參見例 3.277。

3.279　你如果不努力學習，很快就要落在人家後面了。

✔ If you don't study hard, <u>pretty soon</u> you will fall behind the others.

✘ If you don't study hard, <u>as soon as</u> you will fall behind the others.

> as soon as 是從屬連接詞，表示一件事一發生之後，另一件事立即發生，不能當作副詞用來表示"不久"、"很快"。

3.280　你看這本書就會明白一切。

✔　If only you read this book, everything will be clear.

✘　As long as you read this book, everything will be clear.

> as long as 有"只要……"之意，相當於 while，它所引導的子句中的動詞往往是連繫動詞或表示延續動作的動詞。例如：
>
> As long as you are a student here, you must observe the school rules.
> As long as you persevere, you are sure to succeed in the end.
>
> 如果從屬句表示比較短暫或瞬息即逝的動作，最好不用 as long as 或 so long as，而應該用 if only。

3.281　只要我還有一個機會，我一定會做得更好。

✔　If only I can have another chance, I will surely do a better job.

✘　As long as I can have another chance, I will surely do a better job.

> 參見例 3.280。

3.282　他一聽到這個消息，就馬上跑過去看她。

✔　As soon as he heard the news, he rushed over to see her.

✘　He heard the news as soon as he rushed over to see her.

> 不可以把從屬連接詞短語 as soon as 機械地代上中文句子中的"馬上"，as soon as 引導副詞從屬句，說明很短暫的時間。上句中 as soon as 修飾"聽到"，不是修飾"跑過去"。

3.283　我們一做完工作，就跳舞去了。

✔　We went dancing as soon as we (had) finished our work.

✘　We finished our work as soon as we went dancing.

參見例 3.282。

3.284 這個字既可用作動詞，又可用作名詞。

✔ This word may be used both as a verb <u>and</u> as a noun.

✘ This word may be used both as a verb <u>as well</u> as a noun.

both...and... 連用，both 不可和 as well as 連用。

3.285 我們一到家，他們就到了。

✔ <u>No sooner had</u> we reached the house <u>than</u> they arrived.

✔ We <u>had no sooner</u> reached the house <u>than</u> they arrived.

✘ <u>No sooner</u> we reached the house they arrived.

此句等於 They arrived as soon as we reached the house.。用了 no sooner...than，通常用過去完成時態。no sooner 放在句首時，主詞與述詞須倒置。

3.286 我一產生這種念頭，立即想到了老師的話。

✔ No sooner <u>had</u> the idea come to my mind than I remembered my teacher's words.

✘ No sooner <u>than</u> the idea <u>I had</u> come to my mind I remembered my teacher's words.

參見 3.285。

3.287 他不但花光所有的積蓄，還向父母借了很多錢。

✔ He <u>not only spent</u> all of his savings, but also <u>borrowed</u> heavily from his parents.

✘ He <u>spent not only</u> all of his savings, but also <u>he borrowed</u> heavily from his parents.

not only...but also... 是相關連接詞，連接句中結構相似的單詞、短語或子句。

3.288　他不但會説德語，也會説法語。

✔　He speaks <u>not only</u> German <u>but also</u> French.

✔　<u>Not only does</u> he speak German, he speaks French <u>as well</u>.

✘　He <u>not only</u> speaks German <u>but also</u> French.

> 注意：⑴ not only 放在句首，主詞和助動詞應倒置。⑵ also 可用 as well 代替，但 as well 常放在句末。⑶ not only 不可分開，but also 則可。

3.289　我一直等到他回來才睡覺。

✔　I <u>did not</u> go to sleep <u>until</u> he returned.

✔　I went to sleep <u>when</u> he returned.

✘　I went to sleep <u>until</u> he returned.

> until 和 till 都可以作介詞或連接詞用。例如：
>
> I did not go to bed <u>till / until</u> 10 o'clock.
>
> I did not go to bed <u>till / until</u> he came back.
>
> 關於 until 和 till 的用法有四點該注意：
>
> ⑴　從屬句或短語裏面用了 until 或 till，主句裏一般用否定詞或在意義上含有反面的語詞。例如：I sat up till he returned. ＝ I did not go to sleep till he returned.
>
> ⑵　until 和 till 的意義並不與中文"等到"完全相等，它們含有"等到……為止"、"非等到……不……"的意思。例如：I will stay here <u>until</u> I have finished my work.（我將留在這裏，直到工作完成為止。）＝ I will not leave here <u>until</u> I have finished my work.（我非到工作完成才離開這裏。）
>
> ⑶　如主句中的動詞表示延續性的動作，動詞肯定或否定都可以，但意義不同。例如：I worked till he came back.（我工作到他回來為止，即他回來了我就停止工作。）I did not work till he came back.（他回來了我才開始工作。）
>
> ⑷　如主句中的動詞表示一時的動作，則動詞非加否定不可。例如 He did not get up till the sun was high up in the sky. ，決不可説 *He got up till the sun was high up in the sky. ，這裏 till 應改用 when。

3.290 直到我高聲叫了，他才注意。

✔ He <u>did not pay</u> attention <u>until</u> I yelled at the top of my voice.

✘ He <u>paid</u> attention <u>until</u> I yelled at the top of my voice.

> 參見例 3.289。為了加強語氣，這句也可以寫為 <u>Not until</u> I yelled at the top of my voice did he pay attention.。

3.291 不論武裝干涉或者戰爭威脅都不能使他們屈服。

✔ <u>Neither</u> armed intervention <u>nor</u> threat of war can cow them into submission.

✘ <u>No matter</u> armed intervention <u>or</u> threat of war can cow them into submission.

> 如果表示"兩者都不"，要用 neither... nor...。no matter 表示"不管怎樣"，後面接 how, what, when, which, who, where 等。例如：
>
> I shall never consent to it no matter what you say.

3.292 不管前面有多大的障礙，我們都要抗戰到底。

✔ We will resist to the end <u>no matter what</u> obstacles may stand in our way.

✘ We will resist to the end <u>no matter</u> obstacles may stand in our way.

> no matter 後面接 how, when, what 等等作連接詞用，其後再接句中的強調部分。試觀察下列句子。
>
> <u>No matter</u> what he says, I'm still going to do it.
> <u>No matter</u> how well you can manage, you'll still have to be careful.

3.293 不管你怎樣跟他說，他還是不聽。

✔ No matter what you say to him, he won't listen.

✘ No matter what you say to him, <u>but</u> he won't listen.

> 中文往往把"不論怎樣……可是……"連用，但英語用了 no matter how

/ when / who，不可再用 but。no matter 是從屬連接詞，but 為並列連接詞，兩者不可在同一句子中出現。參見例 3.292。

3.294 因為她的丈夫棄她而去，她就得撫養一家人。

✓ <u>Since </u>her husband had deserted her, she had to support her family.

✓ Her husband had deserted her, <u>so</u> she had to support her family.

✗ <u>Since</u> her husband had deserted her, <u>so</u> she had to support her family.

since 是從屬連接詞，so 是並列連接詞，不能在同一個句子中出現。

3.295 他因生病，沒有參加體育課。

✓ He did not attend gym <u>because</u> he was sick.

✗ <u>Because</u> he was sick, <u>so</u> he did not attend gym.

參見例 3.294。

3.296 他雖然長得高，但身體卻很弱。

✓ <u>Although</u> / Though he is tall, he is very weak.

✗ <u>Although</u> he is tall, <u>but</u> he is very weak.

though 和 although 不可與 but 連用，可用 yet 或 still，也可不用。

3.297 甚至到現在他還是不相信我。

✓ <u>Even now</u> he doesn't believe me.

✗ <u>Even if now</u> he doesn't believe me.

even if 是從屬連接詞，不能與副詞 even 混淆。

3.298 我們必須隨時隨地遵守行為準則與紀律。

✔ We must observe code of conduct and discipline <u>everywhere</u> and <u>at all times</u>.

✔ We must observe code of conduct and discipline <u>whenever</u> and <u>wherever we can</u>.

✘ We must observe code of conduct and discipline <u>whenever</u> and <u>wherever</u>.

---

wherever 和 whenever 是從屬連接詞。前者為 where 的強調式，後者為 when 的強調式。例如：

<u>Whenever</u> he comes home, there is great joy in the house.
We will find him <u>wherever</u> he goes.

whenever 和 wherever 也可以個別當副詞用，但把 whenever and wherever 當副詞用是比較不正式的用法。

3.299 他不像你那樣和氣。

✔ He is not as (/ so) friendly <u>as</u> you.

✘ He is not so friendly <u>like</u> you.

---

not so 後面與 as 連用，不能與 like 連用。like 是介詞，as 是連接詞。正句即 He is not as (/ so) friendly as you are.，口語裏 not as... 比 not so... 普遍。

3.300 像他哥哥一樣，他十三歲就參加了賽跑。

✔ <u>Like</u> his brother, he participated in the race <u>as</u> a mere boy of thirteen.

✘ <u>As</u> his brother, he participated in the race <u>when</u> a mere boy of thirteen.

"像他的哥哥一樣"是短語，不是從屬子句，因此應用介詞 like，而不用連接詞 as。

3.301 像我老師那樣，他也把外語看作一項有用的工具。

✔ He regarded foreign languages as useful tools, just <u>as</u> my teacher <u>did</u>.

✔ He also regarded foreign languages as useful tools, just <u>like</u> my teacher.

✘ He also regarded foreign languages as useful tools <u>as</u> my teacher.

參見例 3.300。

3.302 吉美知道老闆會把他像一匹老馬那樣攆出去。

✔ Jimmy knew the boss would certainly turn him out to pasture <u>like</u> an old horse.

✘ Jimmy knew the boss would certainly turn him out to pasture <u>as</u> an old horse.

參見例 3.300。

3.303 儘管已學了五年法語，她的法語還是不太好。

✔ Her French is not very good <u>even though</u> she has been studying it (for) five years.

✘ Her French is not very good <u>even</u> she has studied it (for) five years.

"儘管"、"即使"是 even though 或 even if，不是 even。even 單獨用時，指"甚至於"，是副詞，不是連接詞。

3.304 你想成功的話，就得學習多注意一些細節。

✔ <u>If you</u> want to succeed, <u>you must</u> learn to pay close attention to details.

✘ <u>You</u> want to succeed, <u>must</u> pay close attention to details.

中文往往省略表示"假如"、"假使"等連接詞,而英語往往不可缺少。
下列第二句的錯誤屬於同類性質:

✔ <u>If you</u> prepare your lessons well, you will be able to solve this problem.

✘ <u>You</u> prepare your lessons well, you will be able to solve this problem.

下面的例句是習慣用法:

Work hard and you will succeed.=<u>If</u> you work hard, you will succeed.

Talk of the devil and he <u>will</u> appear.

(說曹操,曹操到。)

Love me, love my dog.(愛屋及烏。)

3.305 我把錢遞給他,他就把它放進保險箱。

✔ I handed him the money, <u>and </u>he put it in his safe.

✘ I handed him the money, he put it in his safe.

中文中兩個意義緊接的句子之間用逗號而不用"和"、"並且"等連接詞,但在英語中,按正規的用法,須用連接詞,這點往往易為一般學生所忽略。同樣的例子有:

布朗老師進來,學生起立道早安。

The teacher came in, and the students all stood up and said, "Good morning, Mr. Brown."

我碰巧有這樣的一本書,就借給他了。

I happened to have such a book and I lent it to him.

Self-test 自測

I. 選擇題

1. 我有六根白頭髮。 (3.7 註)
   I have six grey (　　).
   a) hair　　　　　　b) hairs　　　　　　c) haires

2. 祖父的頭髮已經變白了。 (3.7)
   Grandfather's hair (　　) already turned white.
   a) has　　　　b) have　　　　c) are　　　　d) is

3. 他總能找到許多需要做的事情。 (3.8)
   He always finds a lot of (　　) to be done.
   a) working　　b) works　　c) workings　　d) work

4. 我們是中國人，他們是美國人。 (3.3 註)
   We are (　　). They are Americans.
   a) Chinese　　b) Chineses　　c) Chinaman

5. 壞事傳千里。 (3.11 註)
   Bad news (　　) quickly.
   a) travel　　　b) travels　　　c) travelling

6. 昨天我們買了兩件家具。 (3.5 註)
   Yesterday we bought two (　　).
   a) pieces of furnitures　　　b) pieces of furniture
   c) furnitures　　　　　　　d) furniture

7. 在你和我之間，她比較喜歡你。 (3.29)
   She likes you better than (　　).
   a) me　　　　b) I　　　　c) myself　　　　d) mine

8. 他不是我們的同事。 (3.23 註)
   He is (　　) co-worker of ours.
   a) not a　　　b) not　　　c) not one　　　d) none

9.　像她這樣的好學生應該受到獎勵。　(3.33)

Such a distinguished student as (　　) should be given an award.

a) she　　　　　　b) her　　　　　　c) hers　　　　　　d) she's

10.　這朵花的花瓣已經掉光了。　(3.36)

The flower has shed (　　) petals.

a) their　　　　　　b) theirs　　　　　　c) its　　　　　　d) it's

11.　勞倫斯在他的作品中表達了他的原始主義的理念。　(3.41)

In (　　) works (　　) expressed his ideas of primitivism.

a) Lawrence's; he　　　　　　　　b) his; Lawrence

c) Lawrence; him　　　　　　　　d) its; Lawrence

12.　這是我們所住的地方。　(3.42)

This is the place (　　) we dwell.

a) where　　　　　　b) which　　　　　　c) that

13.　這是她上個星期參觀過的地方。　(3.45)

This is the place (　　) she visited last week.

a) where　　　　　　b) on which　　　　　　c) that

14.　他們遷移到需要熟練技術人員的地方。　(3.44)

They moved to a place (　　) needed skilful technicians.

a) where　　　　　　b) which　　　　　　c) there

15.　這是我所要講的話。　(3.48)

This is (　　) I want to say.

a) that　　　　　　b) all what　　　　　　c) what

16.　我只知道她不久就要出國了。　(3.49)

(　　) I know is that she'll soon go abroad.

a) All　　　　　　b) All what　　　　　　c) That　　　　　　d) Which

17.　他們互換座位。　(3.50註)

They changed places (　　).

a) each other　　　　　　b) one another　　　　　　c) with each other

18. 許教授能將唐詩譯為法文，以土生土長的中國人來説算是很了不起的。 (3.54)

Professor Xu can translate Tang poetry into French, which is amazing for ( ) native Chinese.

a) an   b) a   c) x   d) the

19. 對這件事小題大做是不智的。 (3.56 註)

It is unwise to make ( ) fuss about it.

a) the   b) an   c) x   d) a

20. 船正向北航行。 (3.58 註)

The ship is sailing ( ).

a) north   b) by north   c) northern   d) the North

21. 誰控制媒體就控制民心。 (3.59)

He who controls the media, controls the mind of ( ) people.

a) all   b) the   c) x   d) a

22. 美國人是富於拓荒精神的民族。 (3.61)

( ) American people have a pioneering spirit.

a) An   b) x   c) The   d) A

23. 他決心起來反抗極權主義。 (3.69)

He made up his mind to stand against ( ) totalitarianism.

a) x   b) a   c) the   d) all

24. 那叛國賊被處以絞刑。 (3.73)

The traitor was ( ).

a) hung   b) hang   c) hanged   d) hangen

25. 昨晚她把你的信放在書架上。 (3.75)

She ( ) your letter on the bookshelf last night.

a) laid   b) lay   c) lied   d) lain

26. 他們已經到奧地利去了。 (3.76 註)

They have ( ) Austria.

a) been to   b) been   c) gone to   d) gone

27. 我大學畢業已經三年了。 (3.79 註)

    I have (　　) college three years.

    a) gone out of　　b) been out of　　c) graduated from

28. 他已經醒來一小時了。 (3.79 註)

    He has (　　) one hour.

    a) waken　　b) got up　　c) been up　　d) awake

29. 半小時前我已經把房間清理好了。 (3.84)

    I (　　) cleaning the room half an hour ago.

    a) has finished　　b) have finished　　c) finished　　d) finishes

30. 她的舅舅在第二次世界大戰中負傷過好幾次。 (3.86)

    Her uncle (　　) several times during the Second World War.

    a) wounded　　b) was wounded　　c) had been wounded

31. 他們將在下星期來我家。 (3.88)

    They (　　) to my house next week.

    a) are coming　　b) going to come　　c) will coming

32. 伊士曼太太在一週內將前往孟買。 (3.88 註)

    Mrs. Eastman (　　) for Bombay in a week.

    a) will leaves　　b) going to leave　　c) is leaving

33. 他一走我們就開始玩。 (3.90 註)

    As soon as he (　　) we will start playing

    a) leave　　b) leaves　　c) will leave　　d) is leaving

34. 他把百葉窗關上，開始看那些幻燈片。 (3.92)

    He closed the shutters and (　　) to look at the PPTs.

    a) began　　b) begun　　c) begin　　d) begins

35. 她說傍晚六點之前本來可以完成那幅畫。 (3.94)

    She said that she (　　) have finished the picture by six in the evening.

    a) will　　b) would　　c) must　　d) x

36. 坐在那邊的那個女孩是我以前的學生。 (3.98 註)

    The girl who is sitting over there (　　) my student.

    a) was　　b) were　　c) is　　d) are

37. 前幾天你在體育館遇到的那個男孩是我的班上最好的學生。 ^(3.98 註)

The boy you (　　) in the gym the other day is the best student in my class.

a) have met　　　b) meet　　　c) met　　　d) had met

38. 他的第一次嘗試已經失敗。　(3.106)

He (　　) in his first attempt.

a) had been failed　　　b) had failed　　　c) was failed

39. 傑克的體格檢驗以 A 等及格。　(3.108)

Jack (　　) with a grade of A on his physical examination.

a) passed　　　b) was passed　　　c) had been passed

40. 這城市在革命期間經歷了大變化。　(3.109)

The town (　　) a great change during the period of the revolution.

a) was undergone　　　b) underwent　　　c) undergo

41. 他一點也不適合這個職位。　(3.113)

He is not (　　) suitable for the position.

a) a point　　　b) a little　　　c) at all　　　d) but also

42. 甲：那必定是個錯誤。　(3.115 註)

乙：不，那絕不是一個錯誤。

A: That must be a mistake.

B: No, it (　　) be a mistake.

a) must not　　　b) mustn't　　　c) cannot　　　d) shouldn't

43. 你絕對不可以在地板上吐痰。　(3.115 註)

You (　　) spit on the floor.

a) mustn't　　　b) couldn't　　　c) won't　　　d) wouldn't

44. 昨天他必須還債。　(3.117)

He (　　) pay his debts yesterday.

a) must　　　b) has to　　　c) had to　　　d) needed

45. 她今天不必洗衣服。　(3.118)

She (　　) wash clothes today.

a) must not　　　b) doesn't need to　　　c) cannot　　　d) should not

46. 只要他盡其全力就一定會贏。　(3.119)

He (　　) win so long as he does his level best.

a) is sure to　　　b) will sure　　　c) must　　　d) has to

47. 你要他做甚麼事？　(3.122)

What would you have him (　　)?

a) do　　　b) to do　　　c) doing　　　d) done

48. 我寧願要薄的而不要厚的。　(3.123 註)

I would rather (　　) the thin one than the thick one.

a) had　　　b) have　　　c) having　　　d) to have

49. 我姊姊忘了帶錢包。　(3.124)

My elder sister forgot (　　) her purse with her.

a) take　　　b) taking　　　c) to take　　　d) took

50. 他忘了他曾經向海倫借一支鉛筆這件事。　(3.124 註)

He forgot (　　) a pencil from Helen.

a) borrowing　　　b) to borrow　　　c) borrow　　　d) borrowed

51. 我記得曾在圖書館遇見過你。　(3.125 註)

I remember (　　) you in the library.

a) meet　　　b) to meet　　　c) meeting　　　d) met

52. 要記得寄我的包裹啊！　(3.125)

Remember (　　) my parcel!

a) mail　　　b) mailing　　　c) to mail　　　d) mails

53. 你讀了昨天報章上那篇談著作權的文章嗎？　(3.133 註)

Have you read the article on copyrights (　　) in yesterday's newspaper?

a) appearing　　　b) to appear　　　c) appeared　　　d) that appeared

54. 我厭惡他的偽善。　(3.136 註)

I am (　　) by his hypocrisy.

a) disgusted　　　b) disgusting　　　c) disgust　　　d) to disgust

55. 他的穿著讓我覺得好笑。　(3.136 註)

I am (　　) by his way of dressing.

a) amuse　　　b) to amuse　　　c) amusing　　　d) amused

56. 《新娘不是我》是一部好笑的電影。 (3.136 註)

My Best Friend's Wedding is an (　　) film.

a) amusing　　b) amuse　　c) amused　　d) interested

57. 她居然說這樣的話，真令我錯愕。 (3.136 註)

It is (　　) to me that she would say so.

a) astonished　　b) astonish　　c) astonishing　　d) amazed

58. 他對他的事業感到氣餒。 (3.136 註)

He feels (　　) in his undertaking.

a) discourage　　b) discouraging　　c) discourages　　d) discouraged

59. 他們停下來休息一下。 (3.143 註)

They stopped (　　) a rest.

a) have　　b) to having　　c) to have　　d) having

60. 我爸爸習慣於熬夜。 (3.145)

My father is used to (　　) up at night.

a) staying　　b) stay　　c) stayed　　d) stays

61. 她成功地獲得晉升。 (3.147)

She succeeded (　　) a promotion.

a) to get　　b) to getting　　c) in getting　　d) get

62. 那邊人很少。 (3.153)

There are (　　) people there.

a) a little　　b) little　　c) a few　　d) few

63. 他們幾乎沒有時間把工作做完。 (3.155)

They have (　　) time to finish their work.

a) a little　　b) little　　c) a few　　d) few

64. 她不如她姊姊聰明。 (3.159 註)

She is not (　　) as her elder sister.

a) as smartly　　b) like smart　　c) as smart　　d) smart

65. 在獨裁國家裏，人民沒有任何自由。 (3.163 註)

In dictatorial countries people have (　　) freedom.

a) not　　b) none　　c) no　　d) x

66. 我必須在三點鐘前準備就緒。 (3.166)

    I must (　　) ready by three.

    a) got   b) be   c) have   d) to

67. 他氣得滿面通紅。 (3.168)

    He was flushed with (　　).

    a) angrily   b) anger   c) angry   d) angers

68. 她因數學考試沒能拿高分而悶悶不樂。 (3.171)

    She looks (　　) because she failed to get a high grade in the math test.

    a) not happy   b) unhappily   c) unhappy   d) unhappiness

69. 那歹徒貪婪地看着錢。 (3.171 註)

    The villain looked (　　) at the money.

    a) greedy   b) greedily   c) greed   d) greediness

70. 他被嚇得呆立無言。 (3.172 註)

    Completely taken aback, he stood (　　).

    a) muteness   b) mute   c) mutely   d) muted

71. 他不知道她的住址，我也不知道。 (3.173 註)

    He doesn't know her address; (　　) do I.

    a) so   b) either   c) also   d) nor

72. 我去過德國，她也去過。 (3.174 註)

    I have been to Germany, and (　　) has she.

    a) so   b) too   c) also   d) either

73. 連三歲小孩都不會相信這樣的謊言。 (3.175)

    (　　) three-year-old children will believe such a lie.

    a) Even not   b) Even no   c) Not even   d) No even

74. 我剛吃完午餐。 (3.177)

    I (　　) my lunch just now.

    a) finished   b) finishes   c) have finished

75. 他弟弟去世已久。 (3.180)

    His younger brother (　　) long ago.

    a) has died   b) died   c) has been dead   d) dies

76. 那風景多麼美啊！ (3.187)

    a) What beautiful view that is!
    b) How beautiful that view is!
    c) How a beautiful view that is!

77. 這姊妹倆誰比較美麗？ (3.190)

    Which of the two sisters is (   ) beautiful?

    a) most   b) the most   c) better   d) more

78. 他的新畫和上一幅風格相似。 (3.193)

    The style of his new painting is similar to (   ) his last one.

    a) that of   b) it of   c) one of   d) x

79. 我在回家的路上碰到他。 (3.197 註)

    I came across him on my way (   )home.

    a) of   b) to   c) the   d) x

80. 兩年前她嫁給了摩爾先生。 (3.200 註)

    She was married (   ) Mr. Moore two years ago.

    a) in   b) with   c) for   d) to

81. 蘇菲亞的父母反對他的求婚。 (3.205 註)

    Sophia's parents were opposed (   ) his proposal.

    a) at   b) against   c) to   d) with

82. 她兩三天之後回校。 (3.208)

    She will be (   ) school in a few days.

    a) back on   b) back   c) back at   d) back with

83. 老師在準備期中考題。 (3.209 註)

    The teacher is preparing (   ) his midterm examinations.

    a) for   b) on   c) with   d) x

84. 她正忙於準備期末考。 (3.209)

    She is busily preparing (   ) the final examination.

    a) on   b) at   c) for   d) x

85. 她明天將談法國的情況。　(3.216)

Tomorrow she will speak (　　) the situation in France.

a) of　　　　　b) x　　　　　c) on　　　　　d) to

86. 他決定過田園生活。　(3.219 註)

He decided (　　) leading a pastoral life.

a) to　　　　　b) on　　　　　c) for　　　　　d) x

87. 她妹妹正在玩洋娃娃。　(3.223 註)

Her younger sister is playing (　　) a doll.

a) at　　　　　b) x　　　　　c) with　　　　　d) for

88. 我們決不容忍任何對本公司人事作業程序的干涉。　(3.239)

We will not tolerate any interference (　　) the procedures of the personnel department.

a) with　　　　b) in　　　　　c) for　　　　　d) of

89. 腳踏實地是成功的鑰匙。　(3.252 註)

Being practical has always been the key (　　) success.

a) to　　　　　b) of　　　　　c) with　　　　　d) for

90. 我們的足球隊必定會贏。　(3.261)

Our soccer team is bound to (　　).

a) victory　　　b) win　　　　c) winning　　　d) victor

91. 當她住在鄉下時，她終於靜下心來寫小説。　(3.263 註)

When she lived in the countryside, she finally got down to (　　) a novel.

a) writing　　　b) write　　　c) written　　　d) wrote

92. 我爸爸不但會講英語，還會講德語。　(3.277)

My father speaks German (　　) English.

a) also　　　　b) and　　　　c) as well as　　d) except

93. 他不僅是我的客戶，也是我的朋友。　(3.277 註)

He is not only my (　　) but also my (　　).

a) client; friend　　　　　　b) friend; client

c) guest; friend　　　　　　d) friend; guest

94. 她以好心和勤快著稱。 (3.284)

She is well-known both for her kindness (　　) for her diligence.

a) also　　　　b) and　　　　c) as well as　　　　d) but also

95. 他剛一睡着，門鈴就又響起。 (3.285)

No sooner had he gone to sleep (　　) the doorbell rang once more.

a) x　　　　b) that　　　　c) then　　　　d) than

96. 吉米直到日上三竿才起床。 (3.289 註)

Jimmy did not get up (　　) the sun was high in the sky.

a) till　　　　b) still　　　　c) when　　　　d) since

97. 不論你能處理得多好，你還是必須小心。 (3.292 註)

No matter (　　) well you can manage, you'll still have to be careful.

a) much　　　　b) x　　　　c) what　　　　d) how

98. 既然你這麼忙，我只好自己去。 (3.294)

(　　) you are so busy, I will go alone.

a) Though　　　　b) Since　　　　c) Therefore　　　　d) Anyway

99. 即使他願意，我也不會向他借錢。 (3.303)

I will not borrow money from him, (　　) he is willing.

a) even though　　b) nevertheless　　c) even　　　　d) as if

100. 雖然她已經八十歲了，但仍然充滿活力。 (3.296)

Although she has reached the age of 80, (　　) she is still energetic.

a) however　　　　b) but　　　　c) x　　　　d) even

II.　填入時態正確的動詞

1.　I (　　) the bottle on the table a moment ago. (lay) (3.75)

2.　He (　　) in Africa for five years so far. (live)　(3.80)

3.　She (　　) the picture on her study wall last night. (hang)　(3.73)

4.　We will go for an outing if it (　　) nice out tomorrow. (be) (3.89)

5.　He lost his balance and (　　) down. (fall)　(3.74)

6.　They (　　) Japan some time ago. (visit)　(3.76)

7. He ( ) away from Paris for quite a long time. (be)   (3.79)

8. She ( ) to see you before she leave London. (come)   (3.90)

9. Mr. Lee has been here to see her and he ( ) a package. (leave) (3.77)

10. She ( ) shopping last Saturday. (go)   (3.78)

11. His elder sister ( ) four years ago. (die)   (3.81)

    = His elder sister ( ) dead four years. (be)

    = It ( ) four years since his elder sister died. (be)

12. He ( ) reading five novels during the summer break. (finish) (3.87)

13. How long has it been since you ( ) your parents last? (see) (3.83)

14. Mrs. Lin found her son, who ( ) lost for seventeen years. (be) (3.82)

15. Mr. Brown ( ) here next month. (come)   (3.88)

16. He told me that he ( ) there every winter. (go)   (3.93 註)

17. The boy you ( ) in the gym the other day is the worst student in my class. (meet)   (3.98 註)

18. The girl standing in the doorway ( ) in first in last year's marathon. (come)   (3.99)

19. He said he ( ) the letter yet. (not mail)   (3.96)

20. If she comes, I ( ) her. (tell)   (3.100)

III. 填入適當的介詞(若毋需填任何介詞則填 X 號)

1. We should not interfere ( ) the internal affairs of other countries.   (3.218 註)

2. She married ( ) Mr. Lin three years ago.   (3.200)

3. She spends a lot of money ( ) clothes every year.   (3.255)

4. We got ( ) there at six yesterday morning   (3.196)

5. They are opposed ( ) this plan.   (3.205 註)

6. We oppose ( ) aggressive war.   (3.205 註)

7. Helen burst ( ) tears on hearing the news.   (3.254)

8. We will carry (　　) the new economic policy. (3.234)

9. Even after the king had entered the room she carried (　　) talking. (3.234 註)

10. Sometimes she goes (　　) home (　　) the weekend. (3.197)

11. We are working hard to serve (　　) our clients. (3.199)

12. Don't get angry (　　) trifles. (3.258 註)

13. Are you angry (　　) me? (3.258)

14. You must pay attention (　　) the teacher. (3.264)

15. His brother cannot come (　　) account (　　) illness.
    = His brother cannot come because (　　) illness. (3.250)

16. You have got to face (　　) reality. (3.201)

17. I have heard (　　) him, but I have never met him. (3.211)

18. The killer escaped (　　) the back door. (3.204 註)

19. Nothing escapes (　　) my father's attention. (3.204)

20. The German army searched (　　) the guerrillas in the forest (　　) vain. (3.220)

21. The police searched (　　) the thief but found no weapon on him. (3.220 註)

22. Henry never listens (　　) the teacher when he is talking. (3.214)

23. We discussed (　　) farming techniques several times a month. (3.203)

24. After half an hour's drive, we got (　　) the beach. (3.207)

25. Tomorrow she will speak (　　) the situation in Germany. (3.216)

26. We are going to have a party in my house. I hope you'll come and join (　　) us. (3.202)

27. They arrived (　　) Paris last night. (3.206 註)

28. We arrived very early (　　) the theatre. (3.206)

29. Please knock (　　) the door before entering. (3.212)

30. Knock (　　) before you enter. (3.212 註)

31. I don't want to intrude (　　) your family. (3.222)

32. My mother is preparing (　　) dinner.　(3.209 註)

33. We must prepare (　　) the worst.　(3.209 註)

34. Which room does your brother live (　　)?　(3.210)

35. He asked Michael what tools he had been working.　(3.210 註)

36. The invention of the telegram was (　　) great significance.　(3.213)

37. This article tells us (　　) the enthusiasm of ecologists (　　) protecting our environment (　　) pollution.　(3.215)

38. The farm labourer used to be looked down (　　).　(3.217)

39. I've decided (　　) going there.　(3.219)

40. I thought of him (　　) quite a louse.

　　= I thought him (　　) quite a louse.　(3.221 註)

41. The little girl likes to play (　　) a doll.　(3.223 註)

42. The divorce laws discriminated (　　) women.　(3.225)

43. He went on (　　) reading and never gave us so much as a nod.　(3.224 註)

44. After a brief break they went on (　　) their work.　(3.224)

45. Don't worry (　　) such trifles.　(3.227)

46. She painted (　　) oils.　(3.245 註)

47. We must pass (　　) the forest before dark.　(3.231 註)

48. Any mistakes on our part now may lead (　　) trouble later on.　(3.247)

49. He lost the key (　　) the room.　(3.252 註)

50. The answer (　　) this question is not difficult at all.　(3.252)

51. The working people have a hatred (　　) all forms of exploitation. (3.251 註)

52. Mrs. Lee is not (　　) home.　(3.228)

53. He was late (　　) a result of the snow.　(3.229)

54. What is the difference (　　) meaning (　　) these two words?　(3.230)

55. The teacher wanted them to retell a story (　　) their own words. (3.232 註)

56. He proposed a motion (　　) the meeting.　(3.226)

57. What is the time (　　) your clock?　(3.233)

58. Why do you take me (　　) a fool?　(3.235)

59. She has been busy (　　) Monday.　(3.237)

60. My brother has been sick (　　) three days.　(3.236)

61. A tree stood (　　) the corner of the wall.　(3.238 註)

62. There is a lamp (　　) the corner of the room.　(同上)

63. She put an apple (　　) the corner of the table.　(同上)

64. I am delighted to see you (　　) good health.　(3.240 註)

65. He plans to finish the work (　　) three months.　(3.241 註)

66. The committee consists (　　) eight members.　(3.246)

67. Happiness consists (　　) contentment.　(3.246 註)

68. She prefers cats (　　) dogs.　(3.253)

69. There is a painting (　　) the wall.　(3.242)

70. The thief made a hole (　　) the wall.　(3.242 註)

71. He saw the ad for the apartment (　　) the paper yesterday. (3.243)

72. The government is responsible (　　) the people.　(3.256 註)

73. Roger became familiar (　　) her.　(3.259 註)

74. People living in countries (　　) different climates lead different lives.　(3.260)

75. (　　) the help of a map, I found his house.　(3.257)

76. Despots are doomed (　　) failure.　(3.261 註)

77. We are looking forward (　　) seeing you.　(3.262)

78. I walked (　　) the bridge and soon came to a hut.　(3.270)

79. There will be heavy rains according (　　) today's weather report.　(3.269 註)

80. You must follow (　　) your physician's advice.　(3.269)

81. He went out (　　) spite of the rain.　(3.273)

82. It's 10 o'clock now; we must get down (　　) business.　(3.263)

83. His mother objected (　　) his going abroad.　(3.265)

84. With a view (　　) improving his ability to speak English, he spent most of his holidays in England.　(3.266)

85. Helen is capable (　　) giving brilliant lectures.　(3.267 註)

IV. 請將括弧內的動詞以正確的型態（原形、不定詞、分詞、或動名詞）填入空格

1. That book is not worth (　　). (read)　(3.149)

2. What would you have me (　　)? (do)　(3.122)

3. She reminded me cthe lecture this afternoon. (attend)　(3.126)

4. They stop (　　) at teatime. (work)　(3.143)

5. My father made me (　　) the story. (repeat)　(3.120)

6. My boots need (　　).(mend)　(3.148)

7. There is a long introduction (　　) the book. (precede)　(3.132)

8. Please let me (　　) when the lecture begins. (know)　(3.121)

9. She is beginning (　　) Chinese. (study)　(3.127)

10. Roger began (　　) German. (study)　(3.127 註)

11. (　　) them coming over, he turned pale. (see)　(3.142)

12. You had best (　　) back right now. (come)　(3.123)

13. They are used to (　　) long hours. (walk)　(3.145)

14. My sister spent one day (　　) her room. (clean)　(3.144)

15. You must remember (　　) off the light when you leave the room. (turn)　(3.125)

16. Tell her not (　　) it. (take)　(3.128)

17. All things (　　), I think it is not impossible. (consider)　(3.131)

18. I find that film very (　　). (bore)　(3.134)

19. His speech was dull, and we were (　　) by it. (bore)　(3.134 註)

20. He looks (　　) at losing the race. (disappoint)　(3.137)

21. She is really (　　) in sport. (interest)　(3.135 註)

22. It's a very (　　) question.(interest)　(3.135)

23. Pollution diseases are increasing at an (　　) rate. (alarm)　(3.136)

24. She was greatly (　　) at the news. (alarm)　(3.136 註)

25. Her remark made me (　　). (disturb)　(3.138)

26. He rushed over (　　) the newspaper. (buy)　(3.130)

27. She insisted on (　　) with him. (go)　(3.146)

28. She succeeded in (　　) the driving test (pass)　(3.147)

29. (　　) the good news, he could not help bursting into laughter. (hear)　(3.141)

30. Howard was kept (　　) a long time, but he kept his temper. (wait)　(3.139)

V.　填空（第 I、II 節）

1. 昨天她買了五塊肥皂。　(3.5)
   Yesterday she bought five (　　) of (　　).

2. 他送給海倫一把新剪刀。　(3.15 註)
   He gave Helen a new (　　) of (　　).

3. 許多聽眾參加那次音樂會。　(3.1 註)
   A (　　) audience attended the concert.

4. 人們一致稱頌他。　(3.14)
   (　　) praised him unanimously.

5. 我哥哥的衣服快穿破了。　(3.2)
   My elder brother's clothes (　　) almost worn out.

6. 我是中國人，他們是英國人。　(3.3 註)
   I am (　　). They are (　　).

7. 可以給我三張紙嗎？　(3.6)
   Could you give me three (　　) of (　　).

8. 工人們能在四個半月內造好他們的新房子。　(3.12)

The workers can complete their new house in four and (   ) (   ) months.

9. 我和她相識已經兩年了。 (3.18)

(   ) and (   ) have known each other for two years.

10. 我弟弟咳嗽得很厲害，所以沒有來。 (3.51)

My younger brother had a bad cough. (   ) why he didn't come.

11. 他自己不願意去那家公司工作。 (3.19)

He (   ) is unwilling to work in that company.

12. 我為我自己的用途買它。 (3.21)

I bought it for (   ) (   ) use.

13. 愛麗絲用手遮住了眼睛。 (3.22 註)

Alice covered her eyes (   ) (   ) hands.

14. 那時我們三兄弟正沿着海灘走着。 (3.25)

My two brothers (   ) (   ) were walking along the beach then.

15. 我比她更喜歡他。 (3.30)

I like him better than (   ) (   ).

16. 我愛你勝過愛她。 (3.29)

I love you better than (   ).

17. 他一點也不像我。 (3.32)

He is not at all like (   ).

18. 我們正在交談。 (3.50)

We are talking (   ) each other.

19. 他看過你父母住的房子嗎？ (3.43)

Did he see the house (   ) your parents lived (   )?
= Did he see the house (   ) your parents lived?

20. 你認為誰是他們那隊最好的選手？ (3.34)

(   ) do you think is the best player in their team?

VI. 請填入適當的冠詞，無需則填 X 號。

1. Did he take (　　) part in this fighting?　(3.55 註)

2. She always takes (　　) active part in school activities.　(3.55)

3. My sons are still at (　　) school.　(3.65 註)

4. Yesterday we had dictation in (　　) class.　(3.65)

5. (　　) French people are romantic.　(3.61)

6. He no longer believed in (　　) pragmatism.　(3.68)

7. Jack served as (　　) second mate on the ship.　(3.72 註)

8. (　　) awl is a useful tool.　(3.53)

9. You should never tell (　　) lie.　(3.56 註)

10. She intended to study philosophy in (　　) graduate school.　(3.57)

11. It grows wild in (　　) south of Asia.　(3.58)

12. The park is in (　　) western part of the city.　(3.58)

13. The sun sets in (　　) west.　(3.58 註)

14. His house faces (　　) north.　(3.58 註)

15. He lives in (　　) North of France.　(3.58)

16. My father prefers (　　) rice to (　　) bread.　(3.71)

17. (　　) Smith sisters are two pretty girls.　(3.60 註)

18. They will go for a walk after (　　) dinner.　(3.66)

19. (　　) dinner was a great success.　(3.66 註)

20. Oliver is (　　) tallest boy in his class.　(3.62)

21. Most of (　　) glasses are broken.　(3.63)

22. He is occupied in studying (　　) Shakespeare plays.　(3.64 註)

23. Dr. Lee has agreed to give guest lectures on (　　) political science at our college this year.　(3.70)

24. He was born during (　　) First World War.　(3.67 註)

   = He was born during (　　) World War I.

25. There are thousands of (　　) people living in this town.　(3.63 註)

VII. 改錯（第 V 節；第 IV 節之 D、E；第 VII 節）

1. We should use as <u>few</u> money <u>as possible</u> to <u>economize</u>. (3.157)
                A   B   C

   (   )_____

2. I <u>remember</u> <u>that</u> I <u>ever met</u> her last week. (3.178)
       A   B   C

   (   )_____

3. This newly-constructed computer <u>stores</u> <u>10 times</u> as much
                                      A   B

   <u>informations</u> as the old one. (3.160)
       C

   (   )_____

4. Mary is <u>the</u> prettiest <u>than</u> all the daughters <u>in</u> the family. (3.195)
           A   B   C

   (   )_____

5. The people of <u>North India</u> are different <u>from</u> <u>South India</u>.
   (3.192)   A   B   C

   (   )_____

6. We must produce as <u>many</u> <u>fine</u> silk cloth <u>as possible</u>. (3.151)
                  A   B   C

   (   )_____

7. I <u>have</u> <u>few</u> time to <u>finish</u> my homework. (3.155)
     A   B   C

   (   )_____

8. My mother <u>doesn't</u> <u>like to</u> sit <u>idly</u>. (3.172 註)
              A   B   C

   (   )_____

9. The old man <u>has</u> as <u>a good</u> memory <u>as</u> any youngster. (3.158 註)
            A   B   C

   (   )_____

10. This picture <u>worths</u> ten <u>thousand</u> <u>dollars</u>. (3.167)
                 A   B   C

    (   )_____

11. You must <u>make</u> as <u>little</u> errors <u>as possible</u>.   (3.156)
                A   B   C
(   )_____

12. She doesn't <u>like</u> coffee, and I <u>don't</u> <u>too</u>.   (3.173 註)
                 A   B C
(   )_____

13. She <u>cannot</u> swim; <u>either</u> can her <u>younger brother</u>.   (3.174 註)
            A   B   C
(   )_____

14. This custom <u>was abolished</u> <u>over</u> fifty years <u>before</u>.   (3.181)
                   A   B   C
(   )_____

15. <u>There is</u> <u>no enough</u> food <u>for</u> everybody.   (3.184)
   A   B   C
(   )_____

16. He <u>saw</u> two soldiers <u>standing</u> <u>nearby</u> the river.   (3.189)
       A   B   C
(   )_____

17. He was <u>such</u> excited <u>that</u> he could <u>hardly</u> eat.   (3.186)
        A   B   C
(   )_____

18. Her French is <u>as</u> <u>fluent</u> as her <u>teacher</u>.   (3.191)
          A B   C
(   )_____

19. A <u>funny</u> thing <u>was happened</u> <u>at</u> the party last night.   (3.101)
       A   B   C
(   )_____

20. The First <u>World War</u> <u>was broken</u> out <u>in</u> 1914.   (3.102)
          A   B   C
(   )_____

21. <u>Many</u> new schools <u>have established</u> <u>all over</u> our country.   (3.111)
  A   B   C
(   )_____

22. Doris and <u>her</u> brother <u>are belonged</u> <u>to</u> the Labour Party. (3.104)
     A   B   C

 ( )_____

23. Sixty percent of <u>its population</u> <u>is suffered</u> <u>from</u> malnutrition. (3.107)
         A   B C

 ( )_____

24. His German is not very good <u>even</u> he <u>has been</u> <u>studying</u> it for
           A   B   C
 six years. (3.303)

 ( )_____

25. <u>Only if</u> I can have another chance, I <u>will</u> surely <u>win the day</u>. (3.281)
  A   B   C

 ( )_____

26. <u>As</u> her sister, she <u>participated in</u> the race <u>as</u> a mere girl of
 A   B   C
 twelve. (3.300)

 ( )_____

27. Harry is not <u>so</u> <u>sophisticated</u> <u>like</u> you. (3.299)
      A   B   C

 ( )_____

28. She regarded computer <u>as</u> a useful tool, just <u>like</u> my sister <u>did</u>. (3.301)
         A   B   C

 ( )_____

29. Although he is <u>strong</u>, <u>but</u> he is <u>chicken-hearted</u>. (3.296)
      A B   C

 ( )_____

30. Isabella is a <u>soprano</u> singer. She <u>can</u> sing <u>as</u> a bird. (3.302)
      A   B   C

 ( )_____

VIII. 請改正下列句子的錯誤

1. Yesterday she bought many foods. (3.4)

2. He has won the one-hundred-meters race. (3.16 註)

3. She acquired a great deal of knowledges by reading. (3.10)

4. Robert is an old friend of her.   (3.24)

5. Our problem was the same as their.   (3.35)

6. She lost her usual cheerfulness. It puzzled me.   (3.52)

7. Last week we had visited The Palace Museum.   (3.85)

8. She said that she has never been to Taichung.   (3.95)

9. A great change was taken place in our home town.   (3.103)

10. Do you know anyone who was in the accident happened yesterday? (3.133)

11. He is very much happy.   (3.170)

12. His brother has been dead long ago.   (3.180)

13. Most sick people usually feel better in the morning than the afternoon.   (3.194)

14. There is a desk on the corner of the room.   (3.238 註)

15. They are bound to failure.   (3.261)

16. Because he was sick, so he did not attend gym.   (3.295)

17. He didn't even listen to her, and turned around and left.   (3.276)

18. No sooner I had reached the park than he arrived.   (3.285)

4 **Usage 用詞**

i. Nouns and pronouns 名詞和代名詞

4.1 這本書的作者是誰？

✔ Who is the <u>author</u> of this book?

✘ Who is the <u>writer</u> of this book?

> writer 是"作家"，範圍比較廣；author 是"作者"，指文章、小說、書本的作者，兩者略有不同。

4.2 他們兩人中一個進入屋內，另一個留在外面。

✔ One of the two went inside; the <u>other</u> did not.

✘ One of the two went inside; the <u>another</u> did not.

> another = an + other，不可加 the。提到的人或物只有兩個時，講到"另一個"用 the other，不可用 another。提到的人或物有兩個以上，講到"另一個"則必須用 another，不可用 the other。共有兩個人，"一個在屋裏，一個在外面"，說 <u>One</u> was in the room; <u>the other</u> was outside. 。

4.3 那流浪漢憤怒地向他吼叫。

✔ The bum roared at him in <u>great anger</u>.

✘ The bum roared at him in <u>indignation</u>.

> indignation 是對不正義的事件表示氣憤、憤慨。這裏用 indignation 是錯誤的。在下列情況下，可用 indignation：
>
> Reports of child abuse aroused public <u>indignation</u>.
> She was filled with <u>indignation</u> at the conditions under which miners were forced to work.

4.4 殖民主義者是注定要失敗的。

✔ The <u>colonialists</u> are doomed to failure.

✘ The <u>colonists</u> are doomed to failure.

> colonist 是指移往殖民地居住的人，colonialist 則指殖民主義者，兩者不可混淆，參見例 2.29。

4.5 他們把幾瓶葡萄酒全都搬到地下室去了。

✔ They moved all the <u>bottles of</u> wine into the cellar.

✘ They moved all the wine <u>bottles</u> into the cellar.

> wine bottle 是指 "裝葡萄酒的瓶子"，而不是指 "一瓶酒"。其他類似的例子有：
>
> | | |
> |---|---|
> | a cup of tea | 一杯茶 |
> | a tea cup | 一個茶杯 |
> | a bottle of ink | 一瓶墨水 |
> | an ink bottle | 一個墨水瓶 |
> | a bag of money | 一袋錢 |
> | a money bag | 一個錢袋 |

4.6 全國各地民眾示威遊行，抗議敵軍入侵。

✔ People in different parts of the country held <u>demonstrations</u> protesting (against) the enemy's invasion.

✘ People in different parts of the country held <u>parades</u> protesting (against) the enemy's invasion.

> parade 原意是 "閱兵、遊行"，為節慶活動；demonstration 則是 "集體抗議"，乃羣眾就某一事件表示態度的集會或遊行。

ii. Verbs 動詞

4.7 他馬上就動身。

✔ He is <u>about to</u> go.

✔ He is going at once.

✘ He is <u>about to</u> go <u>at once</u>.

> to be about to start ＝ to be on the point of starting，表示 "正打算動身"，"就要出發"，不能再和 at once, immediately 等時間副詞連用。

4.8　老師要求我們把課文背熟。

✔ The teacher made us <u>memorize</u> the text.

✔ The teacher made us <u>learn</u> the text <u>by heart</u>.

✘ The teacher made us <u>memorize</u> the text <u>by heart</u>.

> to memorize 是 "把……記住"、"熟記"，by heart 即 by memory 或 from memory，不能與 memorize 連用，否則造成語義重複。通常我們 說 to learn（/ say / know 等）something by heart 或 to memorize something。

4.9　請把你的話再講一遍。

✔ I <u>beg your pardon</u>?

✘ Could you <u>repeat</u> what you just said?

✘ Could you <u>repeat</u> what you just said <u>again</u>?

> repeat ＝ say again，本身已有 "再次" 的意思。

4.10　作為主修英語的學生，我們必須精通英語。

✔ As English majors, we must <u>master</u> the language.

✔ As English majors, we must have <u>a good command</u> of the language.

✘ As English majors, we must <u>master</u> the language <u>very well</u>.

> master 已含 "精通" 的意思，不必加用 very well。可以改用 to have a good command of 等慣用語。

4.11　你（比較）喜歡誰，莫札特還是巴哈？

✔ Whom do you <u>prefer</u>, Mozart or Bach?

✘ Whom do you <u>prefer more</u>, Mozart or Bach?

> prefer 是 like better，有對某事物 "比較喜歡"、"更喜歡" 等涵義，所以不可與 more 連用。這個句型現代英語裏也常用 Who 來代替 Whom。

4.12 太陽一出來，我們就起牀。

✔ As soon as the sun <u>rose</u>, we got up.

✘ As soon as the sun <u>raised</u>, we got up.

> rise, rose, risen 是不及物動詞；raise, raised, raised 是及物動詞，如：
> to raise one's hand。

4.13 這一次經驗在我心中留下極為深刻的印象。

✔ This experience has <u>left</u> a deep impression on my mind.

✘ This experience has <u>remained</u> a deep impression on my mind.

> remain 是不及物動詞，有 "留下"、"仍是" 等意義。例如：
> The rest had gone home; he alone <u>remained</u>.
> He <u>remained</u> the same.
> "留下印象" 是 to leave an impression on 或 to give an impression。

4.14 他一天到晚穿着一件皮夾克。

✔ He <u>wore</u> a leather jacket all day.

✔ He <u>had</u> a leather jacket <u>on</u> all day.

✘ He <u>put on</u> a leather jacket all day.

> put on 指 "穿上（衣服、鞋子等）"、"戴上（眼鏡、手套等）"，表示一時的動作。例如：
> He <u>put on</u> a leather jacket before he went out.
> wear 指 "穿着"、"戴着"，表示繼續的動作或狀態。例如：
> Most people <u>wear</u> ready-made shoes.
> He <u>wore</u> a tailor-made suit.
> She <u>wore</u> dark-blue overalls.

4.15 我上星期六帶我妹妹去看電影。

✔ I <u>took</u> my sister to the movies last Saturday.

✘ I <u>brought</u> my sister to the movies last Saturday.

> bring 是 "拿來" 或 "帶來"; take 是 "拿去" 或 "帶去", 或不指明方向。
> 例如:
>> Take this empty bottle away and <u>bring</u> me a full one, please.
>> <u>Bring</u> your younger brother with you next time you come.
>> When you come to class, <u>bring</u> your dictionary with you, please.

4.16 在你來以前，我在找原子筆。

✔ I was <u>looking for</u> a ballpoint pen before you arrived.

✔ I was <u>trying to find</u> a ballpoint pen before you arrived.

✘ I was <u>finding</u> a ball pen before you came.

> find 作 "發現" 或 "找到" 解，是瞬間動詞 (point-of-time verb)，或稱終止性動詞 (terminative verb)，通常不可用進行時態。"找尋" 應用 to look for 或 to try to find。

4.17 他找到他那隻狗了嗎？

✔ Has he <u>found</u> that dog of his?

✘ Has he <u>found out</u> that dog of his?

> find out 指經探索或觀察而發現，通常指發現無形的、隱藏的事情。例如: to find out the truth, to find out how to do something 等。找到失去的書本、鋼筆之類，該用 to find。

4.18 我擔心得睡不着覺。

✔ I was too worried to <u>go to sleep</u>.

✘ I was too worried to <u>go to bed</u>.

> to go to bed 是 "就寢"、"上牀"; 本句中的 to go to sleep 是 "睡着"、"入睡"，兩者不可相混。

4.19 他從不向程度好的同學學習。

✔ He never <u>learns</u> from the better students.

✘ He never <u>studies</u> from the better students.

> "向（某人）學習"是 to learn (something) from（或 of），不是 *to study from。

4.20 我從他那裏知道王先生已在前三天離城。

✔ I <u>learned</u> from him that Mr. Wang had left the town three days before.

✘ I <u>knew</u> from him that Mr. Wang had left the town three days before.

> to learn from someone 表示"從某人那裏聽來"、"從某人那裏得悉"，不可以説 *to know from someone。又 to learn from someone 也可作"向某人學習……"解。參見例 4.19。

4.21 我和她相識已經很久了。

✔ I have <u>known</u> her for a long time.

✔ I <u>got acquainted with</u> her a long time ago.

✔ I <u>made</u> her <u>acquaintance</u> a long time ago.

✘ I have <u>recognized</u> her a long time.

> recognize 是"認出"、"看出"，意為"見了某人而認識"，是瞬間動詞，不可與表示持續時間的副詞連用。to know, to get acquainted with 或 to make one's acquaintance 是"與……相識"。

4.22 我已經學得一點法語知識。

✔ I have <u>acquired</u> a little <u>knowledge</u> of French.

✔ I have <u>learned</u> a little French.

✔ I <u>have</u> a little <u>knowledge</u> of French.

✔ I <u>know a smattering</u> of French.

✘ I have <u>learned</u> a little <u>knowledge</u> of French.

習慣上說 to acquire a good knowledge (/ some knowledge / a little knowledge)。to learn 或 to study 不可以和 knowledge 搭配。

4.23 他給她一杯酒，她接受了。

✔ He offered her a glass of wine, which she <u>accepted</u>.

✘ He offered her a cup of wine, which she <u>received</u>.

receive 是 "收到"；accept 是 "接受"。從下例中可看出其涵義不同：
I <u>received</u> his gift yesterday, but I do not think I will <u>accept</u> it.。酒杯通常用 glass，不用 cup。

4.24 他答應替我做這件事。

✔ He <u>promised</u> to do this for me.

✘ He <u>allowed</u> to do this for me.

allow 作 "允許別人做某件事" 解時，後面接賓語與不定詞。例如：
He <u>allowed</u> me to do so.

作 "允許給某人某一種東西" 解時，後面接 double object。例如：
The teacher <u>allowed</u> us two weeks to write the paper.

promise 表示 "動作的主體向別人允諾將做某件事" 時，後面跟不定詞短語，或跟以 that 引導的賓語子句，例如：
He <u>promised</u> to be here at six o'clock sharp.
I <u>promised</u> him that I would do my best to help him.

注意下列兩句不同的意義：
He <u>allowed</u> me to leave the office. 他允許我離開辦公室。（不是 "他離去"，而是 "我離去"。）
He <u>promised</u> me to leave the office. 他答應離開辦公室。（是 "他離去"，不是 "我離去"。）

4.25 馬先生替他從圖書館借了幾本有趣的書。

✔ Mr. Ma <u>borrowed</u> some interesting books from the library for him.

✘ Mr. Ma <u>lent</u> some interesting books from the library for him.

lend "借給"、"貸"、"借出"；borrow 是 "借自"、"從……借到" 或 "借進"。例如：

> Will you lend me the book which you have borrowed from the library?（你從圖書館借來的書，可以借給我嗎？）

4.26 他要抓那隻貓。

✔ He wanted to catch the cat.

✘ He wanted to catch up with the cat.

catch 是 "捉住"、"抓住"；catch up (with) 是 "趕上"、"追着"。

4.27 我忽然想起了他們所做的事。

✔ Suddenly I recalled what they had done.

✔ Suddenly I was reminded of what they had done.

✘ Suddenly I reminded what they had done.

remind 是 "提醒"、"使想起"；recall 含有 "回想起"、"想起" 的意思。前者指 "某事或某人提醒某人某件事情"，後者為 "某人主動地想起了某事或某人"，試比較下列句子：

> I reminded him that there would be a lecture in the evening.
> （我提醒他晚上有演講。）
> He recalled that there would be a lecture in the evening.
> （他想起晚上有演講。）

4.28 這兩年以來他們創造了許多經濟奇蹟。

✔ They have worked (/ performed / done) economic wonders during the last two years.

✘ They have created economic wonders during the last two years.

中文裏 "創造" 用得較廣泛，但英語裏的 create 不可濫用。例如：不能說 *to create new tools, to create new methods, to create miracles (wonders)；應說 to invent new tools (new methods), to work (perform, do) miracles 或 to do mighty work。下列幾句中 create 的用法是正

確的：
> Dickens <u>created</u> many characters.
> This style of writing <u>was created</u> by a well-known novelist.

4.29 僅僅一年他發明了不少有用的機器。

✔ In one year alone he <u>invented</u> quite a number of useful machines.

✘ In one year alone he <u>discovered</u> quite a number of useful machines.

> discover 是 "發現"，發現的事物是客觀存在，而前所未知的。例如：
> Columbus <u>discovered</u> America in 1492.
> I <u>discovered</u> that it was too late to catch the last train.
> invent 是 "發明"，發明的事物以前並不存在，經人們創造出來的。例如：
> The art of printing <u>was invented</u> in the Han dynasty.
> The model worker <u>has invented</u> a set of farm tools.
> invent 有時指 "捏造"。例如：
> The pupil <u>invented</u> an excuse for his being absent.

4.30 這位技師教他們怎樣操作機器。

✔ The technician taught them how to <u>operate</u> the machine.

✘ The technician taught them how to <u>master</u> the machine.

> to master 一般指 "精通"，是對知識而言，沒有 "操縱機器" 的意義。可以説 to master a language；不可説 *to master a tractor (an airplane) 等等。

4.31 你願意和我在公園裏散步嗎？

✔ Do you <u>care for</u> a walk in the park with me?

✔ Do you <u>care to take</u> a stroll in the park with me?

✘ Do you <u>mind to take</u> a walk in the park with me?

> 徵詢某人是否樂於做某事，或對某物是否感到興趣，應用 to care to do

something 或 to care for (/ about) something。例如：

> Do you <u>care to</u> go to the concert (/ movies) with me?
> Would you <u>care for</u> an orange (/ another cup of tea)?

徵詢某人對做某事是否介意或反對時，才用 mind，例如：

> Do you <u>mind</u> if I smoke?
> Would you <u>mind</u> passing me the salt and pepper?
> I hope you don't <u>mind</u> if I smoke.
> Do you <u>mind</u> if I turn on the radio?

4.32 他太太勸他戒酒，但沒有成功。

✔ His wife <u>advised</u> him to give up drinking, but in vain.

✔ His wife <u>tried to persuade</u> him to give up drinking, but in vain.

✘ His wife <u>persuaded</u> him to give up drinking, but in vain.

> persuade 是 "說服"，沒有說服成功，就不能用 persuade，應用 advise 或 try to persuade，錯句中上下文顯然有矛盾。

4.33 他們難道不準備在會議上說些甚麼嗎？

✔ Aren't they planning to <u>say</u> something at the meeting?

✘ Aren't they planning to <u>speak</u> something at the meeting?

> speak 指 "講" 的發聲；say 指 "講" 的達意。孩子牙牙學語，可以說 The baby is learning to <u>speak</u>, but he is unable to <u>say</u> anything.。啞巴不能 speak，而瘋子能 speak，但不能 say anything sensible。可以說 speak English(/ Chinese / the Shanghai dialect / a foreign language), speak at the meeting, speak to/with someone, speak about / of something, speak on some subject；不可以說 *speak something，應說 say something (或 nothing)。

4.34 我寫那篇報告只用了一個鐘頭。

✔ <u>I only spent</u> one hour (in) writing the report.

✔ <u>It only took</u> me one hour to write the report.

✔ Writing the report <u>only took</u> me one hour.

✘ <u>I only took</u> one hour writing the report.

"用掉了多少時間"，如主詞是人，用 spend... + 動名詞，但如果主詞是事物，則必須用 take... + 不定詞，而不用 spend。

4.35 醫生將在三點給他動手術。

✓ The doctor will <u>perform</u> the operation on him at three o'clock.

✗ The doctor will <u>make</u> an operation on him at three o'clock.

"動手術"是 to perform an operation 或 to operate，不可説 *to make an operation 或 *to do an operation。"為某人動手術治療某種疾病"，應説 perform an operation on someone for some disease。

4.36 我説服她改變主意。

✓ I <u>persuaded</u> her to change her mind.

✗ I <u>convinced</u> her to change her mind.

convince 是"使（人）信服"，即 make one believe；persuade 的第一意義等於 convince，第二意義是"説服（人）"、"勸服（人）"，即 make one act。要使別人有所行動，往往要先使他信服。例如：

We <u>convinced (/ persuaded)</u> him that we were right and he was wrong.

We <u>convinced him that</u> it was his duty and persuaded him to do it at once.

4.37 請你給我介紹一本好的漢英詞典好嗎？

✓ Would you <u>recommend</u> a good Chinese-English dictionary for me?

✗ Would you <u>introduce</u> me a good Chinese-English dictionary?

把某甲介紹給某乙，使他們相識，或把某物、某種風俗習慣傳到另一地方，用 introduce。把某物介紹、推薦給某人，或把某人推薦給某人，應用 recommend，例如：

Can you <u>recommend</u> a good dentist to me?

4.38 他在這次生病以前一向洗冷水澡。

✓ He <u>used to</u> take cold baths before his recent illness.

✘　He <u>was used to</u> take cold baths before his recent illness.

> to be used to 作 " 對……已習慣 " 解，used 是形容詞，to 後面接名詞或動名詞。例如：He <u>was used to</u> cold showers.　He <u>was used to</u> taking cold showers.。若表示過去經常反覆的動作，有 " 過去如此而現在不如此 " 之意，應該用 used to 接動詞原形。例如：
>> He <u>used to</u> take a walk before breakfast.（他現在早餐前不散步了。）
>> He is not what he <u>used to be</u>.（他跟以前不一樣了。）

4.39　史大林利用特務來除去政治對手。

✔　Stalin <u>made use of</u> the secret service to get rid of political rivals.

✘　Stalin <u>took advantage of</u> the secret service to get rid of political rivals.

> to take advantage of something 作 " 利用 " 、 " 趁 " 解。例如：
>> <u>Taking advantage of</u> my spare time, I read widely.
>
> to take advantage of someone 作 " 用手段欺騙某人 " 解。 " 利用某人而自己得利 " 應該用 to make use of。

4.40　我懷疑他騙了你。

✔　I <u>suspect</u> that he tricked you.

✘　I <u>doubt</u> that he tricked you.

> suspect 和 doubt 都可以作 " 疑心 " 解，但 suspect 是 " 有點感覺到 " 、 " 覺得可疑 " 、 " 有點發覺（危險、陰謀、犯罪行為）" ，可能有其事的意味較多。例如：
>> I <u>suspect</u> that he had something to do with this.（我懷疑他與此事有關。）
>> I <u>suspect</u> him to be seriously ill.（我懷疑他病得很厲害。）
>
> doubt 是 " 懷疑 " 、 " 不確定 " ，除在否定句和疑問句裏可接 that 外，後面常接 if, whether, what 等疑問連接詞。試比較：
>> I don't <u>doubt</u> that he was there.（我相信他是在那裏的。）
>> I <u>doubt</u> whether he has lost the package.（我懷疑他未必把包裹弄丟了。）

iii.　　Adjectives and adverbs 形容詞和副詞

4.41 政府號召全國人民拿起武器來抗敵。

✔ The government called <u>the whole</u> nation to arms to resist the enemy.

✘ The government called <u>all the</u> nation to arms to resist the enemy.

> "全國"一般總是用 the whole country / nation；"全民族"用 the whole nation / people；"全城"用 the whole town；不用 all the country, all the nation, all the town（或 city, village 等）。

4.42 他是有錢人。

✔ He is <u>a rich man</u>.

✔ He is <u>rich</u>.

✘ He is <u>a rich</u>.

> rich 是形容詞，the rich ＝ rich people，必須用定冠詞，不可以說 *a rich。屬於同類性質的有：the poor, the strong, the weak, the unemployed, the wounded, the oppressed 等。

4.43 他太老了，不能做太多的工作。

✔ He is too <u>old</u> to do much work.

✘ He is too <u>aged</u> to do much work.

> aged 常用作修飾性形容詞，如 an aged man，讀 ['eɪdʒɪd]；或在名詞之後，如 "He is a man <u>aged</u> seventy."，讀 [eɪdʒd]。它不同於 old，不能作補語形容詞用。

4.44 這張桌子是木頭做的。

✔ This table is <u>made of wood</u>.

✔ This is a <u>wooden table</u>.

✘ This table is <u>wooden</u>.

> wooden 只能用作修飾性形容詞，如 a wooden leg, a wooden box，不可以用作補語形容詞。

4.45 那人喝得爛醉。

✔ The man was dead <u>drunk</u>.

✘ The man was dead <u>drunken</u>.

> drunken 通常作修飾性形容詞用，很少作補語形容詞用；而 drunk 只作補語形容詞用。例如：a drunken fellow, to get drunk, to be very drunk。

4.46 "你不能逼我去打一個貧病交迫的女人！" 湯姆回答説。

✔ "You can't force me to beat a poor <u>sick</u> woman," replied Tom.

✘ "You can't force me to beat a poor <u>ill</u> woman," replied Tom.

> ill 和 sick 都可用作補語形容詞，例如：
> I have been <u>ill</u> / unwell〔英語〕for two weeks.
> I have been <u>sick</u>〔美語〕for two weeks.
> 但作為修飾性形容詞置於名詞之前時，英美都用 sick，不用 ill，如 a sick man / woman, a sick child 等。

4.47 昨天整天都在下大雨。

✔ <u>Heavy rain</u> fell all day long yesterday.

✔ <u>There was heavy rain</u> all day long yesterday.

✘ <u>A great rain</u> fell all day long yesterday.

> 中文裏的 "大"，英語中不可一律用 big 或 great，須視習慣用法，試對照下列中英文：
> 大風：a strong / heavy wind
> 大雪：a heavy snow

4.48 他有好多次因為做錯事被罰不能吃飯，餓着肚子去睡覺。

✔ Many a time he went to bed with an <u>empty</u> stomach, because he misbehaved.

✘ Many a time he went to bed with a <u>hungry</u> stomach, because he misbehaved.

> "餓着肚子" 實際上是 "空着肚子"，應用 an empty stomach。

4.49 學好鋼琴不容易。

✔ It is <u>not easy</u> to master the piano.

✔ It is <u>difficult / hard</u> to master the piano.

✘ It is <u>uneasy</u> to master the piano.

> easy 作 "容易" 解時，它的反義詞是 hard 或 difficult；easy 作 "安心"、"舒適" 等解時，它的反義詞是 uneasy。例如：
> It is an <u>easy</u> chair.
> He leads an <u>easy</u> life.
> He feels <u>uneasy</u> about the result of the examination.
> （他擔心自己的考試成績。）

4.50 這個座位有人坐嗎？

✔ Is this seat <u>taken / vacant</u>?

✘ Is this seat <u>empty</u>?

> empty 是 full 的反義詞，如 an empty box, an empty bottle, an empty pot, an empty cup。vacant 指 "未被（人）佔用" 之意。試比較下列句子：
> We must find a <u>vacant</u> room（指未被佔用的）for the meeting.
> The <u>empty</u> room（指空無一物的）looks especially large.

4.51 他手術醒來時並不覺得痛。

✔ He felt <u>no pain</u> when he awoke from surgery.

✘ He felt <u>painless</u> when he awoke from surgery.

> painless 是 "無痛的"、"不使人感覺痛苦的"，用於事物，如 painless

death（善終）。説人覺得痛或痛苦，須用 to feel a pain；説人不覺得痛或痛苦，該用 to feel no pain。

4.52 侵略者是愛好和平者的死敵。

✔ Invaders are the <u>deadly</u> enemies of peace-loving people.

✘ Invaders are the <u>dead</u> enemies of peace-loving people.

dead 是 “已經死去” 的意思。表示 “不共戴天”、“極兇惡的”、“致命的”，應該用 deadly。deadly 通常作形容詞，例如：deadly poison（劇毒）、deadly hatred（深恨）、deadly enemy（不共戴天的敵人）等。

4.53 他做事很認真負責，頗受同事們的尊敬。

✔ Being a <u>conscientious</u> worker, he is respected by his co-workers.

✘ Being a <u>conscious</u> worker, he is respected by his co-workers.

conscious 是 “有知覺的”、“神志清醒的”。例如：
　　He is <u>conscious</u> of his responsibility. 或
　　He is <u>conscious</u> that he has a responsibility.
　　（他感到他有責任。）

表達 “正直的”、“負責的”、“按良心辦事的” 應用 conscientious，參見 1.1。此外，當代美語裏，除律師、學者外，使用 “同事” 一詞時多用 co-worker，少用 colleague，以免讓人覺得自命不凡。

4.54 我一想起這件事總是感到慚愧。

✔ The very thought of it made me <u>ashamed</u>.

✘ The very thought of it made me <u>shameful</u>.

ashamed 是 “（感到）羞恥” 或 “慚愧”，用於人；shameful 是 “可恥的”，指事情或行為。試觀察下列句子：
　　This is really <u>shameful</u>, and I feel ashamed of it.
　　（這事真可恥，我感到慚愧。）

4.55 “真討厭！” 他帶着鄙夷的語氣説。

✔ “What a nuisance!” he said with a <u>contemptuous</u> snort.

✘ "What a nuisance!" he said with a <u>contemptible</u> snort.

> contemptible 是 "可鄙的"、"無聊的"、"下賤的"。例如：
>
> He is a most <u>contemptible</u> fellow.
>
> contemptuous 是 "傲慢的"、"瞧不起人的"。例如：a contemptuous look, a contemptuous remark 等。
>
> 有些形容詞也含有主動或被動的意味。主動的如：contemptuous（鄙視的）、forgetful（健忘的）、respectful（恭敬的）；被動的如：contemptible（可鄙的）、unforgettable（難忘的）、respectable（可敬的）。

4.56 他的行為令人無法容忍。

✔ His conduct is simply <u>intolerable</u>.

✘ His conduct is simply <u>intolerant</u>.

> intolerant 是 "不容忍的"、"褊狹的"，用於人。例如：
>
> He was so firm in his own belief that he was <u>intolerant</u> of others' opinions.
> intolerable 是 "難受的"、"令人受不了的"、"令人無法忍受的"。例如：intolerable heat, intolerable insult 等。
> Fashion is a form of ugliness so intolerable that we have to alter it every six months.

4.57 這孩子痛改前非，他父母非常高興。

✔ The boy's parents are <u>extremely happy</u> because he has turned over a new leaf.

✘ The boy's parents are <u>very pleasant</u> because he has turned over a new leaf.

> pleasant 表示 "（令人）舒適的"、"（令人感到）有趣的" 或 "令人高興的"。例如：a pleasant companion, a pleasant voice, a pleasant journey 等。說 "自己心裏高興"，應用 happy 或 pleased。例如：
>
> I'm very <u>pleased</u> with what you have done.

4.58 聽了這個消息，他很不愉快。

✔ He was very <u>displeased</u> when he heard the news.

✘ He was very <u>unpleasant</u> when he heard the news.

> unpleasant 是 pleasant 的反義詞；displeased 是 pleased 的反義詞。
> 它們的區別，參見例 4.57。

4.59 你這個月的工作不能令人滿意。

✔ Your work this month has not been <u>satisfactory</u>.

✘ Your work this month has not been <u>satisfied</u>.

> satisfactory 表示 "令人滿意"，用於事；satisfied 表示 "感到滿意"，用
> 於人。例如：
>> The student's answer is quite <u>satisfactory</u>.
>> He <u>was satisfied</u> with my answer.
>
> 參見例 4.57。

4.60 這絕不是甚麼鑽石，它一文不值。

✔ This is no diamond! It is <u>valueless / worthless</u>.

✘ This is no diamond! It is <u>invaluable</u>.

> in- 一般是反義詞字首，如 incorrect, indirect，但 valuable 的反義詞不
> 是 invaluable。invaluable 是 "無法估價的" 或 "無價的"、"非常貴重
> 的"。valueless 才是 valuable 的反義詞，作 "毫無價值的" 解。

4.61 某些國家由於接受了別國的 "經濟援助" 而喪失了獨立
自主。

✔ A number of countries have lost their independence as a result
of foreign "<u>economic</u> aid."

✘ A number of countries have lost their independence as a result
of foreign "<u>economical</u> aid."

> economical 是 "節儉的"、"節約的"、"合算的"。
> economic 是 "有關經濟方面的"，如 economic policies, economic

> history 等。

4.62 他的實驗雖然失敗了，可是他的努力卻值得稱讚。

✔ Though his experiment failed, his efforts are <u>worthy of praise</u>.

✔ Though his experiment failed, his efforts are <u>worth praising</u>.

✘ Though his experiment failed, his efforts are <u>worth praise</u>.

> to be worth 作 "價值" 解時，後面接金額；作 "值得" 解時，後面接動名詞。例如：
>
> The pen <u>is worth</u> 8 dollars.
>
> The book <u>is</u> well <u>worth</u> reading.
>
> to be worthy of 作 "值得" 解，後面接名詞。

4.63 這本書值得你看。

✔ It is <u>worth</u> your <u>while to read</u> this book.

✔ This book is <u>worth reading</u>.

✘ It is <u>worth</u> to read this book.

> worth 作 "值得" 解時，不能單獨在句中作補語形容詞用。在以先行詞 it 引導的句型中，應與 while 連用。例如：
>
> It is <u>worth while</u> to see this film twice.
>
> It is not <u>worth while</u> to bother about such trifles.

4.64 首先，你們都必須用功讀書。

✔ <u>First,</u> you all must study hard.

✘ <u>At first</u>, you all must study hard.

> at first 是 "起初"、"當初" 或 "開始時"，等於 in the beginning，而不是 "首先" 或 "第一"。例如：<u>At first</u> I found French difficult, but I liked it from the start. 。
>
> "首先"、"第一" 是 first, in the first place 或 first of all。例如：<u>First</u>, I will explain my topic. Next, I will give you some background material. 。

4.65 他努力學習日語。

✔ He studies Japanese <u>hard</u>.

✘ He studies Japanese <u>hardly</u>.

> hard 和 hardly 都是副詞，但 hardly 作"幾乎不"解。例如：I could hardly understand him.（我幾乎不懂他的話）。hard 指"努力"、"用功"，兩者絕不可混淆。

4.66 現在颳大風。

✔ The wind is blowing <u>hard</u>.

✘ The wind is blowing <u>hardly</u>.

> "風大"、"雨大"是 The wind blows hard. 、It rains hard. 。

4.67 沒人知道她多麼受苦受難。

✔ No one knows how <u>much</u> she suffered.

✘ No one knows how <u>hard</u> she suffered.

> 可以説 The wind blew hard. It rained very hard. He worked hard. ，不可以説 *He <u>suffered</u> very hard. ，應説 He <u>suffered</u> a great deal / very much. 。

4.68 他成為非常熟練的技工。

✔ He became a <u>highly</u> skilled worker / technician.

✘ He became a <u>high</u> skilled worker.

> high 既可用作形容詞，也可用作副詞；但 highly 只可用作副詞。high 作副詞時，常用在 to aim high, to hold one's head high, the bird flew high, hold high the banner of... 等詞組或句子中。highly 指抽象的 "高"，例如：highly amusing, a highly paid officer, to speak highly of someone, to think highly of someone, He is highly respected. 。

4.69 "昨天你為甚麼沒來上學？"老師嚴厲地問道。

✔ "Why didn't you come to school yesterday?" asked the teacher <u>sternly</u>.

✘ "Why didn't you come to school yesterday?" asked the teacher <u>strictly</u>.

> stern, sternly 含有 "嚴酷" 之意，常用於 a stern look, a stern voice，同義詞是 severe, cruel, pitiless 等。a stern person 的反義詞是 a gentle person。strict, strictly 指要求上的嚴格，常用於紀律、規章制度，例如：
>
> A teacher should be <u>strict</u>, but not <u>stern</u>. (老師要嚴格，不要嚴酷。)
> A director may give <u>strict</u> orders.
> There is a <u>strict</u> rule against smoking.
> <u>Strictly</u> speaking, ... (嚴格地說，……)

4.70 他東西一直都亂放。

✔ He has been <u>leaving things</u> everywhere.

✘ He has been <u>leaving things about</u> everywhere.

> about 在這裏是副詞，作 here and there 解，與 everywhere 重複，應刪去其一。又如：
>
> There are several men lying <u>about</u> (=here and there) on the grass.

4.71 我小女兒以她的年紀算是很高了。

✔ My <u>little</u> daughter is quite tall for her age.

✘ My <u>small</u> daughter is quite tall for her age.

> 小女兒可以說 younger daughter 或 little daughter，但不可以說 *small daughter。

4.72 我大女兒今年十六歲。

✔ My <u>big</u> daughter is sixteen years old now.

✘ My <u>large</u> daughter is sixteen years old now.

> 大女兒可以說 older daughter 或 big daughter，但不可以說 *large daughter。

Self-test 自測

I. 選擇題

1. 他們兩人中一個穿着制服，另一個沒穿制服。 (4.2)

   One of the two was in uniform; (　　) was not.

   a) the one　　　b) the another　　　c) the other　　　d) one another

2. 他們舉行反戰示威。 (4.6)

   They held a (　　) against the war.

   a) demonstration　　　　　　b) threatening show
   c) parade　　　　　　　　　d) intimidation

3. 這本新書的作者會成名。 (4.1)

   The (　　) of this new book will become famous.

   a) writer　　　b) author　　　c) maker　　　d) founder

4. ABC 公司強硬的反應激起了員工的義憤。 (4.3 註)

   The ABC company's strong response aroused its employees' (　　).

   a) rage　　　b) anger　　　c) sympathy　　　d) indignation

5. 他在外出之前穿上一件毛衣。 (4.14 註)

   He (　　) a sweater before he went out.

   a) put on　　　b) wore　　　c) had on　　　d) wore on

6. 他昨天穿着笨重的鞋子。 (4.14)

   He (　　) heavy shoes yesterday.

   a) put on　　　b) wore　　　c) had on　　　d) wore on

7. 她馬上就要出發了。 (4.7 註)

   She is (　　).

   a) going to starting　　　　　b) about to starting
   c) about to start at once　　　d) about to start

8. 他的表演在我心中留下很深刻的印象。 (4.13)

   His performance (　　) a deep impression on my mind.

a) remained   b) left   c) stayed   d) continued

9. 老師鼓勵我們把這首詩背起來。 (4.8)

The teacher encouraged us to (   ) the poem by heart.

a) remember   b) memorize   c) learn   d) recollect

10. 你（比較）喜歡哪一本筆記簿，厚的還是薄的？ (4.11)

Which notebook do you (   ), the thick or the thin?

a) prefer more   b) prefer better   c) prefer   d) likes

11. 她舉起手去按電鈕。 (4.12註)

She (   ) her hand to press the button.

a) raised   b) rose   c) rise   d) uprised

12. 下次來的時候帶你弟弟來。 (4.15註)

(   ) your younger brother with you next time you come.

a) Take   b) Bring   c) Get   d) Put

13. 他上星期天帶他的兒子去動物園。 (4.15)

He (   ) his son to the zoo last Sunday.

a) got   b) brought   c) took   d) led

14. 他興奮得睡不着覺。 (4.18)

He was too excited to (   ).

a) go to sleep   b) fall sleepy   c) go to bed   d) feel asleep

15. 她和我哥哥相識已經很久了。 (4.21)

She has (   ) my older brother for a long time.

a) recognized   b) known   c) acquainted   d) understood

16. 我媽媽叫我的時候，我正在找我的數學筆記簿。 (4.16)

When my mother called me, I (   ) my math notebook.

a) was finding out   b) was finding

c) was looking for   d) was searching out

17. 你可以替我查那班渡輪甚麼時候到達嗎？ (4.17註)

Will you please try to (   ) for me what time that ferry arrives?

a) find out   b) search for   c) find   d) look for

18. 她父親從電視上得知他女兒成功的消息。 (4.20)

Her father (　　) his daughter's success on TV.

a) know   b) known   c) learn of   d) learned of

19. 我們決心在科技上趕上美國。 (4.26註)

We made up our minds to (　　) the U.S.A in the area of scientific technology.

a) catch   b) catch with   c) catch up with   d) hurry up with

20. 她已經學得一點電腦知識。 (4.22)

She has (　　) a little knowledge of computers.

a) acquired   b) learned   c) studied   d) received

21. 我不能借給你那本從圖書館借來的書。 (4.25註)

I cannot (　　) you the book which I have (　　) from the library.

a) borrow; lend   b) lent; borrowed

c) borrow; lent   d) lend; borrowed

22. 我送他一件生日禮物，他收下了。 (4.23)

I gave him a birthday gift, which he (　　).

a) absorbed   b) received   c) took   d) accepted

23. 他提醒我下午跟客戶有約。 (4.27註)

He (　　) me that I had an appointment with my client in the afternoon.

a) reminded   b) recalled

c) was reminded of   d) remembered

24. 我已經想起在哪裏遇見過她。 (4.27註)

I have (　　) where I met her.

a) reminded   b) recalled   c) memorized   d) thought

25. 你願意和我去看電影嗎？ (4.31)

Do you (　　) go to the movies with me?

a) mind to   b) care for   c) willing to   d) care to

26. 我可以開電視機嗎？ (4.31註)

Do you (　　) if I turn on the television?

a) mind for   b) mind   c) care about   d) cares

27. 這兩年以來他們創造了許多經濟奇蹟。 (4.28)

They have (　) economic wonders during the last two years.

a) worked　　　b) created　　　c) invented　　　d) discovered

28. 他們發明了不少有用的機器。 (4.28 註)

They have (　) quite a number of useful machines.

a) create　　　b) invented　　　c) accomplished　　　d) founded

29. 我們發覺他是一個騙子。 (4.29 註)

We (　) him to be a con man.

a) found out　　　b) invented　　　c) thought　　　d) discovered

30. 我花了半個月的時間才使他相信天然飲食有助於他康復。 (4.36 註)

It took me half a month to (　) him that a natural diet can help him recover from his illness.

a) convince　　　b) persuading　　　c) advise　　　d) suggest

31. 她被說服而這麼做。 (4.36)

She was (　) to do so.

a) advised　　　b) persuaded　　　c) submitted　　　d) convinced

32. 我已習慣於洗冷水澡。 (4.38 註)

I (　) taking cold showers.

a) used to　　　b) am used to　　　c) am used　　　d) used

33. 他過去在晚餐後一向會去散步，現在則不去了。 (4.38)

He (　) take a walk after dinner.

a) was used to　　　b) is used to　　　c) used to　　　d) always

34. 她教我怎樣操作咖啡機。 (4.30)

She taught me how to (　) a coffee machine.

a) perform　　　b) master　　　c) control　　　d) operate

35. 我勸我哥哥戒煙，但沒有成功。 (4.32)

I (　) my older brother to give up smoking, but in vain.

a) convinced　　　b) persuaded　　　c) advised　　　d) supported

36. 我能佔用你幾分鐘嗎？我有一些話要對你說。 (4.33)

Could you spare me a few minutes? I have something to (   ) to you.

a) say　　　　　b) speak　　　　c) tell　　　　d) declare

37. 昨天他在一間私家醫院執行了一場重要的手術。 (4.35)

Yesterday he (   ) an important operation at a private hospital.

a) performed　　b) took　　　c) made　　　d) did

38. 他只花十分鐘清理那個房間。 (4.34)

It only (   ) him ten minutes to clean the room.

a) wasted　　　b) spent　　　c) took　　　d) consumed

39. 她利用所有的機會練習英語。 (4.39)

She made (   ) of every opportunity to practise English.

a) advantage　　b) profit　　　c) use　　　d) using

40. 他老是佔我便宜。 (4.39 註)

He always takes (   ) of me.

a) advantage　　b) using　　　c) profit　　　d) cheap

41. 我懷疑這個故事是否真實。 (4.40 註)

I (   ) whether the story is true.

a) suspect　　　b) dread　　　c) doubt　　　d) consider

42. 大雨後河水淹沒街道。 (4.47)

The river flooded the streets after a (   ) rain.

a) great　　　　b) grave　　　c) serious　　　d) heavy

43. 這張椅子是木頭做的。 (4.44)

This chair is (   ).

a) wooden　　　　　　　b) produced by wood
c) made of wood　　　　d) done by wood

44. 一個醉漢躺在街上。 (4.45 註)

A (   ) fellow lay in the street.

a) drunken　　b) drunkard　　c) drunk　　d) drinker

45. 這個座位空着嗎？ (4.50)

Is this seat (　　)?

a) hollow　　　　b) taken　　　　c) empty　　　　d) devoid

46. 拔牙時，她不覺得痛苦，因為麻醉劑產生了效果。(4.51)

Because she had been given an anesthetic, she (　　) when her tooth was pulled out.

a) felt not pain　　b) felt painless

c) felt no pain　　d) spared no pains

47. 這顆頂級鑽石是個無價之寶。(4.60 註)

This top-quality diamond is (　　).

a) invaluable　　b) nonpriced　　c) valueless　　d) unvaluable

48. 砒霜是一種劇毒。(4.52)

Arsenic is a (　　) poison.

a) dying　　　　b) deadly　　　　c) dead　　　　d) death

49. 我相信他是一個認真負責的員工。(4.53)

I believe him to be a (　　) worker.

a) conscious　　b) responsibly　　c) conscientious　　d) responsive

50. 他認為這是一種可恥的行為。(4.54 註)

He considers this kind of conduct to be completely (　　).

a) ashamed　　b) shameful　　c) shamefaced　　d) shame

51. 起初我不喜歡英文，但現在卻喜歡。(4.64 註)

(　　) I didn't like English but now I do.

a) Firstly　　　b) At first　　　c) First　　　d) In first

52. 他對自己的信念是如此地堅定，以致於無法容忍別人的意見。
(4.56 註)

He was so firm in his own belief that he was (　　) of others' opinions.

a) unbearable　　b) intolerable　　c) unendurable　　d) intolerant

53. 我不高興他未經允許就離開。(4.58)

I was (　　) when he went away without permission.

a) unpleasant　　b) displeased　　c) offensive　　d) annoying

54. 這結果毫不令人滿意。　(4.59)

The result is by no means (　　).

a) satisfactory　　b) contented　　c) satisfied　　d) satisfaction

55. 這博物館很值得參觀。　(4.62)

This museum is well (　　) seeing.

a) worthy　　b) worth of　　c) worth　　d) worthy for

II.　翻譯填空

1. 他醉得無法站立。　(4.45)

He is too (　　) to stand.

2. 我哥哥經常空腹去上學。　(4.48)

My elder brother usually goes to school with an (　　).

3. 他因說謊而感到慚愧。　(4.54)

He was (　　) that he had told a lie.

4. 我們必須更省點，因為我們沒有很多錢。　(4.61 註)

We need to be more (　　) because we haven't much money.

5. 老師應該嚴格但要公平。　(4.69 註)

A teacher should be (　　) but fair.

6. 學習四年之後，他精通德文。　(4.10)

After four years of studying, he had a good (　　) of German.

7. 她答應留到我回來為止。　(4.24)

She (　　) to stay till I came back.

8. 我希望你能善用時間。　(4.39)

I hope you can (　　) good use of your time.

9. 這些假珍珠是用塑膠做的，毫無價值可言。　(4.60)

These false pearls are made of plastic. They are (　　).

10. 我的老師十分讚賞我。 (4.68 註)

    My teacher speaks very (　　) of me.

11. 他覺察到他被跟蹤。 (4.53 註)

    He was (　　) that he was being followed.

12. 她對我的解釋不太滿意。 (4.59 註)

    She was not very (　　) with my explanation.

13. 這部電影值得看兩遍。 (4.63 註)

    It is (　　) (　　) to see this film twice.

14. 雖然雨下得很大，他仍然繼續練跑。 (4.66)

    Although it was raining (　　), he continued his running practice.

15. 我們一直到處找你。 (4.70 註)

    We have been looking (　　) for you.

III. 改　錯

1. The students of different universities held parades protesting
   　　　　　　　　　　　　　　　　　　　　　A　　　B　　　　C
   the Prime Minister's visit. (4.6)
   (　　)＿＿＿＿＿＿＿

2. One of the two has come back; the another has not. (4.2)
   　　　　　　　　　　　A　　　　　　　B　　　C
   (　　)＿＿＿＿＿＿＿

3. The teacher made them memorize the whole poem by heart.(4.8)
   　　　　　　　A　　　　　B　　　　　　　　　　　C
   (　　)＿＿＿＿＿＿＿

4. Take this empty bottle away and take me a full one, please. (4.15 註)
   　A　　　　　　　　　B　　　　C
   (　　)＿＿＿＿＿＿＿

5. He was finding something when I came across him. (4.16)
   　　　　A　　　　　　　B　　　C
   (　　)＿＿＿＿＿＿＿

6. He <u>has</u> <u>found out</u> his <u>wallet</u>.   (4.17)
      A   B   C
  (   )_____

7. I <u>got acquainted</u> <u>to</u> him <u>in</u> Thailand.   (4.21)
        A   B   C
  (   )_____

8. She has <u>learned</u> <u>a little</u> <u>knowledge</u> of Italian.   (4.22)
         A   B   C
  (   )_____

9. I <u>allowed</u> her that I <u>would</u> do my <u>best</u> to help her.   (4.24 註)
    A   B   C
  (   )_____

10. Margaret <u>lent</u> some books <u>on</u> art from <u>the library</u> yesterday. (4.25)
        A   B   C
  (   )_____

11. We have <u>created</u> educational <u>wonders</u> <u>during</u> the last four years. (4.28)
        A   B   C
  (   )_____

12. The man <u>who</u> <u>discovered</u> the <u>electric lamp</u> is Edison.   (4.29)
        A   B   C
  (   )_____

13. <u>Painting</u> the room only <u>spent</u> me <u>half an</u> hour.   (4.34)
    A   B   C
  (   )_____

14. <u>Can</u> you <u>introduce</u> me a good <u>electrician</u>?   (4.37)
    A   B   C
  (   )_____

15. I <u>suspect</u> whether she <u>has</u> <u>lost</u> the letter.   (4.40 註)
    A   B C
  (   )_____

16. <u>I'm</u> not used to <u>stay</u> up <u>till midnight</u>.   (4.38 註)
    A   B   C
  (   )_____

17. It is <u>uneasy</u> to <u>master</u> the violin. You <u>have to</u> spend a lot of time
   A   B   C
practising. (4.49)

( )_____

18. <u>Do</u> you know how <u>hard</u> he <u>suffered</u>? (4.67)
 A   B C

( )_____

5　Idioms 慣用語

5.1　他的健康已有好轉。

✔　His health has taken a turn <u>for the better</u>.

✘　His health has taken a turn <u>for better</u>.

> to turn (/ change) for the better (/ worse), a turn (/ change) for the better (/ worse) 都是慣用語。

5.2　徑賽次序如下：

✔　The order of track events is <u>as follows</u>:

✘　The order of track events is <u>as follow</u>:

> 不論句子中的主詞是複數或單數，"如下"都用 as follows，不用 as follow。例如：
>
> 　　The program is <u>as follows</u>.
> 　　The items are <u>as follows</u>.
>
> 也可以説：
>
> 　　The items <u>follow</u>.
> 　　The program <u>follows</u>.
> 　　<u>The following</u> is the program.
> 　　<u>The following</u> are the items.

5.3　要做這一切，精通外語是很必要的。

✔　A good command of foreign languages is necessary to do all <u>this</u>.

✘　A good command of foreign languages is necessary to do all <u>these</u>.

> 總結上文時，"這一切"應説 all this，不説 all these。

5.4　這些照片使我想起我年輕的時候。

　　✔　These photos <u>reminded me of</u> my youth.

　　✘　These photos <u>made me remind</u> my youth.

> to remind one of something 作 "使想起" 解。例如：
>
> The monument <u>reminds us of</u> the heroic deeds of the martyrs.
>
> You <u>remind me of</u> your mother.=When I see you, I think of your mother.
>
> 作 "提醒" 解時，remind of 後面接名詞、動名詞，或用 to remind... to..., to remind... that... 的結構。例如：
>
> He <u>reminded me of</u> my promise.
>
> He <u>reminded me to do</u> the work.
>
> He <u>reminded me to prepare for</u> the test.
>
> He <u>reminded me that I must answer</u> the letters.
>
> He <u>reminded me of what</u> to do.

5.5　因為旱災，農民入不敷出。

　　✔　Because of the drought, the farmers couldn't <u>make (both) ends</u> meet.

　　✘　Because of the drought, the farmers couldn't <u>make their ends</u> meet.

> to make (both) ends meet 作 "收支相抵"、"量入為出" 解。ends 前面從前通常有 both，現在比較少見；間或也有人用 two，但不可加人稱代名詞所有格。

5.6　他一就職，就着手對自己的系務工作做一系列的改革。

　　✔　As soon as he <u>took office</u>, he began a series of reforms in his department.

　　✘　As soon as he <u>took his office</u>, he began a series of reforms in his department.

> to take office 一語裏的 office 具有比較抽象的意義，作 "職位" 解，前面不可以有人稱代名詞所有格。

5.7　他們拿起武器，保衛他們的城市。

✓　They <u>took up arms</u> to defend their city.

✗　They <u>took up their arms</u> to defend their city.

> to take up arms 這一慣用語中不需用人稱代名詞所有格。

5.8　這是我所見過最漂亮的房子。

✓　This is the most beautiful house I have ever <u>set eyes on</u>.

✗　This is the most beautiful house I have ever <u>set my eyes on</u>.

> to set eyes on 這一慣用語中不用人稱代名詞所有格。

5.9　時間已經不早，最好馬上回家。

✓　It is getting dark. You <u>had better</u> go home at once.

✗　It is getting dark. You <u>have better</u> go home at once.

> had better 或 had best 是慣用語，後面接動詞原形。儘管説的是現在或將來，had 也不可改作 have 或 has，在口語裏可以説 <u>Better</u> go at once 或 <u>Better</u> be going。

5.10　時間到了，該回家了吧！

✓　<u>It is time to go</u> home.

✓　<u>It is time we went</u> home.

✗　<u>Time is up. Let's go</u> home.

> Time is up. = The time allowed is at an end. 指"所給的時間完了"。比如，考試時規定兩小時交卷，兩小時完了，學生仍不交卷，老師可以説："Time is up. Hand in your papers, please."。説"……時間到了"、"現在（或那時候）該……了"，常用 It is (high) time... 的句型。例如：
>
>   <u>It is time</u> to go back.
>
>   <u>It is (high) time (that)</u> we went to bed.
>
>   <u>It is (high) time (that)</u> we started our work.
>
> 注意 It is time 中沒有冠詞，括弧裏的 high、that 常常省去，後面從屬句中的動詞屬虛擬語氣，須用過去式。

5.11 是政府採取行動的時候了。

✔ It is (high) time <u>for</u> the government <u>to take</u> action.

✔ It is (high) time <u>that</u> the government <u>took</u> action.

✘ The (high) time <u>for</u> the government <u>to take</u> action <u>is drawing near</u>.

> high time 前面沒有冠詞，一般用在 it is, it was 後面，有 "正是……的時候"、"事不宜遲" 的涵義。

5.12 屋子前面有一個花園。

✔ <u>In front of</u> the house there was a flower garden.

✘ <u>In the front of</u> the house there was a flower garden.

> in front of 是 "在……的前面"；in the front of 是 "在……的前部"，兩者不同。試比較下列句子：
>
> There is a pot plant <u>in the front of</u> the classroom.
> （盆栽在教室內的前部）
> There is a pot plant <u>in front of</u> the classroom.
> （盆栽在教室外的前面）
> The teacher is sitting <u>in front of</u> the students.（不能說 *in the front of）

5.13 我一定見過他，但是一時記不起他的名字。

✔ I have met him before, but his name escapes me <u>for the moment</u>.

✘ I have met him before, but his name escapes me <u>for a moment</u>.

> for the moment ＝ at the / this / that moment，作 "此刻" 或 "當時" 解。
> 例如：
> Well, we are still friends <u>for the moment</u>.（此刻）
> <u>For the moment</u> the troops had stopped firing.（當時）
> for a moment 意為 "一會兒"。試比較：
> <u>For a moment</u> I did not know what to say.
> （好一會兒我不知說甚麼好。）

> For the moment I did not know what to say.
> （當時我不知説甚麼好。）

5.14 救護車及時趕到。

✔ The ambulance arrived in the nick of time.

✘ The ambulance arrived in the nick of the time.

in the nick of time 這一慣用語裏，time 前面不能加定冠詞。

5.15 她非常愛她的家人。

✔ She is devoted to her family.

✔ She devoted herself to her family.

✘ She devoted to herself.

to be devoted to 一語中的 devoted 是形容詞，不是動詞，to 是介詞，後面應接名詞。 devoted 用作動詞時必須有受詞，例如：

He devoted himself to the cause of equal rights for all.
He devoted his life to the cause of equal rights for all.

5.16 我會在一兩天之內把事情做完。

✔ I will be finished in a day or two.

✔ I will be finished in one or two days.

✘ I will be finished in one day or two.

a...or two 不可和 one or two... 相混。例如：a mile or two=one or two miles；a book or two=one or two books，不可用 one...or two 或 a or two...。

5.17 他全心全意愛她。

✔ He loved her heart and soul.

✔ He loved her with all his heart and soul.

✘ He loved her soul and heart.

可以說 put <u>heart and soul</u> into (a thing), to do something <u>with all one's heart</u>。慣用語 heart and soul 通常作副詞用，次序不可顛倒。

5.18 他們兩人毫無共同之處。

✔ The two of them have nothing <u>in common</u>.

✘ The two of them have nothing <u>in common with each other</u>.

"The two of them have <u>nothing in common</u>." 意為 "他們的愛好、興趣等各有不同"。也可以說 "He has <u>nothing in common</u> with him."。to have something / much in common, to have nothing / little in common 後面接 with each other 較少見。

5.19 小偷偷走了我所有的東西。

✔ The thief <u>robbed</u> me <u>of</u> all my belongings.

✘ The thief <u>robbed</u> all my belongings.

rob 是指非法取人財物，可以是搶，也可以是偷，要看上下文決定。"偷或搶走某人的東西" 可說 to rob (someone) of (something) 來表達。注意："The gangsters <u>robbed</u> him."，意思是 "把他的東西搶走"，並不是說 "把人搶走"。

5.20 他們剝奪了這些工人的各項權利。

✔ These workers were <u>deprived of</u> their rights.

✘ They <u>deprived</u> these workers' rights.

參見例 5.19。

5.21 我們大家都不感覺累，因為我們是輪流開車的。

✔ None of us felt tired, as we took <u>turns</u> at driving.

✘ None of us felt tired, as we took a <u>turn</u> at driving.

to take a turn 意義是 "散步一會兒" 或 "短時間騎一會兒馬、划一陣槳"、"做一陣工" 等，如 I <u>took a turn</u> around the campus before I went to bed.（我睡前在校園遛了一圈）。"輪流做某種工作"應為 to take turns at ＋名詞或動名詞。注意：這裏的 turns 是複數形式。

5.22 狼畢竟是狼，儘管偽裝得巧妙，遲早要現原形的。

✓ A wolf, after all, is a wolf. In spite of his artful disguises, sooner or later he will show his <u>true colours</u>.

✗ A wolf, after all, is a wolf. In spite of his artful disguises, sooner or later he will show his <u>true colour</u>.

in one's true colours 中的 colours 不可用單數形式。

5.23 為了不被敵人發現，他爬着走。

✓ To avoid being detected by the enemy, he crawled <u>on all fours</u>.

✗ To avoid being detected by the enemy, he crawled <u>on all four</u>.

on all fours 一語裏的 fours 應是複數。

5.24 不要為這樣的小事傷腦筋。

✓ Don't rack / cudgel your <u>brains</u> over such a trifle.

✗ Don't rack / cudgel your <u>brain</u> over such a trifle.

to rack one's brains 中的 brains 必須用複數形式。

5.25 你喜歡盛氣凌人，自己都不知道。

✓ You <u>lord it over</u> others and you don't even know it.

✗ You <u>lord over</u> others and you don't even know it.

to lord it over 裏面的 it 無所指，僅是約定俗成的一種用法，不能任意略去。

5.26 他寫錯了地址，通知書我沒有收到。

✓ He wrote the wrong address, so the notice never <u>reached me</u>.

✘ He wrote the wrong address, so the notice never <u>reached my hand</u>.

> reached my hand 不合習慣，應改為 reached me 或 came to my hand（或 hands）。

5.27 沒有周密的調查，我們不能做出任何結論。

✔ We cannot <u>come to any conclusion</u> without first investigating carefully.

✘ We cannot <u>make any conclusion</u> without first investigating carefully.

> "做（得）出結論"英語習慣用 to come to a conclusion, to come to the conclusion that... , to reach a conclusion, to draw the conclusion that... 等。

5.28 這位科學家在應用幹細胞方面又有了新發現。

✔ The scientist <u>made</u> another new discovery in the use of stem cells.

✘ The scientist <u>did</u> another new discovery in the use of stem cells.

> to make a discovery 是慣用語，其中的動詞 make 不能任意用其他動詞代替。

Self-test 自測

I. 選擇題

1. 這個紀念碑使我想起這些烈士的英勇事蹟。 (5.4 註)
   The monument (　　) the heroic deeds of the martyrs.
   a) makes me remind　　　　　　b) makes me remind to
   c) reminds me　　　　　　　　d) reminds me of

2. 這是我所見過最大的畫。 (5.8)
   This is the largest picture I have ever (　　).
   a) set eyes on　　　　　　　　b) set my eyes on
   c) set eye on　　　　　　　　 d) set my eye on

3. 他的病情惡化。 (5.1)
   His condition took a turn (　　).
   a) for worse　　b) the worse　　c) for the worse　　d) to the worse

4. 我們現在該就寢了。 (5.10 註)
   It is (　　) time we went to bed.
   a) a　　　　　　b) high　　　　　c) the　　　　　　d) up

5. 要做這一切，精通法語是很必要的。 (5.3)
   A good command of the French language is necessary to do (　　).
   a) this all　　　b) these all　　　c) all this　　　d) all these

6. 我和我太太都必須工作才足以維生。 (5.5)
   My wife and I have to work to make (　　) meet.
   a) ends　　　　b) our ends　　　c) the ends　　　d) the end

7. 老師正坐在學生的前面。 (5.12 註)
   The teacher is sitting (　　) the students.
   a) in front of　　　　　　　　b) in the front of
   c) on front of　　　　　　　　d) on the front of

8. 傑克坐在班上的前排，因為他個子矮。 (5.12註)

   Jack sits ( ) the class because he is short.

   a) in front of   b) in the front of
   c) on front of   d) on the front of

9. 她的煩惱使她不能入睡。 (5.20)

   Her troubles deprived her ( ).

   a) sleep   b) to sleep   c) sleeping   d) of sleep

10. 她現在很忙。 (5.13註)

    She is very busy ( ).

    a) for a moment   b) at the moment
    c) in moment   d) on the moment

11. 好一會兒他不知道說甚麼好。 (5.13註)

    For ( ) moment he did not know what to say.

    a) the   b) x   c) a   d) another

12. 他獻身於世界和平運動。 (5.15)

    He ( ) the cause of world peace.

    a) devoted himself for   b) was devoted for
    c) devoted himself to   d) devoted to

13. 我爸爸全心全意地投入工作。 (5.17)

    My father threw himself into his work ( ).

    a) his heart and soul   b) his soul and heart
    c) heart and soul   d) soul and heart

14. 克萊拉絞盡腦汁想解決這個問題。 (5.24)

    Clara racked her ( ) trying to solve the problem.

    a) head   b) thought   c) brain   d) brains

15. 這兩個士兵輪流挖洞。 (5.21)

    The two soldiers ( ) at digging the hole.

    a) took a turn   b) took turn
    c) took turns   d) took the turn

16. 我們做出證人並非都可靠的結論。 (5.27)

    We ( ) the conclusion that not all witnesses are reliable.

a) came to　　　b) arrived　　　c) made　　　d) took

17. 他在生物學上有了令人驚訝的發現。　(5.28)
He (　) a surprising discovery in biology.
a) had　　　b) made　　　c) found　　　d) did

18. 那個經理經常盛氣凌人地指揮職員。　(5.25)
That manager usually (　) the clerks.
a) lords over　　　　　　b) lords upon
c) lords it over　　　　　d) lords it upon

19. 他趴在地上給他的嬰兒騎。　(5.23)
He got down (　) and gave his baby a ride.
a) all four　　b) all fours　　c) on all four　　d) on all fours

20. 暴民搶走了他全部的食物。　(5.19)
The mob robbed (　).
a) of all his food　　　　b) all his food
c) him of all his food　　d) him all his food

II.　改錯

1. When his <u>trick</u> failed, he <u>showed</u> his true <u>colour</u>.　(5.22)
　　　　　　　　A　　　　　　B　　　　　　C
(　)＿＿＿＿＿＿

2. I usually <u>take turns</u> <u>around</u> the campus before I <u>go</u> to bed.　(5.21)
　　　　　　A　　　B　　　　　　　　　　C
(　)＿＿＿＿＿＿

3. The order of <u>field events</u> <u>is</u> as <u>follow</u>:　(5.2)
　　　　　　　　A　　B　　　C
(　)＿＿＿＿＿＿

4. After he took <u>his office</u>, the <u>efficiency</u> <u>improved</u> remark-
　　　　　　　A　　　　　　B　　　　C
ably.　(5.6)
(　)＿＿＿＿＿＿

5. The doctor arrived in <u>the nick</u> of <u>the time</u> to save my grandfa
　　　　　　　　　A　　　　B

ther <u>from</u> choking to death. (5.14)

       C

( )_____

6. I <u>wrote</u> the wrong <u>address</u>, so my letter never reached <u>her hand</u>. (5.26)

    A   B   C

( )_____

7. I usually <u>take</u> <u>one book</u> <u>or two</u> to my office every day. (5.16 註)

            A   B   C

( )_____

8. Sophia and her sister <u>have nothing</u> <u>in common</u> <u>with each other</u>. (5.18)

                    A   B   C

( )_____

9. Many <u>townsmen</u> <u>took up</u> <u>their arms</u> to protect their proper-
ty. (5.7)   A   B   C

( )_____

10. I <u>have better</u> <u>leave</u> now, or I'll <u>miss</u> the train. (5.9)

    A   B   C

( )_____

6 **Punctuations and Capitalisation**
標點符號和大小寫

6.1　參閱第六十三頁。

✔　See p. 63.

✘　See P. 63.

> page 的縮寫通常是 "p."，通常小寫。

6.2　他住在西部。

✔　He lives in the West.

✘　He lives in the west.

> 一國的區域名稱須大寫，如 the North（北部地方）、the South（南部地方）等。比較：
> He went to the north.（這裏的 north 指方向）
> He lived in the North during his childhood.（這裏的 the North 指地區）

6.3　我寫了一篇文章，題目是〈我的老師生涯〉。

✔　I wrote an article entitled:
　　"My Life as a Teacher."

✘　I wrote an article entitled:
　　"My Life As A Teacher."

> 題目中每一重要單詞開頭都要大寫，但冠詞、介詞、連接詞，只有當它們在題目中是第一字或最後一字時，或分兩行書寫的長題目第二行的第一字時，才可大寫。例如："What We Live For"。

6.4　他們學哲學、心理學等。

✔　They study philosophy, psychology, etc.

✘　They study Philosophy, Psychology, etc.

> 學習的科目一般不大寫，除非 1) 該學科名是由專有名詞演變而來的，如法文、英文、中文（French, English, Chinese）；或 2) 指特別的選課程名稱（specific course titles）時則當專有名詞用，須大寫，如 English Composition, Introduction to Linguistics。試比較：
>
> The courses are Children's Literature, Introductory Economics, and French Composition.（以上皆特定的課程名稱）
>
> They hope to take courses in children's literature, introductory economics, and French composition.（這裏不指實際的課程名稱，只指這方面的科目）

6.5　他是個牙醫。

✔　He is a <u>dentist</u>.

✘　He is a <u>Dentist</u>.

> doctor, professor, general, president 等當普通名詞用時不需大寫。但作為尊稱或職銜而位於專有名詞前面時，應大寫。例如：Doctor Wang (Dr. Wang), Professor Li, President Chiang 等。

6.6　春、夏、秋、冬，你最喜歡哪一季？

✔　Which season do you like best: <u>spring, summer, autumn or winter</u>?

✘　Which season do you like best: <u>Spring, Summer, Autumn or Winter</u>?

> 四季的名稱一般不大寫。秋在美式英文裏通常稱 fall。

6.7　請把窗子關上。

✔　Shut the window, <u>please</u>.

✔　<u>Please</u> shut the window.

✘　Shut the window <u>please</u>.

> 祈使句裏面的 please，若放在句末，用逗號與句子其他部分分開；若放在句首，則不用逗號。

6.8　他會說英、德、法三種語言。

✔　He can speak three languages, <u>namely,</u> English, German, and French.

✘　He can speak three languages, <u>namely</u> English, German, and French.

> namely, that is 等的前面用逗號或分號，後面用逗號。

6.9　a 這個字是不定冠詞。

✔　The word <u>'a'</u> is an indefinite article.

✘　The word, <u>'a',</u> is an indefinite article.

> 同位語之間，如果已用引號，或用不同字體（斜體字或粗體字），或下面劃有橫線加以區別，則不必再用逗號。

6.10　他的妻子安妮和女兒艾瑪還在意大利。

✔　His <u>wife Anne and daughter Emma</u> are still in Italy.

✘　His <u>wife, Anne and daughter, Emma,</u> are still in Italy.

> 名詞後緊接專有名詞，雖屬同位語性質，不必用逗號分開。

6.11　我把蛋糕給了李先生，他帶回家給他太太。

✔　I gave the cake to <u>Mr. Li,</u> who brought it home to his wife.

✘　I gave the cake to <u>Mr. Li</u> who brought it home to his wife.

> 非限定性形容子句前一般要用逗號，在譯成中文時須另起一句。

6.12　到他十二歲，父母才准他晚上出去。

✔　<u>Not until he was twelve</u> did his parents allow him to go out at night.

✘　<u>Not until he was twelve,</u> did his parents allow him to go out at night.

> 表示時間的副詞從屬句放在句首，一般可用逗號與後面的主句分開，
> 但以 till, until 引導的副詞從屬句放在句首時，概不用逗號與後面的主句
> 分開。

6.13 我剛開始演講，他就離開了。

✓ <u>Scarcely had I begun to lecture</u> when he left.

✗ <u>Scarcely had I begun to lecture,</u> when he left.

> 用 scarcely...when (before)..., hardly...when..., no sooner...than... 表達
> 的句子，在 when, before, than 之前一律不用逗號。例如：
> Hardly had I gained my foothold when I was pushed forward violently
> from behind.
> No sooner had the bell rung than the teacher began to lecture.

6.14 王先生一定上廁所去了，因為他不在他辦公室。

✓ <u>Mr. Wang must have gone to the restroom,</u> for he is not in his
office.

✗ <u>Mr. Wang must have gone to the restroom</u> for he is not in his
office.

> for 在此用作並列連接詞，前面常用逗號，在較長的句裏常用分號。
> for-clause 常在主句之後。注意這裏 for 引導一個説明，不可換用
> since 或 as。又如：It must be morning, for the cock is crowing. The
> temperature must have fallen considerably, for I see icicles on the
> trees.。

6.15 一再嘗試後他才成功。

✓ <u>Only after repeated attempts</u> did he succeed.

✗ <u>Only after repeated attempts,</u> did he succeed.

> 在以 only 開始的強調句式中不用逗號。試比較：
> <u>After repeated failures,</u> he succeeded.

6.16 他沒去，因為他病了。

✔ He didn't go, <u>because</u> he was sick.

✘ He didn't go. <u>Because</u> he was sick.

> because 是從屬連接詞，它所引導的句子永遠是附屬子句，不能獨立。
> because 前面可用逗號，也可不用。

6.17 聽了校長的報告，他難過得講不出話來。

✔ On hearing the principal's report, <u>he</u> was too upset to say anything.

✘ On hearing the principal's report. <u>He</u> was too upset to say anything.

> on hearing the principal's report 只是一個介詞短語，不成為句子，後面不可用句號，應改用逗號，與後面句子的主要部分連起來。

6.18 我爸爸會坐在那把椅子上讀報紙。

✔ <u>My father would sit in that chair,</u> reading the newspaper.

✘ <u>My father would sit in that chair</u> reading the newspaper.

> 表示陪襯性動作的較長的分詞短語放在句末時，前面要用逗號。在下列句中，因為只用一個分詞，不必用逗號：
> I stood at the door waiting.
> He sat there reading.

6.19 他在黑暗中摸索，撞到了一樣硬的東西。

✔ <u>Groping about in the dark,</u> he bumped into something hard.

✘ <u>Groping about in the dark</u> he bumped into something hard.

> 分詞短語放在句首時，必須用逗號，與句子其他部分分開。

6.20 我的女婿是個帥哥。

✔ My daughter's husband is <u>a handsome young man</u>.

✘ My daughter's husband is <u>a handsome, young man</u>.

young man, old man，如同 postman, statesman, gentleman，可以看作一個合成名詞。handsome 和 young 並非對等，handsome 修飾 young man，因此不需用逗號分開。又如 a thin old man, an old leather trunk；在 thin, old 後面都不要用逗號。但一系列對等形容詞同時修飾一個名詞時，就要用逗號。例如：an old, low, unpainted house。

6.21 老師問："每個人都做好功課了嗎？"

✔ The teacher <u>asked, "Has</u> everyone done his homework?"

✘ The teacher <u>asked "Has</u> everyone done his homework?"

在 say, ask, demand 等 reporting verb 後面，一般須用逗號，有時候也可用冒號。

6.22 她說："我愛你。"

✔ She said, "I love <u>you."</u>

✘ She said, "I love <u>you".</u>

有引文的句子，句號總是放在引號之內，逗號也是如此。例如：
"I refuse to do <u>it,"</u> she said stubbornly.

6.23 "他是誰？"他問。

✔ "Who is <u>that?"</u> he asked.

✔ He asked, "Who is <u>that?"</u>

✘ "Who is <u>that"?</u> he asked.

問號有時放在引號之內，有時放在外面。放在引號之內屬於引文，例如上列正句；放在引號外面屬於全句。例如：
What is the meaning of "inverted commas"?
感歎號也是如此：
He shouted, "Stop <u>it!"</u>
We are told to "make <u>way"!</u>

6.24 她問我要去哪裏。

✔ She asked <u>where I was going.</u>

✔ She asked <u>me</u>, "Where are you going?"

✘ She asked <u>where I was going?</u>

> 在間接問句後面不能用問號。

6.25 他說他很高興見到他們。

✔ He <u>said that he was happy to see them.</u>

✔ He <u>said</u>, "I am happy to see them."

✘ He <u>said that "he was happy to see them."</u>

> 間接引語不用引號，引號只用於直接引語。

6.26 "你只能怪你自己。"王方反駁道。

✔ "You have only yourself to <u>blame," Wang Fang retorted.</u>

✘ "You have only yourself to <u>blame." Wang Fang retorted.</u>

✘ "You have only yourself to <u>blame" Wang Fang retorted.</u>

> 直接引語若放在句首，在英文引號中不可用句號，也不能沒有標點符號，須用逗號，因整句並非到此結束。若直接引語為問句或感歎句，則引號之內須用相應的問號或感歎號。

6.27 "你應滿足，"他說，"你甚麼都有了。"

✔ "You should be content," he said. "<u>You've</u> got everything."

✘ "You should be content," he said. "<u>you've</u> got everything."

> 第二句中的直接引語與第一句中的直接引語在結構上並無關聯，應以大寫開始，同時在 said 後應用句號。但如果 he said 前後的直接引語在結構上構成一個句子，則 he said 前後應用逗號，引語的後部分就不必以大寫開始。例如：
>
> 　　"Well," he <u>said, "you</u> may come if you want."
>
> 　　"All of you," the boss <u>said, "must</u> be here at seven o'clock sharp tomorrow morning."

6.28 把書打開到四十頁，朗讀第一句。

✔ Open your book to page <u>40,</u> and read the first sentence.

✘ Open your book to page <u>40.,</u> and read the first sentence.

> 指頁碼的數字後面不應用句號，如 page 10 或 p.10 等等後面都不放句號。

6.29 講台上站着校董、校長⋯⋯

✔ On the rostrum stood <u>the director, the principal.</u>...

✘ On the rostrum stood <u>the director, the principal</u>......

> 刪節號的句點，英文中為三個，如果在句尾，則為四點，每個點佔一個字母寬度的空格；中文裏則用六個點，點是居中的，英文裏的則是齊底。這種刪節號常用以表示一段引文的節略處，也用以表示話沒有說完或因故中斷的情況。

6.30 咖啡桌上有書、雜誌等等。

✔ There are books, <u>magazines, etc.,</u> on the coffee table.

✘ There are books, <u>magazines... etc.</u> on the coffee table.

> etc. 是拉丁文 et cetera 的縮寫＝ and the others 或 and so forth。"⋯"是刪節號，表示一個未完的話語。兩者同時使用，顯然重複。

6.31 他可能知道那是甚麼東西。

✔ He might know <u>what it is.</u>

✘ He might know <u>what it is?</u>

> 受詞從屬子句僅是整個句子的一部分，若整個句子不是疑問句，從屬子句即使有疑問口氣仍不應用問號。

6.32 我們雖然遭受嚴重的天然災害，但一定能克服困難。

✔ Though we suffer from serious natural <u>calamities, we</u> are sure to overcome all difficulties.

✗ Though we suffer from serious natural <u>calamities</u>
, <u>we</u> are sure to overcome all difficulties.

> 英文在一行的開頭除了引號外，不能有其他標點符號，包括逗點、句點、感歎號等。也許是受了中文排版的影響，一般學生有時因為行尾沒位置了，而將這些標點符號移到下一行的行頭，但在英文裏是絕對不行的。另外將引號的前半部放在行尾如：
>
> *The man went over to the receptionist and asked, "
>
> Is there any message for Mr. John White? "
>
> 這也是錯的。引號的前半部不能放在行尾，引號的後半部也不能放在行頭。

小結

　　關於標點符號的用法，有幾點難免是有爭議的。特別是逗號，它的用法較多，往往因各人的看法而有所不同，沒有絕對的標準。近代趨向於少用標點，只要意義明晰，以少用為宜，切忌濫用。讀者於閱讀名著時不妨多多觀察。

Pronunciation of punctuations
標點符號的英語讀法

Symbols commonly used 常用符號

,	comma 逗號
.	period, full stop, dot 句號
?	question mark 問號
:	colon 冒號
;	semicolon 分號
!	exclamation mark (Br.) exclamation point (Am.) 感歎號
-	hyphen 連字號
—	– n dash (with spaces) (Br.) — m dash (no spaces) (Am.) 破折號

_	underscore 下劃線，底線
'	apostrophe 撇號，所有格符號
' '	single quotation marks 單引號
" "	double quotation marks 雙引號
&	ampersand, and, reference, ref 和；(程式語言) 參照
`	backquote 反引號或倒引號
~	swung dash 代字號
~	tilde 波浪號
...	dots / ellipsis 省略號
"	ditto 雙點號
/	slash, divide, oblique 斜線，斜槓，除號

\	backslash, sometimes escape 反斜線，有時表示轉義符號或續行符號
//	slash-slash, comment 雙斜線，註釋符號
*	asterisk, star 星號 (美語)，（程式語言中表示 multiply）
( )	brackets / parentheses 圓括號
(	left parenthesis, open parenthesis, open parenthesis, opening parenthesis 左圓括號

)	right parenthesis, close parenthesis, closing parenthesis 右圓括號
{	open brace, open curly, brace left 左大括號
}	close brace, close curly, brace right 右大括號
[ ]	square brackets 方括號
[	bracket left, opening bracket 左方括號
]	bracket right, closing bracket 右方括號

Mathematical symbols 數學符號

+	plus 加號；正號
−	minus 減號；負號
±	plus or minus 正負號
×	multiplied by 乘號
÷	divided by 除號
=	is equal to 等於號，等號
≈	is approximately equal to 約等於號
≠	is not equal to 不等於號
≡	is equivalent to 全等於號
≌	is equal to or approximately equal to 等於或約等於符號
√	(square) root 平方根

<	is less than 小於號
>	is more than, greater than 大於號
≤	is less than or equal to 小於或等於號
≥	is more than or equal to 大於或等於號
≮	is not less than 不小於號
≯	is not more than 不大於號
%	percent (sign) 百分之……；百分號
‰	per mill 千分之……
⊥	perpendicular to 垂直於
π	pi 圓周率
○	circumference 圓周
⊙	circle 圓
⌒	semicircle 半圓；arc 弧
△	triangle 三角形
∠	angle 角
°	degree 度
∪	union of 並；合集
∩	intersection of 相交；交集
∫	the integral of ……的積分
Σ	(sigma) summation of 總和
∞	infinity 無限大號
∝	varies as 與……成比例
∷	equals, as (proportion) 等於；成比例
∵	since; because 因
∴	hence 所以

Other symbols 其他符號

@	at / at the rate of
#	number sign, hash (Br.), pound (Am.)，音樂裏作 sharp，如 C#
$	dollar (sign)
℃	degrees Celsius 攝氏度
℉	degrees Fahrenheit 華氏度
/	virgule 斜線號
‥	tandem colon 雙點號
^	caret 插入符號
		bar, vertical bar, vertical virgule, upright slash, vertical slash 豎線

‖	parallel 雙線號；平行號
§	section; division 分節號
→	arrow 箭號；參見號
《 》	French quotes 法文引號；guillemets 書名號
'	minute 分；feet 呎
"	second 秒；inches 吋

Notes 備註

www	讀 WWW / ˈdʌbljuː / （重複三次），不讀 "triple W"
000	讀 "triple /əu/"
4 × 4	讀 "four by four" "four times four" "multiply four by four"

Answers 答案

第 1 章

I.

1. c	13. d	25. b
2. b	14. d	26. a
3. d	15. b	27. d
4. a	16. a	28. c
5. b	17. c	29. d
6. c	18. b	30. a
7. d	19. d	31. d
8. c	20. a	32. b
9. a	21. c	33. c
10. b	22. a	34. b
11. c	23. b	
12. a	24. b	

II.

1. How; What
2. for
3. conscientious
4. beat
5. bothers
6. what
7. sick / ill
8. about; over
9. do, think
10. another
11. spite
12. improve, consult, encounter
13. spare
14. much; much, cost; price
15. No, isn't
16. Yes, will
17. No, matter; Wherever
18. high; expensive
19. lectured, on
20. in; to
21. of, going
22. catches, cold; liable,to; subject, to
23. could
24. It, for, him
25. out, of; in
26. have, in
27. for, stupidly
28. led, in

III.

1. A, conscientious
2. C, sick
3. B, x
4. A, beat
5. C, they have

6. A, territorial area
7. A, The hearts
8. B, of going
9. B, could not
10. B, to master

IV.

1. How much is the car?
2. He wanted to learn another instrument.
3. Let me think it over.
4. I appreciate your kindness, but I cannot accept your offer.
5. It is three o'clock now.
6. What do you think of the movie?
7. We'll have a test in chemistry Tuesday.
8. He is very tall.
9. Does he like that girl? Yes, he does.
10. She is doing her work.
11. We know each other well.
12. Professor Lee lectured to the students....
13. The transportation is very convenient here.
14. My wife criticized me for behaving so stupidly.
15. This old friend of John's is a carpenter.
16. Andrew is liable to catch cold.
17. The price of this table is too high.
18. It is difficult for him to do this job alone.
19. In spite of difficulties, he got the job done.
20. Thank you for your assistance.

第 2 章

I.

1. d	18. b	35. a
2. a	19. b	36. b
3. c	20. a	37. c
4. b	21. b	38. a
5. a	22. d	39. d
6. d	23. c	40. c
7. b	24. c	41. b
8. c	25. d	42. b
9. a	26. b	43. c
10. b	27. a	44. d
11. d	28. d	45. c
12. c	29. d	46. c
13. b	30. c	47. a
14. b	31. a	48. d
15. d	32. c	49. b
16. a	33. b	50. d
17. d	34. c	

II.

1. Either	14. the, before
2. Many, a	15. how, it, is
3. has	16. None, of
4. all; that	17. either; neither
5. what	18. hardly
6. that	19. never; always
7. that; to; of	20. such, a; no
8. it, together	21. either, or
9. it, there	22. which
10. as, if	23. came, across
11. not; that	24. manners; ill-mannered
12. Not, having; As	25. has, forgotten
13. has, it	

III.

1. B, is
2. C, they could catch
3. B, which
4. B, struggled
5. B, that
6. B, that
7. B, and
8. C, cost
9. A, proud
10. C, be strictly
11. B, will they
12. A, As he was weak
13. A, what was
14. B, not to
15. C, haven't they
16. C, can I
17. C, become
18. B, or

IV.

1. He asked them where they were going.
2. Neither of them is to blame.
3. No one will be admitted while the meeting is in progress.
4. Seven minus four is three.
5. Her heart sank and she could hardly remain standing.
6. The singers are singing well, aren't they?
7. The news came that men were stranded on the beaches.
8. He asked her why she looked so sad.
9. I don't understand why you don't trust him.
10. He pretended not to know about it.
11. The whole nation mourned its dead heroes.
12. They will go to see the house where you lived last year.

第 3 章

I.

1. b	5. b	9. a
2. a	6. b	10. c
3. d	7. a	11. b
4. a	8. a	12. a

13. c	43. a	73. c
14. b	44. c	74. a
15. c	45. b	75. b
16. a	46. a	76. b
17. c	47. a	77. d
18. b	48. b	78. a
19. d	49. c	79. d
20. a	50. a	80. d
21. b	51. c	81. c
22. c	52. c	82. c
23. a	53. d	83. d
24. c	54. a	84. c
25. a	55. d	85. c
26. c	56. a	86. b
27. b	57. c	87. c
28. c	58. d	88. b
29. c	59. c	89. a
30. b	60. a	90. b
31. a	61. c	91. a
32. c	62. d	92. c
33. b	63. b	93. a
34. a	64. c	94. b
35. b	65. c	95. d
36. a	66. b	96. a
37. c	67. b	97. d
38. b	68. c	98. b
39. a	69. b	99. a
40. b	70. b	100. c
41. c	71. d	
42. c	72. a	

II.

1. laid
2. has lived
3. hung
4. is
5. fell
6. visited
7. has been
8. will come
9. left
10. went

11. died; has been; has
    been
12. finished
13. saw
14. had been
15. is coming

16. goes
17. met
18. came
19. hadn't mailed
20. will tell

III.

1. in
2. x
3. on
4. x
5. to
6. x
7. into
8. out
9. on
10. x, on
11. x
12. at
13. with
14. to
15. on, of; of
16. x
17. of
18. through
19. x
20. for, in
21. x
22. to
23. x
24. to
25. on
26. x
27. in
28. at

29. on / at
30. x
31. on / upon
32. x
33. for
34. in
35. with
36. of
37. about, in,
    from
38. on / upon
39. on
40. as; x
41. with
42. against
43. x
44. with
45. about
46. in
47. through
48. to
49. to
50. to
51. for / of
52. at
53. as
54. in, between
55. in

56. at / in
57. by
58. for
59. since
60. for
61. at
62. in
63. on
64. in
65. in
66. of
67. in
68. to
69. on
70. in
71. in

72. to
73. with
74. with
75. with
76. to
77. to
78. across
79. to
80. x
81. in
82. to
83. to
84. to
85. of

IV.

1. reading
2. do
3. to attend
4. working
5. repeat
6. mending
7. preceding
8. know
9. to study
10. to study 或 studying 皆可
11. Seeing
12. come
13. walking
14. cleaning
15. to turn

16. to take
17. considered
18. boring
19. bored
20. disappointed
21. interested
22. interesting
23. alarming
24. alarmed
25. disturbed
26. to buy
27. going
28. passing
29. Hearing
30. waiting

V.

1. cakes, soap
2. pair, scissors
3. large
4. People
5. are
6. Chinese; English
7. sheets, paper
8. a, half
9. She, I
10. That's

11. himself
12. my, own
13. with, her
14. and, I
15. she, does
16. her
17. me
18. to
19. which, in; where
20. who

VI.

1. x
2. an
3. x
4. x
5. The
6. x
7. x
8. An
9. a
10. x
11. the
12. the
13. the

14. x
15. the
16. x, x
17. The
18. x
19. The
20. the
21. the
22. the
23. x
24. the; x
25. x

VII.

1. A, little
2. C, met
3. C, information
4. B, of
5. C, those of South India
6. A, much

7. B, little
8. C, idle
9. B, good a
10. A, is worth
11. B, few
12. C, either

13. B, nor
14. C, ago
15. B, not enough
16. C, by
17. A, so
18. C, teacher's
19. B, happened
20. B, broke
21. B, have been estab lished

22. B, belong
23. B, suffers
24. A, even though
25. A, If only
26. A, Like
27. C, as
28. B, as
29. B, x
30. C, like

VIII.

1. Yesterday she bought a lot of food.
2. He has won the one-hundred-metre race.
3. She acquired a great deal of knowledge by reading.
4. Robert is an old friend of hers.
5. Our problem was the same as theirs.
6. She lost her usual cheerfulness. That puzzled me.
7. Last week we visited the The Palace Museum.
8. She said that she had never been to Taichung.
9. A great change has taken place in our home town.
10. Do you know anyone who was in the accident that happened yesterday?
11. He is very happy.
12. His brother died long ago.
13. Most sick people usually feel better in the morning than in the afternoon.
14. There is a desk in the corner of the room.
15. They are bound to fail.
16. He did not attend gym because he was sick.
17. He didn't even listen to her, but turned around and left.
18. No sooner had I reached the park than he arrived.

第 4 章

I.

1. c	20. a	39. c
2. a	21. d	40. a
3. b	22. d	41. c
4. d	23. a	42. d
5. a	24. b	43. c
6. b	25. d	44. a
7. d	26. b	45. b
8. b	27. a	46. c
9. c	28. b	47. a
10. c	29. d	48. b
11. a	30. a	49. c
12. b	31. b	50. b
13. c	32. b	51. b
14. a	33. c	52. d
15. b	34. d	53. b
16. c	35. c	54. a
17. a	36. a	55. c
18. d	37. a	
19. c	38. c	

II.

1. drunk	9. valueless
2. empty, stomach	10. highly
3. ashamed	11. conscious
4. economical	12. satisfied
5. strict	13. worth, while
6. command	14. hard
7. promised	15. everywhere
8. make	

III.

1. B, demonstrations
2. B, other
3. B, learn
4. C, bring
5. A, looking for
6. B, found
7. B, with
8. A, acquired
9. A, promised
10. A, borrowed
11. A, worked
12. B, invented
13. B, took
14. B, recommend
15. A, doubt
16. B, staying
17. A, difficult
18. B, much

第 5 章

I.

1. d	8. b	15. c
2. a	9. d	16. a
3. c	10. b	17. b
4. b	11. c	18. c
5. c	12. c	19. d
6. a	13. c	20. c
7. a	14. d	

II.

1. C, colours
2. A, take a turn
3. C, follows
4. A, office
5. B, time
6. C, her
7. B, a book
8. C, x
9. C, arms
10. A, had better

Index 索引

* 英文字或短語後為單元碼。

False Friends
似識而非的 "假朋友"

蘇正隆

　　我們在學英文或從事翻譯的時候，最容易的是中文裏有對應（equivalent expression）或極為類似（striking similarity）的說法。譬如："蛙人"英文叫 frogman，"鐵人"英文叫 iron man，這種詞彙學起來、譯出來輕而易舉，不費工夫。比較麻煩的是似 "識" 而非，英文表面上和中文看起來極為類似，但意思卻差十萬八千里的詞彙，如 green bean 字面上有 "綠" 有 "豆"，指的卻是 "四季豆"，bald eagle 不是 "禿鷹"，而是 "白頭海雕"。這種情形就好像遇見似曾相識的人，以為 "他鄉遇故知"，結果卻是被擺了一道而不自知。英文裏像這種我們自以為認識，似 "識" 而非的詞彙，語言學上稱之為 false friend（假朋友）或 false cognate（假同源詞）。例如：英文的 eat one's words 不是 "食言"（go back on one's word / break a promise），是 "認錯；道歉"（to admit that they were wrong about something they said）；或法文的 pain 是 "麵包"（bread）不是 "痛苦"，experience 是 "實驗"（experiment）而不是 "經驗" 等。類似這樣的 "假朋友" 在英文裏比比皆是，我們不提高警覺，很容易就會掉入陷阱而不自知。以下就是一些 false friend 的例子：

armchair 單人沙發；loveseat 雙人座沙發；sofa 長沙發

　　armchair 是單人座沙發，不是有扶手的椅子都叫 armchair，必須是 upholstered，通常指客廳單人座沙發，雙人座沙發叫 loveseat，只有三人座長沙發叫 sofa 或 couch，跟有無靠背沒關係，中文的沙發泛指以上三種 upholstered chairs。

at the end of the day 總之

常有人誤以為是 * “一天終了時”，其實是 “總之”，請見下例：

It's just that, for all the sound and fury, not a lot seems to really happen, and at the end of the day I felt that I wanted something that wasn't there. Perfect vacation or travel-time reading.

bald eagle 不是 “禿鷹”，是白頭海雕。

鷹是 vulture，而 bald 在生物上常指白色或白色斑點。

bank holiday 不是 Bankers Day，是公共假期 (public holiday)。

在一影集裏，男主角與另一位男士邊走邊談，一位提到明天是 bank holiday，電視中文字幕赫然出現 “明天是 * 銀行節”。在英國國定假日叫 bank holiday，也許銀行與英國人關係太密切了，是生活中不可或缺的，所以國定假日銀行不開門，就稱之為 bank holiday。

bargain hunter 不是獵人，是撿便宜者。

我們從學英文開始，就強調背單字，而每個英文單字往往只附一個、頂多兩個中文解釋。如：hunter 是 “獵人”，worker 是 “工人”，business 是 “商業”，對許多學習者，像這些初學英文時所學到的中文意思往往跟着他們一輩子，不加質疑。因此 conscientious worker（做事很認真），就有人把它翻成 “誠實的工人”，又如：on a business trip（出差），很多人就會譯成 * 做商業旅行”；get down to business 其實是 “言歸正傳”、“談正事”之類的意思，當然也可能包括談生意在內，但不一定只是 “談生意”。

以 Last minute bargain hunters flocked to the shop. 為例，句子裏 bargain hunter 無關打獵，是店家大廉售，想要在最後一刻撿便宜者蜂擁而至的意思。當然，喜歡瘋狂採購（on a shopping spree）的人，往往見 “獵” 心喜，不過到底自己是獵人或為商家所獵，就見仁見智了。

board of directors 不是導演的板凳，是董事會。

有次一位同學把 sitting on the board of directors（擔任董事）翻成 " 坐在板上的指導者 "，我看了忍俊不住，想 served on our board of directors in recent years 這樣的句子，説不定會譯成，" 近幾年拿來作為導演的板凳 " 吧！

bookmaker 不是 publisher / bookseller，是賭注業者。

現在俗稱 " 組頭 "，接受賭注的莊家。英國人賭注的名堂很多，除了彩券（lottery）以外，從賭馬到賭球，甚至哪一球隊下任教練人選是誰，都可以下賭注，稱為 bookmaking。大街小巷到處都可見投注站，掛着 bookmaker 的招牌。不知情者還以為是書店或印書的地方呢。bookmaker 口語裏常簡稱 bookie。

美國大部分地方賭博是非法的，他們的 bookmaking 以球賽或賽馬為主，賭六合彩之類押數字的賭注則稱為 numbers。

boot camp 不是賣馬靴的地方，是新兵訓練中心（training centre）。

boot 是長統靴，camp 可以是露營區、軍營、夏令營（summer camp）、難民營（refugee camp）、集中營（concentration camp）、訓練營（training camp）等。至於 prison camp 在美國指沒有危險的輕罪犯人拘留的地方，可以容許犯人外出工作。但在英式英文裏，則指戒備森嚴，關政治犯、戰犯的地方。

boot camp 在美國本來是指新兵訓練中心，現在一般大企業培訓新進員工的訓練營或講習所也流行用這詞彙。

boot fair / car boot sale 不是 shoe fair，是類似跳蚤市場之類的市集。

car boot 在英式英語裏是指汽車行李廂。有人覺得買舊衣、舊地毯之類的東西，難免會附贈跳蚤若干，因此賣二手貨、廉價品的市集，就被謔稱為跳蚤市場（flea market）。在英國，稱這種市集為 boot fair 或 car boot fair。行李廂在美國稱 trunk，在英國稱 car boot。有東西要賣的，可在週末把車子開到指定場地,打開行李廂,把物品陳列出來賣。

bootleg 不是 the leg of a boot,是製造或者販賣非法商品,如 CD 或私酒之類。

在 1920-33 年間,美國實施禁酒令(Prohibition),走私者往往用扁瓶(flask)裝酒,藏在靴子裏。所以製造販售私酒或非法物品就叫 bootleg,可作動詞、名詞、形容詞。如:bootleg whisky, bootleg CD, bootleg tapes 等。

building society 不是 builders association,是銀行的一種,以房地產貸款為主。

society 可以是協會或學會,如:歷史學會(the historical society);但 building society 在英國是銀行的一種,原來係以建築融資、房貸為主的合作社,就像台灣的土地銀行、合作金庫,現在也與一般銀行無異。

chamber of commerce 不是 department of trade,是商會。

曾有報紙把 Chamber of Commerce of the U. S. 誤譯為 "美國貿易總署",其實應該是 "美國商業總會"。chamber of commerce 是各鄉鎮、城市商人的公會,又稱 board of trade, merchants' association 等。

cheerleader 不是 captain of the cheerleaders,是啦啦隊裏面的一員,或任何搖旗吶喊,為人加油的人。

大概受到 leader 一字的誤導,幾乎海內外的英漢詞典都把 cheerleader 為 "啦啦隊長"。在比賽時,任何帶領觀眾喊加油的人都是 cheerleader,所以出現在報章雜誌上往往用複數形式。

中文裏啦啦隊的意思比較廣泛,除了上面提到的,也可以指拿着有羽毛或花邊裝飾圓圈(pompom)表演助陣的 pompom squad,甚至包括 marching band。啦啦隊長可稱為 captain,如果是 marching band 的指揮,稱為 drum major 或 majorette。

coming of age 不是 coming of an epoch，而是成年（become adult / mature）。

　　以往在歐美滿 21 歲算成年（of age），現在大多數國家則以 18 歲為成年。許多文化裏都有成年禮（coming of age ceremony 或 rite of passage）來慶祝生命中這一重要時期的來臨。因此 coming of age 及 rite of passage 又有"重要階段，轉捩點"的意思。epoch（時代）則是指一段相當長的時期。

crow's feet 不是 feet of a crow，是魚尾紋。

　　年紀大了眼角產生皺紋，中文叫"魚尾紋"，英文叫 crow's feet。愛美女士必慾去之而後快，早年有訴諸拉皮（facelift）等美容手術（plastic surgery），前些年流行注射肉毒桿菌毒素（botulin）製品 Botox，近年來則流行注射玻尿酸（hyaluronic acid）。

crow's nest 則是指十字路中央供警察指揮交通的高台，或船艦上的瞭望台。

cupboard (as in *Harry Potter*) 小儲藏室

　　cupboard 不一定是"碗櫥"，在英國一般是指樓梯旁的"小儲藏室"，如《哈利波特》第一集：

> *Until Harry's 11th birthday, he is forced to sleep in a cupboard under the stairs.*

date, date palm 海棗，椰棗 vs. jujube 棗子

　　date 一般常誤為"棗子"，其實是棕櫚科的"海棗"，或叫"椰棗"，jujube 才是"棗子"。

eat one's words 承認失言

　　eat one's words 是"承認失言"，go back on one's word 才"食言"，見下例：

Ullrich keen for Armstrong to eat his words German rider Jan Ullrich has reacted angrily to criticism from American rival Lance Armstrong that he does not train hard enough.

flat footed 不一定是扁平足，有可能是手足無措。

扁平足英文叫 flatfoot 或 splayfoot。扁平足的人腳弓 (instep arch) 直接觸地，不利於行，因此 flat footed 常用來指笨手笨腳，手足失措。如：不久前的旱災讓政府窘態百出，束手無策，就可以説 A recent drought caught the government flat footed.

fourth estate 不是第四筆地產，是指記者或新聞界。

estate 有地產、遺產、地位等意思。歐洲傳統上認為社會由貴族、教會、平民三大階層構成，就是所謂的 estate of the realm；近代新聞記者自成一個勢力，則是傳統三大階層以外的第四階層，稱為 fourth estate，有人把它譯成第四權。

full of beans 不是到處都是豆子，是精力充沛 (energetic)。

英語裏 bean 字通常指的是四季豆，大概是豆子營養豐富吧，full of beans 意指精力充沛，如：After a siesta he was full of beans. (午睡後他精神十足)。不過在美國俚語裏 full of beans 另有 "錯誤連篇" 的意思。另外，spill the beans 則是指洩漏機密。beanbag 除了指做為遊戲丟擲用的裝乾豆小布袋，現在一般用以指俗稱 "懶骨頭"，裏面裝泡棉的變形椅，全名叫 beanbag chair。

go back on his word 食言

Once you have a signed contract from a dealer can the dealer go back on his word (食言)？

注意 go back on one's "word"，不是 "words" (cf. eat one's words 承認失言)。

gray matter / grey matter 不是 grey material，是指頭腦（brain）。

大腦裏有所謂的 "灰質" 與 "白質"（gray matter & white matter），白質主要是神經纖維構成，灰質是由能解讀訊號的神經細胞組成的，因此用來喻指大腦。如：她花不少時間絞盡腦汁想解決那問題，可以説 That problem has caused her gray matter to work overtime. 。

green bean 不是 mung bean，是四季豆。

這是一個最典型的 false friend，因為字面上剛好有 "綠" 及 "豆" 兩字。

我們拿來做綠豆湯，綠豆芽的豆子英文叫 mung bean。green bean 是四季豆，又稱敏豆。

hard shoulder 不是 bony / strong shoulder，是路肩。

正規道路的邊緣，也就是路肩，在美國稱為 shoulder，可供緊急停車或急救車行駛。在英國，只有高速道路（motorway）設有路肩，稱為 hard shoulder。高速公路在美國通稱 expressway，不收費的叫 freeway，大多在美國西部，收過路費（toll）的叫 turnpike，大多在東部。

headhunt 不再是 cannibalistic act，是當前流行的 "挖角" 行為。

培養人才要花時間，所謂百年樹人。現代企業流行撿現成，從別公司找現成人才最方便省事，就是所謂挖角（headhunt）。譬如，聖巴伯拉加州大學曾想把牛津大學某位教授挖過來，報導上説：UCSB attempted to headhunt Professor Cheetham, who had been at Oxford for 26 years… 。負責挖角的人或尋才公司就叫 headhunter，有人硬生生把它譯成獵人頭公司。

提到人頭，現在有人心存不軌，出資找貪圖小利者或欺騙無辜，取得他們的身份證、印章，搞假結婚販賣人口或成立空頭公司來行騙斂財，這些被利用的人頭，英文叫 puppet。

heavy-duty 不是 heavy burden，是耐用（durable / powerful）。

　　duty 除了職責外，還有稅的意思，如 customs duty（關稅）、import duty（進口稅）等。但 heavy-duty 並非重稅，也不是職務繁重，而是耐用，如：heavy-duty battery（強力、耐用電池）。順便一提，免稅是 duty-free，不是 free duty，但香港回歸中國後，機場免稅店招牌全部卻從 duty-free 改成中式英文 free duty。

hobby horse 不是愛馬，是別人早就聽膩，自己卻樂此不疲、老愛談起的話題。

　　hobby 一般翻成嗜好，但跟中文嗜好的意思稍有不同。學生在會話及作文課時，如果提到 hobby，常會說 watching TV, sleeping, eating, window shopping 是自己的 hobby。但在英文裏這些活動不能算 hobby。中文有所謂的不良嗜好（addiction），英文裏不止沒有不良 hobby，連不夠正面、積極的嗜好也不能算 hobby。看電視、吃飯、睡覺、逛街不需要刻意去學，也不用培養興趣，所以都不算。相對的，bird-watching（賞鳥）、gourmet cooking（美食烹飪）、meditating（打坐）等則算。

　　騎馬（horseback riding）可算是一種 hobby，但 hobby horse 與馬無關，是別人早就聽膩，自己卻樂此不疲、老愛談起的話題。

holdup 持械搶劫

　　英文裏搶劫因類型不同而有不同的單詞，持刀槍械搶劫叫 holdup，在街上行搶叫 mugging。

industrial action（英）/ job action（美）不是 activity undertaken by industry，是罷工之類的手段。

industrial dispute 不是 dispute between industries，是勞資（management and workers）之間的爭議。

killer whale 虎鯨，不是 "殺人鯨"。

labour of love 不是 love is hard work，是為了興趣嗜好而無怨無悔去做的事。

linden / lime 椴樹，不是菩提樹 pipal。

lightning rod 不是 electric cudgel，是避雷針（lightning conductor）。

living room 不是 the room where people live?，是客廳。

loose cannon 不是 stray cannonball / stray bullet，而是非常脫線，不按牌理的危險人物（a reckless person）。

　　cannon 通常指架在砲車、艦艇或軍機上，機動性高的火砲，如果沒固定好（loose），當然會有危險。八十年代末期美國政界、新聞界開始流行 loose cannon 一詞。尼克森時代的海格將軍，雷根時代的諾斯上校（Oliver North）都常被指為 loose cannon。

loveseat 雙人座沙發，不是 "情人座"。

milk run 不是 milk has run out，是旅行坐的飛機或火車停很多站，不是直飛或直達。

the milk round 不是 surrounded by milk，是每年大公司到各大學徵才的活動。

A miss is as good as a mile. 反正沒中；幸虧沒事

　　不是 "失之毫釐，謬以千里"，是 "反正沒發生" 或 "幸虧沒發生"，見以下兩例：

I was just one number away from winning big on the state lottery. But a miss is as good as a mile.
（反正沒中）

Back from a wonderful trip in Florida, where we slid between hurricanes into fabulous weather—A miss is as good as a mile.
（幸虧沒事）

moonshine 不一定是 moonlight，是私酒（illegal alcoholic drink）或餿主意，愚蠢的評論（silly remark or idea）。

在十四、十五世紀，moonshine 只是 "月光" 的意思，在現代英式英語裏，它仍有月光的意思。但在美語裏，月光一般用 moonlight 一字，moonshine 則用來指私酒，特別是烈酒，尤其在 1920-33 美國禁酒時代（Prohibition），這字更大為流行。

此外，moonshine 在英美都有 "餿主意"，"愚蠢的評論" 之意。如：

It was all moonshine.（都是些餿主意。）
Simply moonshine!（根本就是愚蠢的評論！）

mug shot 不是 shooting of a mug，是（嫌疑犯）拍照存檔。

mugging 街上行搶

參見 holdup 條及下例：

Police charge man with York Street mugging. Bike-riding suspect matches description of 4 other purse grabs.

mung bean 即 "綠豆"，請參見 green bean 條。

no love lost 不是 the love is not diminished，是彼此不喜歡（used for saying that two people do not like each other），見下例：

There is no love lost between John and Mary.

not that I know of 不是 I don't know，是就我所知不是這樣。

oak 櫟，俗誤為 "橡"。

olive 齊墩果，油橄欖，西洋橄欖

　　olive 是木犀科的 "齊墩果"，但譯成 "油橄欖"、"西洋橄欖" 也無妨。它與橄欖科的中國的橄欖 (canarium) 是完全不同科也不同目的植物。

on the couch 不是 on a sofa，是看心理醫師 (shrink, psychiatrist)

operating theatre 不是 theatre for the performance of plays，是手術室，見下例：

　　Conversation in the operating theatre as a cause of airborne bacterial contamination.

own goal 不是 life ambition，是烏龍球或自打耳光。

　　He scored an own goal. 他踢進一個烏龍球。或，他打了自己一個耳光。

pet peeve (美) / pet hate (英) 不是 dislike pets，是你最不喜歡的東西。

press conference 不是 conference on journalism，是記者招待會。

press gang 不是 gang of journalists，是從前英國專門上街抓人去當兵的人，中文稱為抓壯丁。

red herring 不一定是 smoked herring，常用來指轉移焦點，無關宏旨（a false lead / a distraction）。

> *He is trying to draw a red herring across the track.*

rite of passage 不是 opening ceremony of a road / bridge，是成年儀式。

rob / steal 是搶或偷。

> mugging：在街上搶劫；robbery：以暴力或威嚇搶劫。

rocket science 很困難的事。

> 往往用在 It's not rocket science. 這樣的句型中。

secretary 不一定是 assistant / clerk，有時是部長（minister）。

> 如 transport secretary。

self-styled 不是 has one's individual style，是“自命為”。

> 如 a self-styled educational expert。

show stopping 不是 stop the show，是表演精彩。

Siamese twins 不是 twins from Thailand，是連體嬰。

sing a different song 不是 to deliberately oppose，是迎合別人，改變自己的主張。

sofa 長沙發，參見 armchair 及 loveseat。

sound bite 不是 shrill noise，是電視或新聞廣播中所播出的公眾人物講話的片段 (brief recorded speech)。

spin doctor 不是治 your head spins 的醫師，是政客的化妝師，負責和媒體打交道，提供有利於政客或機關的消息。

stepbrothers 不一定是 half brothers，有時既不同母又不同父 (may have no blood ties at all)。

stop press 不是 out of print，是最新消息，最新出版，號外 (latest edition)，見下例：

> *If it's hot off the press, it's here. For in depth information on the latest Puffin news, visit our online Press Office. What's on Stop Press?*

talk shop 不是 talking about shopping，是三句不離本行。

> *For Martin did not see why a man should not talk shop.*

talking shop 光説不練

> *Is politics a science or just a talking shop?*

tax return 不是 refund of tax，是報税。

technically 嚴格説來

> 在下列兩例中都是 "嚴格説來"，但往往誤譯為 "從技術上説"。
>
> *I am a doctor (which, technically speaking I am not, though I have finished medical school).*
>
> *"Welcome to our village. Well, technically speaking, I am not from here either."*